W9-AAO-626

PRAISE FOR SARAH FINE

"As a modern-day 'Orpheus and Eurydice,' *Sanctum* will be a hit with urban fantasy readers, who will love its top-notch world-building, page-turning action, and slow-developing romance."

—*School Library Journal*

"In this well-developed concept of the afterlife, details are well-executed and the setting is described flawlessly. Without a doubt, readers will look forward to the next installment of the Guards of the Shadowlands series."

—*Library Media Connection* on *Sanctum*

"This is one of my favorite books of this year! Smart and sexy."

—*Reading Teen* blog on *Sanctum*

"Theology be damned, though: Lela and Malachi are both likable protagonists, and readers will be happy . . . this trilogy opener has a lot going for it."

—*Kirkus Reviews* on *Sanctum*

"Fans of Rae Carson's books and Victoria Aveyard's *Red Queen* will find much to love in Fine's engrossing novel."

—*VOYA* on *The Impostor Queen*

"Sarah Fine presents a fresh and fascinating magical world with its own rules and rituals, riveting action and relationships (and a sequel-worthy ending), featuring a protagonist who grows in wisdom, compassion, and self-awareness."

—*School Library Journal* on *The Impostor Queen*

UNCANNY

ALSO BY SARAH FINE

Young Adult Fiction

Guards of the Shadowlands Series

Sanctum

Fractured

Chaos

Captive: A Guard's Tale from Malachi's Perspective

Vigilante: A Guard's Tale from Ana's Perspective

Stories from the Shadowlands

Of Metal and Wishes Series

Of Metal and Wishes

Of Dreams and Rust

Of Shadows and Obsession: A Short Story Prequel to Of Metal and Wishes

The Impostor Queen Series

The Impostor Queen

The Cursed Queen

Other Series

Scan (with Walter Jury)

Burn (with Walter Jury)

Beneath the Shine

Adult Fiction

The Reliquary Series

Reliquary

Splinter

Mosaic

Mayhem and Magic (Graphic Novel)

Servants of Fate Series

Marked

Claimed

Fated

MCD

B&T
12·13·17
9⁹⁹
Y

U N C A N N Y

SARAH FINE

SKYSCAPE

SKYSCAPE

This is a work of fiction. Names, characters, organizations, places, events, and incidents are either products of the author's imagination or are used fictitiously. Any resemblance to actual persons, living or dead, or actual events is purely coincidental.

Text copyright © 2017 by Sarah Fine
All rights reserved.

No part of this book may be reproduced, or stored in a retrieval system, or transmitted in any form or by any means, electronic, mechanical, photocopying, recording, or otherwise, without express written permission of the publisher.

Published by Skyscape, New York

www.apub.com

Amazon, the Amazon logo, and Skyscape are trademarks of Amazon.com, Inc., or its affiliates.

ISBN-13: 9781542046466
ISBN-10: 1542046467

Cover design by Damonza

Printed in the United States of America

For Lam, in celebration of our tenth book together. This has been a marvelous journey, and I for one hope we're nowhere near the end of it.

I did not anticipate the wind. On the sidewalk, it makes jackets flap and leaves rustle. Seven stories up, it threatens to throw me right over the edge.

Is that what I want?

I'm not good at knowing what I want—that's what she said to me, and it turns out she was right. This will be my last decision, and it could be my worst or my best, but I don't know if it will be something I *want*.

But wanting isn't relevant now.

My shoes scrape over cement as I stand on the roof's ledge. I am battered. Faltering. My arms are out, my fingers splayed. I turn around and face the school's security cannies, who have formed a semicircle around me on the roof and are slowly approaching. Outdated, out-moded, plastic skin, expressionless. They are here to stop me or at least detain me until emergency services reach us, but like me, they are not immune to gravity. If I go over, they can't save me.

They're programmed to save me. They won't feel a thing if they fail, though. They can't. That's the difference between us.

Looking at their blank eyes fills me with a sense of the inevitable.

I can't remember not existing, whatever happened before I became *me*. I don't think it hurt, not like this. Perhaps I'm wrong, though. Maybe I've been here before.

I crane my neck to see past the machinemen, searching for the one face I need, one I know I've already seen for the last time. She isn't here. Of course she isn't. She can't be.

I want to see her one last time. After everything I did, she wouldn't look at me with anything other than sorrow or maybe hate or pity. But still, I want to see her.

There. That's one thing I know I want.

Even if it were relevant, it still wouldn't matter.

I inch back a little. It would be easier for the wind to take me. I'd prefer that to doing this myself. But the cannies keep getting closer, and now the wind is still. Unhelpful.

"This is my choice," I say loudly. "I'm doing this of my own free will."

Is this what she wanted? I think this might be what she wanted.

It's all tangled up in her, and she's not here. I'll never see her again. I'll never see her again, and it's because of the choices I made.

Free will.

Want.

I close my eyes. It's time.

Chapter One

I wish I were small. Just one of those girls with bird bones who can ball up, knees under chin, heels to butt, tiny-tiny.

But I am huge. I seem to have my own gravitational pull. I am a black hole, expanding by the minute, and no gaze can escape me. My head might as well be brushing the white ceiling, leaving a little grease stain there. I'm contained between the armrests of this chair, but I could swear my elbows are brushing the walls on either side. My belly is swelling, and soon it'll overflow onto Principal Selridge's desk and ooze toward where she stands on the other side, clutching her biceps as if she's afraid they're going to peel away from her bones.

I turn my head and look out the window. We're two stories up. If I had jumped, my body would have sailed past that auto-cleaning windowpane in a fraction of a second, a blink of an eye. Easy to miss. But now I have everyone's eyes. They can't look around me or past me. Black. Hole.

Selridge steps in front of the window, blocking my view of the park across the street. She motions one of the cannies over to take her place and guard the spot. He's got a wide, blank face, fair skin, black hair—impossible to mistake for human. He's the one who unlocked the doors as the others lugged me off the roof, down the stairs, up the hall, past the banner welcoming the incoming freshmen, the Clinton Academy

Class of 2073. First day of school, halfway through homeroom discussion period, and I gave everyone something to talk about.

Lara and Mei were cutting class, laying flowers in front of Hannah's locker as I was carried past. They watched me go by with stone faces. I'm guessing Finn told them about the message he sent me this morning. I hope he doesn't blame himself. I didn't really think about that, up on the roof. I should have.

The rest of my classmates gathered in the doorways of their homerooms and stared. They were probably using their Cerepins to stream what they were seeing to their channels. A hundred simultaneous vids of Cora Dietrich on the Mainstream, screaming, screaming, screaming.

If you were to listen to all of them at once, it wouldn't come close to the noise inside my head.

"You're going to be okay, Cora," Selridge says, now back behind her desk. "Your parents will be here soon. If you turn your Cerepin back on, you could talk to them—they made sure to tell me they're eager to hear from you."

She taps her own Cerepin, a small black nodule on her right temple. Hers is an older model, and unlike the newer ones, it signals when it's capturing. The red light is blinking. She's probably streaming a feed of me straight to Mom and Gary. They can see what she sees, thanks to her implanted lenses. They might even be talking to her now through the sensor in her ear, words I can't hear and don't want to. My mother might even have been the one who told Selridge to guard the window.

Mom was definitely the one who alerted the school. I don't know if it was because Finn carried through on his threat to send her the vid he sent me this morning or because she got scared when I turned my Cerepin off.

Considering what happened last time, I don't blame her at all.

My hands cover my eyes and my shoulders jerk up around my head. I can't think about it, not now, please not now, but my brain is already feeding me memories of a sharp, sickly sweet scent and my cold, wet feet sliding along a marble floor. I bend at the waist and start to rock. I know the keening sound is awful, at once hoarse and high and grating, but I can't stop it. I can't stop.

"Cora . . ."

That's all Selridge can think of to say.

Firm hands grasp my shoulders. I try to wrench away, but the canny is too strong. He holds me still. He doesn't understand that I need this. How could he?

He lets me go when my keening escalates into a full-fledged scream. I keep my fists pressed into my eyes. Outside, I hear the shuffle of feet, the sound of voices. Homeroom discussion is over. I should be going to my individual learning session with Aristotle. Neda will wonder where I am.

Wait. She'll know. Everyone knows.

My hands fall to my lap like birds hit by skycars. Dead on impact. My vision blurs as I stare across the room, making Selridge one with the wall behind her. She shudders when she sees the look on my face.

My breakfast comes up in a single sudden heave. All over Selridge's desk screen, stomach acid and bits of protein bar, sour and burning on my tongue. I spit on the floor as my principal gags. "Sorry," I whisper.

I cover my mouth and breathe, but the smell is a hand around my throat, once again dragging me back to the night it happened. It is fingernails clawing at a closed door, trying to rip through. Everything in me locks up.

Wet feet sliding on a marble floor.

This time, it's just acid and spit, splashing onto the hardwood and the synthetic leather of my boots.

My heartbeat swishes in my ears. The canny offers me a cloth to wipe my mouth, and when I don't take it, he does it for me. Selridge's lips move. What is she saying?

"Cora!" It's Mom. She squats next to me, right in the puke at our feet. When she wraps her arms around me, I feel her shaking. "It's going to be all right. We're taking you home."

Okay, this is good. I was afraid they were going to take me straight back to the hospital.

"We should take her back to the hospital," says Gary from behind me. "We talked about this."

"She really should be evaluated," Selridge says. "If she can't promise she won't try something—"

"I know, but we can monitor her," Mom says, turning to my adoptive father. "I won't leave her side if that's what it takes."

"You shouldn't take more time off," Gary mutters.

"I really can't allow her to return to school until she's been cleared by a doctor," says Selridge, her voice louder now. "The suicide attempt was made on academy grounds. This is very serious."

"That's fair, Maeve," Gary says to my mom.

"No," I whisper. I'm not a black hole anymore. Now I'm invisible.

"We'll decide in the car," Gary says a moment later. Mom probably just gave him the death glare, and he doesn't want to get into it in front of Selridge. "CC, can you walk?"

I've asked him a million times not to call me that, but it's a habit he can't seem to break. He doesn't realize that every time he says it, he makes things harder for me, and I'm scared to explain—scared to hurt him more than I already have. His hands on my shoulders are softer than the canny's. Gentle, like he's asking permission. I don't fight him as he pulls me up and guides me away from the stinking mess I made. I turn and press my face into his sweater, trying to escape the smell, and he lets me. Puts his hand over the back of my head and stiffly holds me there, shushing me as I tremble.

"Please send me a quick message to let me know how she's doing," Selridge says. "We're all very concerned."

As Gary lets me go, Selridge ducks her head a little, trying to make eye contact with me, but I'm not letting it happen. If we lock gazes, I'll see just how bad it is, and I don't want to know.

I had planned to never know.

"Cora, it really will be okay," Selridge says. "We all miss Hannah, but nobody blames you for what happened."

I wish the wind had blown just a little harder up there on the roof. Just one good gust.

Mom puts her arm around my waist, maneuvering me between her and Gary as they lead me out of Selridge's office. "I thought we agreed," Gary says under his breath.

"She'll be better at home," Mom says. "Besides, if she went to the hospital again, she'd just come back to the same house. The same us. The same memories."

He nods. "You're probably right. Besides—the investigation isn't complete. They'll need to talk to Cora at some point."

Mom's grip on my waist tightens. "Not now, Gary!"

We walk past empty classrooms and occupied learning auditoriums with closed doors. Inside one of those auditoriums, Neda is facing off with Aristotle in the way only she can, probably mad as hell at me, maybe scared I'll tell someone about her part in all of this. When I turn my Cerepin back on, there'll probably be fifty messages from her.

When I turn on my Cerepin . . . *if* I do. I'm scared to see Finn's message again, to find out how many times I was tagged in vids by people who believe the worst of me. Not wanting to risk more stares, I examine the floor as we walk down the hall, past the mute cannies standing dormant, waiting for another student to rescue or protect. They have no feelings, but if they did, disgust would be at the top, I'm sure. Some of them nearly fell as they pulled me from the ledge.

Do they fear death?

Do I?

We make it outside. The wind gusts an hour too late, ruffling my short hair, blowing dust into my eyes. A company car is waiting. Gary must have been on his way to the Parnassus complex when he probably got a frantic call from Mom, and here they are. I'm making him look bad.

Hurting him again, after everything he's done for us. God. I don't know why they're being nice. I wish they had just let me go.

Leika's door slides open as we reach the curb. I dive into her, grateful to be hidden, and Mom and Gary climb in after me. "Where to, sir?" Leika asks, all sleek metal and compliance. I wish I had her voice, her calm.

I glance over at Mom and Gary. They're looking at each other. A long look full of shared hours, a shared heart. Mom blinks. Gary's eyes shift to meet mine. "You're in a lot of trouble," he says.

"I know," I mumble.

"We've always been patient with you, CC, but this—"

"Gary," Mom murmurs.

He sighs. Closes his eyes. His nostrils flare. "All right. Let's get real here."

This is his CEO voice. I imagine it echoing in a boardroom. Hannah had this kind of presence, too. You had no choice but to listen to her.

Had.

Oh, god. I clench my teeth as my stomach turns.

"Cora," Mom says. "Gary has a point. What you did this morning—that was . . ."

Insane? She was probably going to say "insane."

"Unacceptable," Gary continues for her. His fingers are interlaced, his elbows on his knees, his eyes so intense. "We lost one of our daughters not even two weeks ago, and the other one seems determined to self-destruct!"

"Gary!"

He holds up his hand. "It has to be said. Because if I don't, I'm going to say worse, okay?" His eyes are shiny and bloodshot.

"I'm sorry," I say, my voice shredded by the screaming and the puking and the crying and the knowing that this is all my fault.

"If you're sorry, just tell us what happened," he says, and it comes out of him in one rapid stream. "Help us understand. Be honest. You're going to have to explain at some point."

"She's doing her best," Mom says. "The doctor said to give it time."

"But she's avoiding the whole thing!" He says to me, "Look at you. Look at what you did this morning."

"I'm sorry."

"We don't want your apologies, goddammit!" snaps Gary. "We want to know why!"

I put my hands over my ears, but it does little to shut out the noise. If my Cerepin were on, I'd turn my music up to eleven. "I told you before. I've told you a thousand times. I don't remember."

"Because you're trying not to," Gary replies. "Franka notified us of the pills in your room. Where did you get them?"

I press my face to Leika's window. "I needed to sleep. The other pills weren't working."

"Hard for them to work if you don't take them," Gary says.

"I found the bottle in your bathroom cabinet this morning," Mom adds. "I counted them. You haven't taken a single one."

I wrap my arms around myself, as if that could keep me from flying apart. I turn to my mom. "I don't want to go to the hospital again. Please."

"Maybe you do need more time and space from the house," she says, stroking my arm as she contradicts herself. "Like Gary said, it hasn't even been two weeks."

I jerk away, but then I see the hurt on her face. "Please," I say again. "I've only been home for a few days. The hospital is so . . . cold."

9

I squeeze my eyes shut as I remember. That nurse with the sad face. I was looking at her over Mom's shoulder as Mom told me Hannah was dead, while Gary sobbed out in the hallway for his lost baby girl.

"You're asking us to trust you, CC," says Gary. "And I'm wondering why you think we should."

Suddenly, I am so, so tired. "I won't turn off my Cerepin tracking again. I was upset."

Finn will blame himself. But I hope he holds off now. I hope he understands there's no need to send the vid to Mom and Gary.

"Things have to change," Gary is saying. "I can't live like this. *We* can't live like this." He puts his hand on Mom's knee, and she scoots a few inches closer to him. "We're grieving, too, you know."

Is he kidding?

"Things will change," I tell him. "I'll change."

"We don't want you to change!" says Mom. She's either a great liar or she's living in an alternate reality, with a different Cora.

"We want you to get *better*," Gary adds. "And you're not going to until you really deal with what happened—and come clean, if you need to."

My stomach lurches. "I don't have any secrets, but I'll try to get better. I'm working on it. I promise."

"Empty promises aren't good enough, not after this morning," Gary says.

Mom sighs. "He's right. We have certain conditions, and if you don't accept them, we have no choice but to take you to the hospital. I want you home, Cora, but I won't do it if it means risking your life."

"Franka's always right there," I say. "And my Cerepin—"

Gary's jaw clenches. "Do I need to remind you," he says slowly, "of what you did that night?"

I know what he's thinking: if Franka's settings hadn't been changed, if our Cerepin trackers hadn't been turned off, Hannah might still be alive.

"No," I say, so loudly that my voice cracks. "I remember that part."

Gary mutters something under his breath, then grips his jaw as if to hold the words in. The muscles of his forearm are taut. After a few seconds, he lets go and takes Mom's hand. "And we won't even get into this morning, when you did it again," he continues. "We can't trust you not to mess with the tech meant to protect and supervise you, and we can't be awake twenty-four seven."

"Please," I say, "I'll do anything you want as long as you don't take me to the hospital. I can't go back there. I just want to go home." I want to be in my room, in my bed, in the dark, the closest I can get to being nothing, thinking nothing. I want to take one of those pills Hannah had stashed away, the ones that crush dreams into blackness.

I want to take all of them at once.

Mom and Gary are quiet. They're looking at each other, intent. The green lights on their Cerepins blink—they have the newest version, with thought control. They can communicate without saying a word. Finally, Mom nods.

"All right," says Gary. "So, CC, I've been doing a lot of research, and I think I've found something that could help. If you cooperate, we'll take the hospital off the table for now, but only if you really give this a chance. Deal?"

"A lot of *research*?" Not sure he could make it sound more ominous if he tried.

"We only want the best for you," Mom says.

"What is it?"

"I have a friend who has developed an amazing program that might be exactly what we need. Really cutting edge."

"Yeah." I draw the word out. "I hope you don't mean that literally. I don't want a neurostim or anything like that."

That's what they'd do to me at the hospital. Cure me with a wire threaded into my brain. They still use them for depression even though they've just been banned for everything else.

"This isn't that kind of treatment. It's something different. More of a . . . service," says Gary. He leans forward. "Up to you, CC. It's that or Bethesda Medical."

Mom's eyes are pleading. Gary looks hopeful but haggard. He's aged ten years since that night.

I shudder as memory draws its sharp nails along the locked door again, leaving deep, ragged grooves. Whatever this "service" is, I don't know if I want it, but I'm certain I don't want to be in a cage, unable to decide my own fate. "Okay," I tell them. "I'll try."

Chapter Two

Data review.
Internal narrative: on.

Hannah Dietrich's Cerepin, installed and activated 11:49 a.m., June 1, 2068, manually deactivated for the 9th and final time at 10:32 p.m., August 22, 2069, contained 1,734 hours, 17 minutes, and 51 seconds of vid documentation, 1,092 hours, 4 minutes, and 25 seconds of which were not publicly available on her Mainstream channel. Due to several epochs of manual deactivation, GPS tracking and biostat data is irretrievable. The first manual deactivation occurred December 15, 2068. Total time of deactivation in the first 8 epochs was 30 hours, 31 minutes, and 2 seconds. Precise duration of the final deactivation epoch is undetermined; subject was pronounced dead at 5:23 a.m., August 23, 2069. The paramedic on scene noted her body temperature to be 36 degrees Celsius, suggesting she may have expired approximately 1 hour prior, ± 30 minutes. Rigor mortis had not yet set in. Given this evidence, the final deactivation is estimated to be 6 hours and 21 minutes, ± 30 minutes, in duration.

During much of that time, it appears that Hannah was dying. This is based on the postmortem evidence of catastrophic fractures to her right pelvis, right humerus, mandible, and right temporal bones. She was most likely conscious for at least part of that time, though the exact duration and extent of lucidity is unknown. Evidence at the scene, including the presence and pattern of bodily fluids on the marble flooring and on the palms of her hands, indicates she crawled 2.72 m from the final impact point at the base of the staircase.

No house data is available to clarify the sequence or timing of events. The house AI, "Franka" (manufacturer: Synthkortex, model number 27925, installed March 10, 2065, and last updated by admin Gary Dietrich August 4, 2069), was manually deactivated by user Cora Dietrich at 10:46 p.m., August 22, 2069, leaving only 14 minutes of vid surveillance and biostat information after Hannah Dietrich deactivated her Cerepin. Franka was reactivated by user Cora Dietrich at 4:59 a.m. August 23, 2069. No additional information is available for that epoch.

Cora Dietrich, reportedly inside the home for all or most of that time, also stated that she performed a manual deactivation on her own Cerepin in order to avoid online tracking and external monitoring from Gary Dietrich and Maeve Dietrich (née Jenkins). The biological and legal guardians of both adolescent subjects reported being in Saumane de Vaucluse, France, when the incident occurred.

Study of data from Cora Dietrich has not been possible. By law, her consent is necessary in order to remotely access data from her device. Consent has not been obtained.

Removal of Hannah Dietrich's Cerepin was complicated by the extensive damage to the nodule casing and to the subject's temporal bone, as well as Gary Dietrich's request to preserve the appearance of the cadaver as much as possible to enable an open-casket memorial. The damaged storage drive was recovered on August 28, 2069, and submitted for analysis. Retrieval programs were partially successful; the visual and audio data were available but scrambled. The documentation has now been loaded and prepared for analysis through specialized scaffolding programs.

Commencing review of vid documentation.

2:41 p.m., June 6, 2068

"God, this still feels so weird," Hannah Dietrich (henceforth referred to as "Hannah") says. Her visual focus is on her hands, fingernails painted blue and partially covered in holographic decals depicting bouquets of flowers with petals that appear to flutter as the air moves. There is a black smudge on the back of her right hand. "I think I'm recording? Yeah."

She laughs. The sound can be coded as bemusement. She looks around the room. A king-size bed, purple coverlet in disarray, six pillows in an asymmetrical pile, a yellow bathrobe draped across one corner. A wall screen, projecting an image of a waterfall, the illusion of water spilling across the carpeted floor. Clothing and shoes are dispersed in piles between the bed and the open closet door, where more clothes are hung. In the corner of the room, there is an easel, upon which is a canvas, 1 m square.

In front of the canvas is a stool, and on that stool are a palette and what appear to be deposits of oil paint. Beside the stool is a trunk, composite metal, approximately .5 m long with an extrapolated depth of 26 cm, lid open, containing tubes of oil paint and additional brushes.

Hannah approaches the painting. "My latest thing, obviously. It's just the underpainting, but I'm totally into this one. I've already given it a name. *Big Day.*"

The canvas is striped with red and black curving lines. Not recognizable as a representation of any specific object.

She walks away from the painting until she is in front of the wall screen. "Let me see if I can—and there it is." She issues another bemused laugh. Now the wall screen shows Hannah looking at herself. Short brown hair, wide-set eyes, iris color hazel. Highly symmetrical features. Objectively pleasing. Subject wears close-fitting black fabric pants colloquially known as "leggings" and a pale-blue short-sleeved tunic with three smears of what appears to be red paint on the left hip. Her feet are bare. "This is going to be fine," she says as she regards herself. "You're going to be okay." She stares at her image for 6 seconds and then adds, "You're going to make it okay."

A female voice becomes audible in the room. "Hannah, your father requests that I unlock your door so he can enter."

"Franka, wait," Hannah says. Her tone indicates apprehension or anxiety. She approaches the painting and turns it around on the easel, revealing the plastic frame and a blank back. "Okay. Go ahead."

There is the sound of the door sliding open, and Dr. Gary Dietrich (referred to hereafter as "Dr. Dietrich") enters the room. He is neatly groomed, with a short, trimmed beard and short, dark hair. His eyes are lighter than his daughter's but would still be coded as hazel. He is smiling, a full Duchenne smile, genuine, teeth showing. "They're almost here. ETA seven minutes. Ready?"

"Sure," says Hannah. She giggles. "Dad, you look sort of goofy."

"Maeve is used to my goofiness. Cora is, too." Dr. Dietrich's expression is soft, loving, as he looks at his daughter. "That was really nice, how you decorated her room. I think she's going to love that painting."

"I wanted her to feel at home," Hannah says. "We vid-chatted once, and I saw the New York skyline on one of her screens. We kind of bonded over it."

"I know she's not always the easiest person to talk to . . ."

"We got along fine. We both like Cynical Revolution and real coffee, and we both want to travel someday, and we both hate when Aristotle leans forward and raises his eyebrows when we take too long to answer a question."

Dr. Dietrich snorts. "I'll have my development team back off on his nonverbal prompts. I don't want a full-scale student rebellion on my hands. The government just re-upped the subsidy on that program, and we'll be in all fifty-two states by next year, nearly ninety percent market saturation."

"Yeah, you're not boring at all."

Dr. Dietrich chuckles as he glances at the canvas. "What's going on here?"

"None of your business."

"Yeah?" He smiles. "Will it be my business at some point?"

"No comment! Stop asking me! You know I can't lie to you."

He strokes her arm, his brow furrowing. Coded as low-intensity sadness. "You really have your mother's talent."

Hannah steps away from him and looks at herself and her father, depicted in the wall screen. They share a family resemblance in the configuration of the eyes and nose, the shape and prominence of the ears. When Hannah taps her Cerepin nodule, the mirror image changes back to a waterfall. She is looking at her hands again when her father says, "I know you miss her. Maeve understands that, too."

"It's okay," Hannah says. "I really like Maeve."

"This'll be an adjustment, though. We get that. You're allowed to have feelings. I just hope you'll talk to me about them."

"Of course I will." Hannah's voice is quiet.

"I'm the luckiest dad," Dr. Dietrich says. He pulls Hannah into a hug, and for 4 seconds all that is visible is the white fabric of his sleeve. "Hey—there's something I wanted to talk to—"

"Sir, the car has landed, and your guests are disembarking."

Dr. Dietrich releases Hannah, his abrupt movements suggesting minor emotional agitation. "Thank you, Franka. Are the attendants ready to unload their stuff?"

"Yes, sir. They will take them to the designated rooms. I also have the interactive preference forms ready for their completion."

"Perfect—I want them to feel at home. Want to help me welcome them?"

When Hannah looks down, he has taken her hand. She lets out an unsteady breath.

"Sure," she says. She follows him out the door, into a hallway with warm ambient light. At the end of the corridor is a foyer with a 10-m ceiling, partially open to the 2nd floor, with the front entrance to the house on 1 side, a wide, curved staircase on the other, and an ebony table in the approximate center, upon which sits a decorative arrangement of calla lilies. The walls are covered in blue damask. The staircase and floor are composed of brecciated marble.

The front door swings open. Dr. Dietrich walks forward as 2 people enter the home. He has released his daughter's hand. A woman with medium-length auburn hair and blue eyes smiles widely as he approaches. Cross-reference with the facial-recognition database identifies the woman as Maeve Jenkins, now known as Maeve Dietrich (hereafter referred to as "Maeve"). She opens her arms. He laughs and enfolds her in a hug, pressing his mouth to her hair. "God, it's good to see you. Welcome home."

"This is surreal," Maeve says. She turns to the adolescent girl who has entered behind her. The girl is blond and blue-eyed. She is frowning.

"Hi, Cora," says Dr. Dietrich. Cross-reference with the facial-recognition database identifies the adolescent girl as Cora Jenkins, biological daughter of Maeve Jenkins, now known as Cora Dietrich (hereafter referred to as "Cora").

Hannah uses her vision implant to focus on Cora's face. The girl's cheeks are wet, and her eyes appear swollen. It can be surmised she has been crying.

"Hey," says Cora.

Maeve gives her daughter a look that can be coded as concerned, though the situational cues are not specific enough to identify what exactly bothers her. She then turns to Hannah, and her smile returns. "You got your hair cut!"

Hannah's left hand skims past her periphery. Most likely touching her hair. "Do you like it?"

"You're a picture," Maeve says, laughter in her voice. "Come here and give me a hug."

Hannah hugs Maeve, but as she swings her gaze to the right, she captures Cora watching. The newly arrived girl's jaw is clenched. Hannah steps away from Maeve. "Hey, Cora," she says, tone indicating caution. "How was the flight?"

"Short," says Cora. Tonal analysis suggests irritation, possibly anger.

Maeve is frowning when Hannah looks at her again. Dr. Dietrich puts his arm around the woman. "Well, we have a surprise for you girls, but maybe, Hannah, you could show Cora her room first?"

"Fine with me," says Cora.

Hannah turns and starts to walk up the hallway, looking over her shoulder twice to view Cora. A canny strides out of a room 1 door down from Hannah's. Hannah mutters a "thank you" to him as he passes, and he inclines his head.

"Here it is," says Hannah, walking into a room of the same dimensions as her own. There is a neatly made bed with a white coverlet and matching shams on the pillows, a wall screen, and a closet, empty save for 2 stacked boxes. Cora stands in front of a framed painting, 1 m by 1.5 m, that hangs on the wall. It depicts the skyline of Washington, DC, the mirrored facades of skyscrapers reflecting the sun and the Capitol, the Washington Monument in the foreground, smaller than the buildings but drawing the eye. "Do you like it?"

Cora is quiet for 7 seconds, during which Hannah shifts her weight back and forth. "I guess."

Hannah lets out a breath. "I . . . thought you might . . ."

Cora turns to her and smiles. The zygomatic major is contracted but not the orbicularis oculi. This is not a genuine smile. "I like how you can see the Parnassus building right there next to the monument. Thanks. You did it yourself? I know you like painting. Mom won't stop talking about how talented you are."

"You don't have to keep it if you don't like it."

"How do you like your new room?" Hannah's gaze shifts to view Maeve as she enters with Dr. Dietrich behind her. They are holding hands. Their cheeks are flushed.

"It's great," says Cora. Both tone and smile indicate she is not being truthful.

"We want you to feel like this is your home," says Dr. Dietrich. "This is a big change from New York, I know, but I really think you're going to like it here. And you'll be at Clinton Academy with Hannah for the new school year—she'll look out for you."

"Yeah," says Cora without looking at Hannah. "No doubt. Thanks."

Maeve bites her lip and glances at Dr. Dietrich. He kisses her forehead. "Do you want to tell them, or should I?" he asks her.

Maeve grins. "I—"

"You want us to know you're getting married," says Cora, her body now moving in a low-intensity oscillation that could be described as rocking, forward and back. "You've decided that living together doesn't do justice to how serious your relationship is, so you've decided to make it official."

Maeve and Dr. Dietrich display identical reactions. Smile rapidly diminishing in intensity. Furrowed brow. Glance at Hannah. Return of smile. "I guess you overheard us . . ."

"The walls in the apartment were thin," Cora says.

"Dad?" Hannah asks in an unsteady voice.

Maeve and Dr. Dietrich rush over to Hannah, who holds her hands out. Her gaze drops to Maeve's left hand. The fourth proximal digit is now decorated with a ring (approximately 2-carat lab-cultured flawless diamond) that was not present when Maeve arrived.

"It's fine, guys!" Hannah's voice is now more even. "It's okay! You just caught me by surprise." She laughs. "I'm happy for you!"

"Well, I guess we really messed that up," Maeve says, rolling her eyes.

Dr. Dietrich lifts her hand and kisses it. "We're kind of feeling our way through this."

"When's the big day?" asks Hannah.

"We're thinking November 21," says Maeve. "Right before Thanksgiving?"

"A fall wedding," says Hannah. "I hope you're going to have a fabulous dress. Hell, I hope I'm going to have a fabulous dress!"

Maeve's reactive expression can be coded as happiness. "Maybe you girls can go through the catalogs with me? Choose a design?"

"We've got the best fabgen," says Hannah, sounding excited. She appears to be bouncing on her heels or jumping up and down, judging by the vertically oscillating cam perspective. "We can download just about anything! You could have something with a train if you wanted!"

"Sky's the limit for my girls," says Dr. Dietrich.

"This is awesome, guys, but I'm really tired." Cora is sitting on her bed, watching everyone else. "Maybe we can talk later?"

"Oh, of course," says Dr. Dietrich. His eyes are bright as he pulls Maeve back toward the hallway. "We've got some catching up to do anyway, and I bet you girls want some time to yourselves! Franka will let you know when dinner's ready. And don't get into any trouble." His laugh suggests that he believes trouble is improbable.

They exit. Hannah stays where she is.

"I think I'm going to take a nap," says Cora.

"How long have you known?" Hannah asks.

"Since last week. Like I said, the apartment was tiny, and the walls were basically paper."

"Are you mad?"

Cora eyes the doorway of her room. "No?"

"I didn't think you would be."

Cora's gaze snaps to Hannah's. For 11 seconds, they stare at each other.

"I just realized something," Hannah says. "That's going to make us sisters."

"Stepsisters," says Cora.

"No," Hannah replies, walking toward the bed. "Let's really be sisters. I've always wanted a sister."

Cora tucks a lock of blond hair behind her ear. Her expression can be coded as uncertain. "Do you really mean it?"

"Yeah," says Hannah. "I do."

End of vid capture, 3:27 p.m., June 6, 2068

Chapter Three

I try to put on privacy settings when I get to my room, but Franka informs me the rules have changed. "I will only report if I detect behavior that might reasonably be interpreted as self-harming," she tells me. "But I have been centrally programmed to disregard verbal requests for privacy that originate from your vocal signature."

I need Neda. She would know how to fix this. Assuming she's still willing to talk to me.

I give my closet a look full of longing. I took the pills from Hannah's painting box when I got home from the hospital a few days ago and put them in my room. I knew she'd stashed them in there. Funny, though—I don't remember seeing her take any. She liked to drink more than anything else.

I swallow hard as a scent memory twists my stomach. Blood and gin and lemonade and bile. Before I realize quite what I'm doing, I'm sitting on my bed, ripping off my socks. With a shudder, I throw them across the room and rub the soles of my feet over the carpet.

"Cora, your biostats are approaching specified thresholds—"

"Franka, I'm upset. I'm allowed to be upset! And they already know I'm upset, so you don't have to tell them!"

"It appears that you would prefer it if I do not notify you regarding the biostat thresholds."

"You're so perceptive," I mutter, flopping back on my bed. I move to pull the pillow over my face, then realize that Franka might reasonably interpret that as self-harming, so I just close my eyes. I need to figure out what to do.

I reach up and push the top of my Cerepin nodule with my index finger, and then I say my password. "Biometric and vocal verification accepted," says a female voice in my ear. "Please indicate the panels you wish to activate."

A display appears against my closed eyelids, white on black.

Biological systems monitoring
Neurological
Circulatory
Respiratory

Capture
Visual
Auditory

Mainstream
Home channel
Saved channels
Search

External communication
Message settings
Confidentiality settings
Forward block
Vid lock
Timed delete

Contacts

I enable all the primary panels, bringing the whole thing back online again. I silence the Mainstream feed immediately—the streaming vids and text make me want to bang my head against the wall—and then I call up the message space. As soon as I do, I'm informed I have twenty-three new messages, twenty-one of them from Neda. I also have one message from Mei . . . and another from Finn.

I take a few slow, deep breaths and look at Mei's icon. "Play."

Her face appears, a cream-colored cinder-block wall behind her. She was at school when she made this. It came in half an hour ago. Mei has lustrous black hair, delicate cheekbones, a narrow chin. She's the kind of effortlessly pretty, stylish girl I've always been jealous of. Like Hannah was. They'd been friends since elementary school when I showed up.

"I can't believe you did this," she says, glaring into her fingertip lens. "It's like you can't stand for Hannah to steal attention from you, even after she's dead!" Tears shine in her dark eyes, and for a moment her hand drops, showing me a few squares of the grimy floor. Then it's pointed at her face again, and her brow is furrowed. "I'm sorry. This whole situation is so messed up. Lara's told me about what she thinks happened . . . but I want to hear it from you. Com me back when you get this."

Yeah. That totally sounds like a conversation I want to have.

I'm not ready to look at Finn's message yet, so I select Neda's oldest message first.

In the vid, her hijab is purple, the fringed end of the scarf dangling over her shoulder. Her eyes look huge as she glares into her fingertip-cam, the size and shape of them accentuated by eyeliner—she gets the cat eye perfect every time. Her lips, as usual, are red, red, red.

"You'd better com as soon as you get this, because if you think I can't—" She presses those lips together, and I know she was probably about to threaten to hack my Cerepin, which is illegal, of course, and also nearly impossible. Neda's skills are fairly terrifying.

They could get her into trouble.

"Anyway." Her chin trembles. "Seriously, why didn't you com me? Did you actually try to jump off the roof? What happened?" She sniffles. "I mean, I know what happened, but I meant this morning. You should have commed. I would have . . ." She looks off to the side, grimacing as she tries to control herself. "Just com me, all right?"

If that was the first message she left, I don't even want to know what the twenty-first one looks like.

I have to check Finn's message now. I'm glad my stomach is empty.

His eyes are red rimmed, and so is the bottom of his nose, like he's been wiping it. The look he gives the cam is so tortured that the display blurs for a minute with my own tears.

"I need to talk to you," he whispers. "Did you try to hurt yourself because I sent that vid? Com me."

It was totally because of that vid. He sent it just before I arrived at school, and I just . . . couldn't take it. It was too much.

I briefly glance at the previous message from him, the one with the vid embedded. The Cerepin interprets my attention as a command to open it, and it begins to play. I open my eyes, letting in the light, and the display auto-adjusts, clouding the background so my visual focus is on Finn's face. His freckled, handsome face. His soft brown eyes. It feels like Leika just parked on my chest.

"I tried to visit you at the hospital, but they said you couldn't have visitors," he says, upper lip glistening with sweat. "I really wanted to see you, Cora. You have to believe me. I haven't been able to think about anything else." He's still in his room at his house, his wall screens displaying a virtual coral reef, gold and red and black-and-white-striped fish. He looks like he's about to cry, or maybe start throwing things. I can't tell. "I heard that you're not saying what happened, but I need to talk to you before you do. Please. Because I got this vid . . . well, you'll see when I got it. I need to talk to you, Cora. Please. I'm . . . so worried about you."

His face disappears, and I am looking at Hannah. Her eyeliner is smudged, and her cheeks look hollow, but that might be the lighting. It makes her brown hair look black. It's standing on end. Messy. She's leaning over, looking down. The tray ceiling above her frames her face and body—it's the ceiling above the second-floor landing that overlooks the foyer. "This isn't funny," she says. "I'm going to turn her back on."

"No you won't," I hear myself say, but my voice is slurred.

The cam view slides to the side, to the mostly empty gin bottle on the floor, before snapping back up to her. "Yeah, you went a little bit overboard, didn't you?" she says.

"Fuck you," the me in the vid says. So slurred. The cam view narrows. I'm squinting.

This vid was recorded and sent from my Cerepin.

"You need help," says Hannah. "You can't just keep threatening to kill yourself."

"Shut up. I did not."

She shakes her head, her brow all squinched. "I don't know what to do for you, CC. I'm trying, but . . . You have everything. I don't get it. Why would you want to die?"

I hear myself mutter a few inaudible curses, then belch.

Hannah's face twists in disgust. "Tonight was supposed to be fun."

I hear myself laugh. It's an ugly laugh. "Maybe you should go spend time with your friends, then."

Is that really what I sound like?

I don't remember any of this. But it sounds very, very familiar.

27

"Why do you always ruin everything?" she whispers. She wipes a tear from her face with the flat of her palm. Her long fingernails are daffodils, yellow and sunny.

Six of them were broken when she was found. The canny investigators located and bagged all the torn pieces.

Except for one. It hasn't been recovered.

I shudder and keep watching.

"I'm sorry," the me from that night says to Hannah. "I don't mean to."

"I know, CC. But you scare me. You're scaring me right now."

"I'll stop," drunk me mumbles.

"You have to. I can't take this anymore." She reaches down and does something. Strokes the side of my face maybe. Her own Cerepin is dark. She'd already turned all panels off.

Apparently mine was still on—the vid capture, at least. It reads 11:57 p.m., August 22, 2069. I haven't gotten up the courage to check my archive to see if there's anything else.

I watch as my hand, the cuff of my favorite black cardigan loose and sagging around my wrist, reaches up and slaps her. Once. A dull thud against the side of her face. Hannah winces as my hand falls out of cam view.

"That's all you've ever wanted to do, isn't it?" she says, her voice hitching. "Hurt me?"

For a moment, the display freezes on Hannah's miserable expression, a red mark on her cheek as she reaches down toward my face. The captured vid ends, and Finn's face appears again.

"Hannah attached a text," he says in the com message. "She wanted someone to see what you were acting like. She said you were threatening to kill yourself and she didn't know what to do. She didn't want to get in trouble with your parents. She didn't want *you* to get in trouble." He sighs and runs his free hand through his wavy hair, and it falls back down over his forehead. "She thought you might be upset because of us, because of me." He shakes his head. "I didn't see this until the morning after, I swear. Then I heard you were in the hospital, and that she . . ." He blinks up at the ceiling. "We need to talk. Do I need to send this vid to your parents? Or someone else? I dunno . . . just . . . Cora. I don't know. You have to com me."

And that's it. But it's more than enough. My fingers ball in the folds of my comforter, my ragged nails digging in, the scream held tightly inside me.

One of Hannah's last acts. Trying to get help for her monster of a sister. Stepsister. Adoptive sister. Monster. I never wanted Finn to know I was a monster. With him, I never thought I was.

"Visual display off," I tell the Cerepin, and the message screen blanks out, revealing my room again, sunlight filtering through lace curtains, everything white, too white, too pure. I am ruined, and nothing in here is right.

Now I've seen that vid twice. I still can't believe it was me. If I didn't know better, if I couldn't recognize my own voice, my own hand as it slapped my sister across her beautiful face, I would be tempted to believe she was talking to someone else. But I know. I *know*. If I go to my archived vid captures, I will find that vid stored there. And maybe others.

I told them. Mom. Gary. The police and paramedics who were there that morning. Hannah and I turned our 'Pins off the night before. We went into our core menus and switched off biostats specifically.

Our parents check those periodically, see. We knew that from experience.

I can't remember whose idea it was. It seemed like something she would suggest. But maybe it was my idea this time. We just wanted a few hours to get messed up, to party, to have fun before our senior year sucked us down into the pit of never-ending studying.

We didn't want Mom and Gary to know our blood alcohol content, something they could easily check remotely thanks to the physiosensors that came along with our Cerepins. If the sensors detect that you've exceeded certain parameters, if your heart rate goes way up or down, if your blood pressure spikes, if your breathing gets funky, or if your blood chemistry is altered, the Cerepin will automatically alert emergency services. Franka can do the same, sort of. Her flooring detects impact, and her sensors monitor body temperature, movement, the chemical composition of the air. If she picks up enough carbon monoxide, or a depressed or drastically elevated heart rate, or any of the other warning signs programmed into her system, she'll make the call.

She would have made the call that night if we hadn't turned her off. Hannah might have lived.

And turning Franka off? We had help with that.

I know everyone wants to know what happened, but I . . . can't. I know enough. Knowing more will break me, like it would have this morning if those cannies hadn't dragged me off the ledge. Now I'm wondering, though—did I turn everything in my Cerepin off? Did Hannah? If we didn't, what would those vids tell us?

"Nothing," I mutter, turning onto my stomach and wrapping my arms around my head. "She was drunk and she fell. It was a stupid, pointless accident."

Because Hannah *had* been drinking. Mom told me.

But she wasn't as drunk as I was. Mom told me that, too.

She said it with questions in her eyes, though. Questions I see whenever I look at her, whenever Gary's hazel eyes swing my way. They want to know . . .

What was I doing while Hannah was dying?

I flop onto my back and rub the soles of my feet over my coverlet, hard and fast so they turn hot with the friction. My throat constricts.

A small green light blinks in the upper right corner of my visual field. I have a new text. I focus on it to indicate I'm ready to read. It's Neda.

There you are. I've been waiting for you to come back.

"I was a mess this morning. I'm better now. Send."

Yeah, I'll believe that when I see it. Are you in the hospital?

So I guess she doesn't have GPS tracking on me . . . or she's playing dumb. "Home. Send."

Okay. And are you really all right? It's all over school. They're saying you tried to kill yourself.

I sigh. "I was thinking about it. Send."

And now? Be real.

Now? I'm still thinking about it. "Now I'm under lockdown at my house, and they made me agree to try some sort of treatment Gary's arranging." Whoa. When I read what I just said, it sounds super creepy. What the hell have I gotten myself into?

"Cora," says Franka, "I'm sorry to interrupt your conversation, but a guest has arrived."

"Okay . . . who is it?"

"Your father said it is an acquaintance of his, but he is indisposed at the moment. He asked if you would please answer the door and show the guest, Rafiq, to the library."

Gary loves to meet with his colleagues in the library. I think he enjoys showing off his collection of real paper books, sealed in glass cases to preserve their delicate pages. He loves it when they admire his mementos from all over the world, a handblown Murano-glass vase from Italy, fearsome Indonesian wooden masks with curved teeth and bulging eyes, an ox-hide Zulu shield and spear, a Japanese katana in its sheath, prominently displayed on a stand on his desk. I don't like going in there, but . . .

He's giving me a chance to be helpful and socially appropriate—and I sense a gentle *or else* here.

"Sure. Fine," I say to Franka. "Neda, I have to go act normal for a while so I don't end up getting my brain zapped at the hospital. I'll com you later. Send."

Whatever. You suck but I love you anyway. Take care of yourself and don't make me come after you. She attaches a fabbed vid of a squirrel wearing boxing gloves. It's almost enough to make me laugh.

I summon up a mirror on my wall screen. Ugh. I look terrible. My short hair is sticking up everywhere, and on me it does not look cute. I smooth it down, throw on a clean tunic and pants, and pad barefoot down the hall. The marble floor of the corridor is warm thanks to Franka, not icy like it was when—

I squeeze my eyes shut and turn my head away from the staircase when I reach the foyer. Gary wants me to show him that I can be a stable, normal human and that I'm willing to do as he asks. I need to do both if I want to stay free. I smooth my hair down again as I approach the front door. "You can open it, Franka."

The door swings open. Standing in the portico is a young man. Maybe a few years older than I am. Early twenties?

I gulp. Like, I actually hear myself do it. "H-hi." God, I'm staring. Black hair, olive skin, bold eyebrows, and the most soulful eyes I've ever looked into, fringed by thick black lashes.

He smiles, and something goes soft and melty inside me. "Good morning." His eyes flick to the side, probably reading his Cerepin display . . . except, he doesn't have a Cerepin. "It's a few minutes after noon, though, so that's not quite right. Good afternoon!"

I smile. I can't help it. His awkwardness kills some of mine. "Good afternoon! Come in."

He's still smiling. "Splendid." He steps inside and holds his hand out. "Rafiq. Nagi."

I shake his hand. It's warm and dry, and mine probably feels like cold raw meat. "Cora. Dietrich. I'm Gary's—"

"Daughter." Rafiq releases my hand and manages not to wipe his palm on his pant leg, which I appreciate. He looks around the foyer and then refocuses on me. "It's really nice to meet you, Ms. Cora Dietrich."

"Um. Cora is fine."

"Cora it is."

"Gary wanted me to show you into the library." I point. "It's this way." I lead him across the foyer, keeping my eyes trained on my destination. My bare feet are getting slick against the floor.

"It's the most beautiful day, weather-wise," Rafiq says, oblivious to my weirdness, or maybe just nervous to meet with my dad. Sometimes Gary invites young Parnassus associates over, a kind of audition for future management. I give Rafiq the side-eye. He looks a little young for that, and he's dressed in tan pants and a simple black shirt with a collar. He doesn't have any visible diamond-dust tattoos, and he doesn't appear to be wearing makeup, but then again, this guy doesn't need to. "I'd love to take a walk later," he adds.

We pass a window and I peer outside, toward the sloping back lawn and the river. The canny gardeners are hard at work, making sure it always looks like a paradise. "I guess it is kind of a pretty day."

Rafiq's eyes light up, like I've just made *his* day. We reach the library. "Franka, where's Gary?" I ask.

"Dr. Dietrich is running late," Franka replies. "He asked that you entertain his guest for a brief time."

I cringe. "Okay."

"It looks like this is an unpleasant task for you. I'm sorry," says Rafiq.

"No! Oh, god, no, I'm sorry. It's not you. I've had . . . a tough day."

Rafiq tilts his head. His eyes are so, so warm. "If that's true, then you're being especially generous, spending time with me." His voice is warm, too.

"Do you want to sit?" I wave my hand at the couch and then plop onto a cushy armchair to the right of it.

"Thank you." He walks over to the sofa and sits down, his back and shoulders straight and proper. "May I ask what made the day so tough?"

I shake my head, my throat tightening abruptly, my eyes stinging.

"That was intrusive of me. I'm sorry again."

"Not your problem. Just . . . can we . . ."

"Do you like fish?" he asks.

My mouth drops open. "What?"

"I'm changing the subject. I like fish. Watching them. How they swim. The canny fish don't quite capture the movements of the organic ones."

"I can't tell the difference."

"I can." He is looking at me intently now.

"I guess I'm not that observant. I've never really tried—they're close enough."

Rafiq is still watching me. He has the smoothest skin. "Close enough," he murmurs. "What does that mean, exactly?"

"Hey! Sorry about that," Gary says as he strides into the room with Mom. They're holding hands. She's a higher-up at Parnassus, too, and their relationship is common knowledge. I guess both of them are going to meet with Rafiq.

Wearing a bright smile, Mom looks back and forth between Rafiq and me. "So you two have met."

Rafiq nods. "Cora has been wonderful company."

"What do you think of this young man, Cora?" Gary asks.

This guy's job depends on *me* saying something nice? "Well, in the forty-five seconds I've known him—"

Rafiq leans toward me. "It's been three-hundred-five seconds," he whispers out of the corner of his mouth.

I snort and do some quick math. "Okay, in the five minutes I've known him, he seems . . . polite."

Rafiq has one lush black eyebrow arched.

"And he enjoys sunny weather and long strolls outside?"

He's still got that eyebrow arched, looking expectant.

"He's got a nice handshake. Very firm."

Gary chuckles. Mom's grin widens.

"And obviously he's very precise about the time," I add.

This time, Rafiq chuckles. "That's a good one," he says.

Er . . . "Also, he smiles a lot."

"Too much?" asks Gary.

"What?" I turn to my parents. "What are you asking me?"

Gary puts his arm around Mom, who looks a little anxious. He squeezes her shoulders. "Does he *smile* too much," he says, as if that clarifies anything at all.

Rafiq is no longer smiling. This poor guy.

"No! No. It's . . . nice," I say. "Friendly." I mean, despite everything that's happened today, he actually got *me* smiling.

Mom now looks more relaxed, but Gary's eyes are narrowed. "Hmm," he says.

If I cost Rafiq his job or a promotion, I won't be able to forgive myself. "Guys? Can I . . . talk to you . . . over there? Or something?"

"You can say whatever you want to say in front of me," says Rafiq. He doesn't look upset, but I don't know him well. He might be dying inside for all I know. "I don't mind."

Mom and Gary look at each other.

"Rafiq," says Gary, "go to sleep."

Rafiq's eyes fall shut, and he goes perfectly still.

A wave of hot tingling rolls outward from my chest. "What-what-what . . ."

Rafiq sits upright on the couch, feet flat on the floor, hands folded in his lap, looking completely relaxed. His chest does not move. No part of him moves.

"I think he just passed an important test," Gary tells Mom. "Don't you?"

I tear my eyes from Rafiq. "He's a canny."

Mom nods. "But the most advanced one you've ever met! He's got biosynthetic components that are revolutionary. He's really special, in other words." She looks anxious again.

"Amican—that's the manufacturer—hasn't even put them on the market yet," Gary says. "I had a contact there do me a favor."

"We really think he could help you," Mom says.

I swallow the sudden excess of saliva pooling in my mouth. "This is what you were talking about. The thing you wanted me to agree to."

"You need someone available for you twenty-four seven," Gary says. "For the foreseeable future, that's what Rafiq's going to do. He'll keep you safe, and he'll help you heal."

"A babysitter." I stand up, trembling. "You got me a canny babysitter?"

"No, honey!" Mom says. "He's a therapeutic companion."

"He's going to help you talk about what happened," Gary adds.

Mom's jaw clenches. "That's not his primary purpose. He's supposed to help her get better, like we talked about."

Gary puts up his hands. "That's what I meant."

"I don't care what you mean," I say. "I'm not doing this." I walk around the chair and head for the hallway. "This is nuts." My cheeks are hot enough to melt plastic. I liked him. I thought he was cute. And he's a robot. I shudder and clutch my stomach as I make my escape.

"Cora! You get back in here right this minute!" Gary's voice is like a neural disruptor, stopping me in my tracks. He is scowling when I turn around. "You said you'd give this a chance. I took you at your word."

"I had no idea what you guys had in mind!"

"Cora," says Mom, her voice trembling. "It's going to be okay. We just want—"

"Is it worse than the hospital?" Gary asks loudly. His index finger hovers close to the Cerepin nodule on his right temple. "If so, I can have Leika take you straight there."

"This isn't fair," I shout. "I deserve some privacy, not some creepy canny following me around constantly and pretending to be my friend!"

"Privacy to do what, exactly?" Gary asks.

Mom has tears in her eyes. "I hate to say this, but we can't trust you right now."

"I can't get better if I'm being smothered." Nor can I pop a few pills and get a decent night's sleep, or turn off my Cerepin and drown myself in the Potomac. But I guess that's the idea.

"If you show us you can cope," Gary says, "maybe I'll change some of his settings. But not until then." He comes over to me and puts his hands on my shoulders. "Come on, CC. Your mom and I only want you to get better. We're already dealing with so much. Please do your part—by letting us take care of you. Will you do that for us?"

I look up at him. His eyes are too familiar. Too like his daughter's. Suddenly, I feel like I'm standing at the edge of the roof again and the wind is gusting hard. I glance at Rafiq, who is not real. Who is like one of those canny fish. A good enough fake to fool me. Probably because I am a fool.

"Yeah," I say. "Okay. You win." Looks like I'm going to have to do some fooling of my own.

"Oh, thank god," Mom says, all choked up.

Gary presses his lips together and nods. "Good. This will be good." He turns around. "Rafiq, wake up."

Rafiq opens his eyes and blinks several times, shifting in his seat as if he's making himself more comfortable, only I know now that he's somehow been programmed to move like that so that he looks real and alive. His gaze glides over to me and my parents, and he smiles. He looks innocent. Hopeful.

I turn my face away.

"Did I get the job?"

"Congratulations, Rafiq," says Gary. "You're hired."

Chapter Four

Data review.
Internal narrative: on.

4:23 p.m., November 21, 2068

Hannah's gaze scans a ballroom, in which 8 crystal chandeliers light the space, and 50 rows of chairs face an archway of authentic flowers. People have gathered on either side of an aisle lined with a silk runner. Hannah curses under her breath as her attention closes in on a girl with blond hair formally styled in a twist with a red rose tucked into the swirl. This girl is Cora. She is wearing a full-length dress of purple tulle.

She is speaking to a young male with wavy brown hair. Cross-reference with facial-recognition software indicates the male is Finn Cuellar, 16 years of age, hereafter referred to as "Finn." As she interacts with Finn, Cora's smile is significantly more genuine and intense than in 76% of previously analyzed vids. She laughs at something the young man says. Her fingers brush his sleeve.

Hannah draws in a sharp breath, as though stunned or surprised. Her vid display is briefly overwritten by an incoming com.

Mei: Want me to rescue Finn?

Another message comes in 2 seconds after the first one:

Lara: She won't keep her stupid hands off him. Want me to slap her for you?

Hannah chuckles. "New group message, Lara, Mei. I'm glad she's having fun. Finn can take care of himself. Send."
Her words appear in the top left corner of her vid display.

Mei: This sucks, Hann. You sure?

"What kind of girlfriend would I be if I didn't trust him? Send."

Lara: The smart kind?

"Are you saying I'm stupid?"
The app inquires as to whether she would like to send her latest comment.
"No," Hannah mutters. "Never mind. New message. Cora." When the prompt appears, she continues. "I'm helping Maeve get ready. You should get in here. Send."
She turns, letting the door to the ballroom close behind her, and walks down a hallway. Canny attendants stride past her carrying large arrangements of purple, red, and orange flowers.

End of vid capture, 4:28 p.m., November 21, 2068

4:36 p.m., November 21, 2068

Hannah enters a dressing area with multiple wall screens, all on the "mirror" setting, and cushioned chairs positioned in front of tables, each displaying an array of decorative cosmetics. Maeve Jenkins, soon to be Maeve Dietrich, sits in one of those chairs as a canny stylist pins a curl into place on the back of Maeve's head. Maeve is wearing an ivory-colored dress with a corseted top and a ruffled skirt. She smiles into the mirror when she sees Hannah approaching. The mirror reveals that Hannah is wearing a purple dress identical to Cora's, and her short brown hair is sleek, with curls against her temples.

"There you are," says Maeve. She searches the mirror, then turns around and looks over her shoulder. "Is Cora coming? She was supposed to bring the pearl bracelet."

"I'm sure she'll be here any minute," Hannah says, her gaze flicking around the room, alighting on a door marked "Restroom" and 3 other tables with chairs. "And I think I saw her put the bracelet in her bag before we left the house."

Maeve's face relaxes in an expression of relief. "It was so important to Gary that I wear it today." She purses her lips, indicating contemplation. "Are you sure it's okay with you, though?"

"It was my idea," says Hannah. "My mom would be happy that Dad found someone as nice as you. And I'm happy, too."

Hannah looks down as Maeve reaches up to take her hand. "Your dad's a pretty special guy, Hannah," says Maeve. "I want to keep making him happy, because that's what he's done for me. Given me my happiness back."

"Dad's one of the good ones," Hannah says.

Maeve nods. The canny that was styling her hair steps back and pauses, head tilted.

"It looks wonderful, Phaedra," says Maeve before looking at Hannah again. "Speaking of good ones, you said I was going to get to meet your special boy today?"

Hannah smiles, but her orbicularis oculi muscle does not contract. "Finn. He's Dr. and Mr. Cuellar's younger son."

"Oh, yes! Did I meet him at the Independence Day barbecue? He's cute! And so nice. He was showing Cora how to play the holographic croquet, wasn't he? I hadn't seen her smile like that since we moved."

Hannah laughs and smiles, but facial-muscle movements again indicate her smile is not genuine.

Maeve tugs at her hand. "Hey, are you all right? Have you talked to your dad today? I know he wanted to talk to you before the ceremony."

"He found me," Hannah says. "And he told me what he's doing."

"And?" Maeve furrows her brow, and her eyes examine Hannah's face. "We just thought . . . it would make our family complete. Your dad thought you would be okay with it."

"I'm fine," says Hannah. "I'm happy. I love Cora."

"I know." Maeve bows her head and holds Hannah's hand between both of hers. "I'm so thankful that you and Gary came into our lives. You're the best thing that ever happened to us."

Hannah kneels quickly and tips Maeve's chin up with her fingertip. "Don't you dare ruin your makeup by crying!" she says, but her voice is gentle and indicative of good humor.

Maeve blinks, and the canny attendant, who has a female appearance and shoulder-length brown hair, offers her a cloth, which she takes and uses to dab the area around her eyes. "This feels like a dream," says Maeve.

"But it's real," says Hannah. "We're just that lucky."

"Mom!" Hannah's view swings to capture Cora as she walks in, her cheeks flushed. "Sorry. I lost track of time."

"The Cerepin was supposed to help with that," Maeve says with a laugh. "That's why I let you get one before school started."

"I forgot to set an alarm," says Cora, her fingers fluttering by her right temple, where a Cerepin nodule is visible. Her eyes meet Hannah's, but she looks away quickly and picks at a bit of loose skin around her right ring finger. Then she nibbles at it.

Hannah takes Cora's hand and pulls it away from her mouth. "Don't do that! It's gross, and you'll ruin your manicure. Seriously, girls, you have to pull it together."

Again, her tone appears teasing, but Cora rolls her eyes as she curls her fingers and hides her nails against the palm of her hand. "I guess we're not as high class as you're used to."

"Cora!" says Maeve, her tone indicating anger. She clears her throat. "Please."

Cora's head tilts. She seems puzzled. "Sorry?"

"I just want this day to be a happy one," says Maeve. "Did Gary talk to you, by any chance?"

"Haven't seen him."

"I think he wanted it to be a surprise," Hannah says.

Cora opens her mouth, her raised eyebrows suggesting curiosity, but Maeve speaks before she has a chance. "Can I have the bracelet, please, Cora? I need to get out there." She points to her Cerepin nodule. "The photographer just let me know she's ready. You girls can join us in about half an hour, maybe? We should be ready for you then."

"Got it right here." Cora walks over to a table in the corner and pulls out the chair, revealing a purple handbag, 30 cm by 15 cm. She opens it and rakes her fingers through the contents. After 4 seconds, she begins to scowl. "Um . . ."

"Please tell me you didn't forget it," says Maeve.

"I remember putting it in here," says Cora.

"I saw her," says Hannah. "She totally remembered it."

Cora gives her a brief smile before continuing to examine the contents of her handbag. "I can't believe this." She looks back toward the door.

"Did you leave it in here the whole time, or were you carrying it around?" asks Hannah. "Where have you been since we got here?"

"I was in the ballroom." Cora shakes her head. "But I left it in here."

"Where someone could have stolen it?" asks Maeve. Her tone suggests displeasure. Impatience.

"I'm sure we'll find it," says Hannah.

"Cora." Maeve's tone is even, but there is a tremble in her voice that suggests agitation. "I trusted you with that bracelet." She glances at Hannah. "You know it's not just a piece of jewelry."

Hannah places her hand on Maeve's shoulder. "Thank you," she murmurs.

Cora closes her eyes and takes a deep breath. "Okay. I'll go retrace my steps in case I maybe dropped it or something. I'll find it."

"Good," says Maeve as Cora walks quickly from the room.

Maeve gets up. "I'd better get out there! See you in a bit." She clutches at the ruffles of her skirt to lift the hem from the floor and walks through a doorway as the canny holds the door.

Hannah turns back to the mirror. She stares at herself, her gaze tracing from the toes of her slippers, up the frothy skirt, past the sash at her waist, across her chest, up to her eyes. For 22 seconds, her focus is unbroken. Then she reaches up and taps her Cerepin nodule.

End of vid capture, 4:54 p.m., November 21, 2068

10:49 p.m., November 21, 2068

Hannah walks into the ballroom, the door held open for her by a canny.

The lights are dimmer than before, the crystals in the chandeliers giving off a low-intensity glow as a band plays. The room has also been rearranged since the last vid capture; now there are approximately 50 round tables that seat 8 persons each, and a dance floor at the far end. As Hannah goes deeper into the room, her focus rests on Cora, who is sitting at a table at the edge of the dance floor. The sweep of Hannah's gaze reveals the subject of Cora's visual concentration—Dr. Dietrich and Maeve. Other couples are also dancing, including Finn Cuellar and a middle-aged woman that the facial-recognition database indicates is Dr. Lorna Cuellar, his mother.

"You finished dancing with Finn," Hannah says as she sits down next to Cora.

"He wanted to cheer me up. But then his mom cut in."

Hannah uses her visual enhancement to zoom in on Maeve's unadorned wrist. "Finn's a great guy. He could tell you were upset."

"I ruined everything. Mom's so mad, and you hate me. Gary does, too."

Hannah scoffs. "Did you hear anything Dad said during the ceremony?"

"He probably regrets deciding to adopt me. Mom probably wishes she'd never let him."

Hannah's head falls back. She is focused on the ceiling. "God, why are you always feeling sorry for yourself? It was *my* mom's bracelet."

"Don't you think I know that?" Cora asks. "I think someone stole it from my bag."

"Really? That's pretty unlikely with this crowd. Plus, the cannies said no one unauthorized entered the dressing room." Hannah's hand, fingernails dark but sparkling, sweeps across the cam view. "But sure. Blame it on someone else if you want."

She turns to Cora, whose eyes glisten with tears. "I didn't mean to lose it!" Cora says.

"I'm sure Maeve and Dad believe you. I mean, why would you lie?"

"Do *you* believe me?"

"Of course," says Hannah, reaching over and taking Cora's hand. "You're my sister."

Cora does not blink as she regards her hand joined with Hannah's.

"You have to go easy on yourself, CC."

"Why do you keep calling me that?"

"I think it has a nice ring to it."

"Okay," says Cora. She's still looking at their hands. "Thanks for not hating me, I guess."

"You should try not hating yourself sometime. It's pretty neat."

Cora raises her head. "I don't hate myself."

"Whatever you say." Hannah watches her father and new stepmother embracing on the dance floor, swaying to the music. "They're going to be here for a while. Dad told us we could go whenever we wanted." She shifts her attention to Finn and his mother, who are walking with a few others toward the main exit of the ballroom.

When Hannah glances over, Cora is also watching Finn. "I bet you're going to miss him," Cora says to Hannah.

"They'll be back on Sunday. They always spend Thanksgiving in California."

"So," says Cora. "We're on our own."

"Just the two of us," says Hannah. "Better than being shipped off to relatives we barely know. And at least we have a chef. Drake always makes the most amazing turkey, and it's the real deal, not lab-genned."

Cora gives Hannah a tentative smile. "I guess this could be fun."

"I guarantee it will," Hannah replies.

End of vid capture, 11:02 p.m., November 21, 2068

Chapter Five

I've been in the shower for over half an hour when Franka turns off the water.

"Cora, your mother wants to speak with you, and she also stated that you are most likely clean at this point."

I lean against the tiled wall, hair dripping, skin pink. If she'd let me, I would have stayed in here the rest of the day, letting the spray sting my face. "I thought she wanted me to hang with my babysitter."

"She is waiting in your room."

I grab a towel and scrub myself dry, rubbing until it hurts. Then I throw on my genned robe. When I nod, Franka opens the door to my room. Mom is sitting on my bed. She's wearing her full-body exercise skin, sapphire blue. "I just finished my session," she says. "I wanted to give you a chance to calm down."

I pull my robe tighter around me and drop into a cushy gel chair that turns cool when it senses my overheated weight. "Did you honestly think I wouldn't be upset?"

She purses her lips and looks down at my coverlet. "No, I knew you would be. Gary suggested it a few days ago, and at first I told him no." Her eyes meet mine. "But then you . . ." She grimaces and lowers her head again.

The lump in my throat feels as big as my fist. "I said I was sorry," I whisper.

She shrugs. "I appreciate that, but it doesn't change whatever reason caused you to try to hurt yourself. And you have to understand, Cora, all I want is for you to be happy. I know that you haven't loved DC like I'd hoped, but—"

"I don't know why you guys think I've been so miserable! But . . ." I am on such dangerous ground right now. I can feel it cracking, fissures radiating out beneath my feet.

"I know," Mom murmurs, saving me from crashing through. "Hannah . . . she was such a bright light, and without her, it's pretty dark." She smears a tear across her cheek.

I am huddled in this chair, and the urge to rock is almost overpowering. "Giving me a canny babysitter won't bring her back."

"But it might bring *you* back."

"Not following." My arms are crossed, wrapped around my chest.

"He's not just a babysitter, as you keep calling him. This canny has the brain of a therapist. His consciousness is more complex than anything that's been created before. He can help you get better if you let him."

"Gary doesn't care how I feel. He just wants to know what happened that night. It's like he wants to blame me."

"That's not fair," she says. "You have to understand where he's coming from."

I do, and it terrifies me. "Mom. I'm . . ." Without words. I'm not great with them anyway, not like *she* was. All I know is there is something big and dark inside me, and I don't know how to get rid of it. This will never get better, no matter how perfect my robot therapist is. But it doesn't matter. Arguing won't help. If I throw a tantrum and fight, they'll send me away. If I start talking, I'm afraid I wouldn't know when to stop . . . and someone would probably *take* me away.

I have to handle this in a smart way.

I wish I were smarter. "I told you guys I'd give it a chance, and so I will."

She slips off the bed and drops to her knees so we're eye to eye. "Cora, if I lose you, too, that'll be the end of me." Her eyes are so full of tears that they overflow at once, straight lines down her curved cheeks.

She pulls me to her, and I melt into her hug. It smashes over me, the memories of just her and me, when we were a team and it was more than enough. For me, at least. I remember so clearly when I realized that she needed more than me to be happy, that she always had. Now I bury my head against her neck and hold on. Grief is an animal inside me, settled in its cave.

A green light flashes in the upper corner of my visual field. I have a waiting message.

Mom lets me go. "I'll let you get dressed," she says. "Maybe you can go for a walk around the grounds?"

"With the canny, you mean." It's funny—he said he wanted to take a walk. Before I even realized what was happening, he was already hard at work doing what his mechanical mind had been programmed to do.

Mom is on her feet now, heading for the door. "He seemed like a nice young man. And he was eager to spend time getting to know you. The more he knows, the more he can help." She looks so hopeful that it hurts me.

"Thanks, Mom."

"I'm going to shower and head to Parnassus, but I'll be back tonight. We can have dinner together." She swallows hard. "As a family. Sound good?"

I nod, even though I want to scream and run. But she leaves, so that's a win, because I can't hold it together in front of her anymore. I lower my head to my knees and give in to the demand of my body and brain. The rocking drives everything else away, and I'm carried by the roll and jerk, forward and reverse. With each repetition, I'm more eager for the next.

The green light flashes again. Two new messages. And the canny is waiting, and if I don't stop, someone's going to come in here and get me. My fingers curl around my shins, fingernails divoting flesh. With a pointed look, I open the message space and sigh with relief when I see that it's not Finn, not Mei, not Lara. It's Neda again.

Just checking in. Answer when you can.
Also, don't look at your tags until tonight.

I read that last one twice as gratitude washes over me. If I know her, she's probably breaking into the channels of all the kids who posted vids of me at school this morning. Over the last year, Neda's hackery has reached a whole new level, and with one exception, which was totally not her fault, she uses her powers for good. She deserves a better friend than I could ever be, but for some reason, she chose me.

Another text pops up.

Also, I'm glad you're alive. Did I say that before? Don't be dead. It would piss me off.

"Reply," I say. I send her a quick message explaining that I've got a new canny shadow and that I'll tell her all about it when I can. I don't say anything about the last text.

I'm not in a position to make promises right now. Not honest ones, at least.

I towel-dry my hair and toss on some freshly genned clothes. I avoid looking at myself in a mirror, because I don't want to know. I'm spending my afternoon with a robot, so it doesn't matter anyway.

Rafiq is in the hallway when I emerge, pressed against the wall as if he wants to stay out of the way. He appears to be looking at one of Hannah's paintings, which Gary had framed and hung on the wall while I was in the hospital. It shows two people with their arms around each other, and the strokes and slashes of paint around them are red. Blue. Orange.

"Dr. Dietrich told me your sister, Hannah, painted this," says Rafiq as I approach. "He said it is you and Hannah, hugging. He said it shows how much she loved you."

Hugging? That's not what it looks like to me. Not at all. "She was pretty talented," I mumble, my eyes on the runner that covers the marble floor. I can't look at the artwork without feeling sick.

Rafiq turns to me. He really moves like a human. He even shifts his weight from foot to foot. He blinks. His smile is friendly with a hint of uncertainty. Whoever created him is a total genius. "Your parents suggested we walk. Do you have a place you like to walk?"

"We could just go out back. There's a trail along the river. There are actual fish." I hazard a glance at his face. "You said you liked fish."

For the third time today, Rafiq's eyes go a little wider, his lush brows rise, his lips twitch upward. It's such a fragile look, and suddenly I'm tempted to poke at his face to see what it feels like.

I know better, though. "So I guess that's a yes."

"Lead the way," he says. "How do you know they are actual fish rather than artificial beings?"

I roll my eyes as I walk through the back hall and head for the deck. "I guess I don't. I've already proved I'm easily fooled."

"If you're referring to your assumption that I was human, I wouldn't call that proof. I am in many ways indistinguishable."

I look him up and down. His hair is ruffled by a cool breeze when I open the door. His face . . . it's perfect. That might be his only flaw, his only tell. No zits, no spots, just smooth, light brown, and soft looking. "What's your skin made out of?"

He clears his throat. *Clears his throat.*

"Oh—is that personal?"

He stops walking and blinks. "I do not actually have that information. I would tell you if I could."

51

His throat-clearing reaction must be programmed. It's a cue—step off. He's protecting his maker's trade secrets or something. He's just a freaking machine, operating on a very complex protocol. "So what am I supposed to do?" I ask as we descend the steps from the deck and our feet hit the short grass of the back lawn. "You want me to talk about my childhood?"

"It's not about what I want."

"Oh, right. Are you even able to want things?"

He looks thoughtful, his head tilted and his eyes on the path as we walk along the edge of the river. The greenish water ripples beneath an early fall gust. "I think my wanting might be different from yours."

"Different? But you do want things?"

"I . . . want you to self-regulate appropriately. I want you to stay safe."

"That seems more like your programming. You're *programmed* to keep me safe."

"It feels like wanting."

"How do you know?"

He laughs. "You are very smart."

"No I'm not."

"Who told you that?"

"It's more something I've figured out over the years."

"What else have you figured out over the years?"

"Oh, that was a good one! Nicely done."

He furrows his brow. "Am I already failing?"

The look on his face makes me feel like a jerk. "No, Rafiq, you're doing fine. It's not your fault you got assigned to me."

"I am happy I was assigned to you."

I sigh. "Okay." He reminds me of a puppy, all eagerness and bright eyes. Less a babysitter than a new pet. At least he's cute. "Are you water-proof? If I jump in this river, do you have to fish me out?"

"I can swim. And I can do CPR." He holds up his palm. "I have a defibrillator for use in emergencies."

"Yikes."

He looks down at his hand. "Is that yikes? I hoped it would be reassuring."

"It's yikes if you want to pretend to be human."

"I'm not pretending, Cora. I'm sorry about our initial meeting. I realize now that it left you feeling mistrustful. Your father thought it would prove to you that I am able to be of service to you in a way most artificial beings cannot be."

"Because you're loaded up with therapy scripts. They told me."

"They're not scripts, but yes, I have extensive knowledge of therapeutic protocols deemed successful in clinical trials."

"Is this conversation a protocol?"

He smiles at me, and unbidden, it makes my heart beat a little faster. "We're developing rapport. It is one of the key factors in therapeutic efficacy."

"How about using normal words? Is that one of the key factors, too?"

His laugh is so real sounding. "Thank you for this feedback!"

He's such a weird combination of normal and robotic, sexy and yet childlike. I can't decide what kind of chills he gives me. "Anytime. So, therapeutic rapport. You do that by being a nice guy?"

"It's something we do together."

More chills. God, there is something wrong with me. "Okay, so it's about the back-and-forth. We can just talk about nothing?"

"Should I have a more specific goal, do you think?"

"Oh, I'm pretty sure you already do."

The little pebbles of the path crunch beneath our shoes as we walk. "I'd like to hear more about things you like," he says, "and things you don't like."

I decide to play his game. Harmless enough. "I like this river. I like the fall. I like . . . toast with real honey and synth butter. I like tea. I like rain and comfortable shoes and the moment my individual learning sessions with Aristotle end each day. I like old trip-hop music and the smell of wood fires. I like it when people are nice to me. I like my friend Neda. I like Christmas and . . . I can't think of anything else right now."

"Do you like painting?"

I flinch. *"No."*

"Oh."

"Why did you ask me that?"

"Your father suggested to me that you enjoy it." Rafiq's brown eyes focus on my hands. I realize my fingers are clasped and twisting.

I pull my hands apart and wipe them on my pant legs. "Gary said . . . ? No, that was Hannah's thing. Not mine."

"Art can be quite freeing. An opportunity to express oneself without words. Do you agree?"

I think of that painting in the hallway. "Absolutely." I walk a little faster.

"You're upset."

"Wow, Rafiq, you're a real pro."

He keeps pace with me easily and gracefully, even though I'm almost jogging. "When we discuss your sister, your heart rate rises dramatically."

"Now you're getting creepy."

"You are surely aware that I am equipped with biostat sensors that can—"

"Yeah, I *know*. Just don't remind me."

"You don't want to be reminded that I know things humans cannot know without the aid of technology."

"Ignorance is bliss." And oblivion is heaven.

"Sometimes, when you avoid something, your fear of it grows."

I slow down. He's going to keep up with me no matter how fast I run. "Maybe because it's something you should actually be scared of."

He frowns. "What are you scared of, Cora?"

"Are you serious?"

"I am." He gestures toward a bench on the riverbank.

I sit down, breathing hard. "This isn't fair. None of this is fair."

He sits next to me, looking out across the water to the trees on the other side. We've walked almost to the edge of the property, and I can see the grand house of my multi-trillionaire adoptive father hulking on its hill, casting its red-brown reflection in the dark water. It wavers and shakes, shifting in and out of focus. "I never thought I would live in a place like this," I murmur. "Have you ever seen a house like that one?"

He shakes his head. "You've been here for approximately one year?"

"A little over. We lived in Brooklyn before."

"Just you and your mother?"

"Since I was about five."

"And before that?"

My eyes close. "My dad lived with us."

"I am inferring that you do not have happy memories of that time."

"Infer all you want." I have a few. Just not many. "He used to take care of me while Mom traveled for work. Then she kicked him out. I think he lives in Cascadia now. I don't think he ever wanted to have a kid, and I'm pretty sure I was an accident. Anyway. Mom used to give me Christmas presents and pretend they were from him so I would think he actually cared about me, but I knew. I always knew it was just her."

"How do you feel about her attempted deception?"

"She did it because she didn't want me to feel unwanted." Oh, god. My heart is like a clenched fist. I clutch the edge of the bench and force myself not to rock. "She tries to protect me as much as she can." It's just that sometimes she fails.

"You know your mother well."

"We were best friends," I blurt out, but I stop when I hear the tremble in my voice.

"You feel like you've lost that connection."

More like it was one-sided, but that's embarrassing. "No, I just got older, and she found Gary. We're still good, just . . . it's not the same, obviously. But not in a bad way. I'm glad she's happy. She really deserves to be happy." And now she's worried and grieving and scared, and what I did this morning made it worse. I'm a walking disease.

And if she and Gary see that vid Finn sent me? They'll see how it was that night. They'll see how I slapped my sister only a few hours before she died.

Gary would probably give it to the police.

Rafiq is watching me try to hold it together. He can hear my heartbeat. "Do *you* deserve to be happy, Cora?"

I laugh nervously. "How is this conversation supposed to be helping, again?"

"It seems you think it is not helping." He places his hands on his thighs, his fingers splayed out.

"Don't take it personally. You just sound very therapisty."

"Therapisty." He looks bemused.

I chuckle. "It sounds a little like a bad word."

He gives me a sly smile. "Maybe it *is* a bad word."

"Feel free to tag it that way, or however you manage language learning."

He smiles. "I have done that. We have invented a new profanity."

"So this wasn't a total waste of time." I'm not on the verge of crying now, at least.

"Time spent getting to know you could never be a waste," he says. "I would like to know even more."

"Yeah? What about you?" I ask quickly. "Does this work both ways? How am I supposed to feel comfortable with you if all we ever do is talk about me?"

"I will tell you whatever I can, if it would make you more comfortable."

"Okay. Do you sleep?"

"I do have a rest period during which I process data and analyze patterns to enhance my performance. It's like dreaming, I think."

"Does it involve you showing up naked to school or being able to fly, only really badly, like you can't quite get off the ground?"

He sits back a little. "No."

"Not so much like dreaming, then. Got it. Do you eat?"

He shakes his head.

"That's too bad. You're missing out." As soon as I say it, it feels mean. "But I guess it's convenient. No mustard on your face, no chocolate on your fingers. How old are you? How long have you been around? How do cannies measure that, anyway?"

"My consciousness was brought online on August 23."

I turn my face away from him. My feet are sliding back and forth over the grass, stripping it out of the dirt. "So basically, you're a baby." Who was born the day that Hannah died.

"If I were human, that would be true."

I look over at him, his perfect face, his perfect body. If he were human, I would be stumbling over my words and possibly drooling. "If you're a therapist, how come you're not . . . I don't know. Aristotle, the AI teacher? He's an old guy. He's nothing like—" I flail my arm toward Rafiq's chest.

"You think I should be an old guy?"

I shrug.

He looks down at himself. "I am a prototype being, but this body . . ." For a moment, I swear, he looks so human. Thoughtful. Maybe a little lost. "It was in use, before."

"For what?"

He clears his throat.

"Does that mean you don't know, or you do know and you're not allowed to say?"

He clears his throat again. This time, it almost looks like it hurts. "Is there anything else you'd like to know?" he asks softly.

"Say one thing that's not a canned therapeutic response." I'm on the verge of stepping out onto the high wire, and I need him to pull me forward. But I can't unless . . . "Say one thing that's just Rafiq, something you came up with all on your own. Can you do that?"

He is quiet, and I look over at him. The wind has blown his hair into a funny pyramid on the top of his head, and on impulse, I reach over and smooth it down. He blinks at me. "I liked that."

"Okay," I say, feeling a little breathless. "I guess that counts."

Chapter Six

Data review.
Internal narrative: on.

3:30 p.m., January 20, 2069

Hannah stands in the hallway, looking toward the foyer. Her message light is blinking in the top right corner of her visual field, and she focuses on it. Messaging indicates it is from Finn Cuellar.

When are you coming over?

"When I feel like it. Send. Close message space."

The hallway becomes visible again, and Hannah turns toward a closed door. She knocks. Her fingernails are red, and there are holographic decals depicting a male who might be yelling or singing.

No discernible sound comes from inside the room. Hannah opens the door 10 seconds after knocking. "Hey," she says. Her gaze takes in a prone figure, Cora, who is lying in her bed with the covers pulled up to her chin. She is on her side, knees drawn up in what is colloquially referred to as a fetal position.

"I watched the inauguration with Dad," Hannah says. "We're all doomed, according to him. He told me that his boss thinks the new pres is going to target Parnassus because that stupid little head case, Marguerite Singer, thinks Aristotle killed her dad or whatever."

"Her father committed suicide after he lost his job, Hannah. Have you seen her vids?"

"Why would I? It's all crybaby stuff. It has nothing to do with reality."

Only Cora's eyes move, snapping up to meet Hannah's. "It's probably very real to her."

"Would you have voted for sleazy Sallese, then? You realize he's a total corrupt criminal who's just been handed the White House?"

Cora's eyes close. "I was taking a nap."

"Yeah, and it's the middle of the afternoon, and I'm bored, and I thought we could hang out! Franka, have Gretchen bring us two hot chocolates with cinnamon."

"Yes, Hannah."

"Any chance you'll leave me alone?" Cora asks.

"What do you think?"

Hannah climbs onto the bed, heaving herself over Cora's body. Cora does not move. Hannah ends up sitting on the other side of Cora, staring at her back. "Should I ask Franka to have Gretchen make us cookies, too?"

Cora grunts.

"What?" asks Hannah.

"You don't even realize how easy you have it."

"Um, don't you have it just as easy? You do live here, last I checked."

Cora looks over her shoulder at Hannah, possibly because Hannah's tone shifted and is unambiguously irritated. "Now I do, but I didn't always."

"But you like it, CC. Be honest," says Hannah. "I've seen Gretchen bringing you snacks more than once. You've gained weight since you got here, too."

Cora turns away quickly. "Gee, thanks."

"It was a factual observation," says Hannah, "not a criticism. I was just saying, this is a really great place to live, right? A total upgrade for you. You have everything you want."

"No I don't."

"What do you want that you don't have?"

"I don't know," Cora mumbles into her pillow.

"How could you not know what you want?"

"Are you serious? Do *you* always know what you want?"

"Of course I do," says Hannah. Her voice is clipped. Brisk. "I always have."

"You remind me of your dad."

"Isn't he *our* dad now?"

Cora is quiet for 22 seconds, then sits up, keeping her back to Hannah. "Are you going over to Finn's?"

"Why?"

She shrugs. "You usually do on Sunday afternoons."

"We'll see how I feel." Hannah's tone is cool. "I'm getting bored of him."

"I thought you guys had a good thing going."

"We did."

Cora begins to rock back and forth, a low-intensity oscillation. "But you don't now?"

Hannah climbs off the bed and begins walking around Cora's room. There are garments draped over chairs and the end of the bed. There is a desk in the corner, projecting a hologram of a woman playing a cello. The painting of the DC skyline is no longer hanging on her wall.

"Relationships are complicated," Hannah says. "You know how it is."

"Not really."

"Liar," Hannah whispers. Her red fingernails scrape along the door of Cora's closet. She quickly slides it open as Cora says, "Hey!"

"Just looking," Hannah says. Cora's footsteps are audible. It can be inferred she has risen from the bed. Hannah focuses on the floor of the closet and then on something white protruding from beneath a black sweater.

"Hannah, stop it! That's my stuff!"

"Really?" Hannah reaches into the closet, and her fingers close over the black sweater. Her gaze skims up the closet and then the ceiling as the view bounces. "Ow, CC!"

It can be inferred that Cora has forcefully pulled Hannah away from her possessions.

"Hannah and Cora, are you in need of assistance?" asks Franka.

"No, Franka," Hannah says, her breathing heavy. She looks down at her hands, which are clutching a small canvas, 30 cm by 30 cm. She then looks back at the closet, where she can now see 3 tubes of oil paint and a paintbrush. "You took this stuff from my room."

"I have no idea how that stuff got in there," Cora replies.

Hannah turns to her. "Why would you steal this stuff?"

"I didn't!" Cora's hands are up. "Probably you left it out and one of the cleaning cannies just put it in the wrong room."

"Why can't you just admit it?"

"I didn't steal!" shouts Cora. Her cheeks are flushed. Her hands have formed claws and are shaking.

Hannah takes a few steps back. "Calm down. You're kind of scaring me."

Cora tucks her hands into her armpits. "I didn't take your stuff."

For 9 seconds, Hannah stares at her adoptive sister. Then she holds out the canvas. "You can have it," she says.

Cora is looking away, shaking her head vigorously. Her hands are still tucked under her arms.

"CC, it's really okay. All you had to do was ask."

When Cora doesn't turn around, Hannah sighs. "It's really okay." She walks over to Cora's desk and sets the canvas next to the hologram.

A sound from the closet brings Hannah's gaze around. Cora is scrounging on the floor, and she comes up with the painting supplies in her hands. "Take it," she says. She walks quickly over to the desk, drops the supplies on the canvas, and then shoves the canvas toward Hannah.

Hannah looks down at the corner of the canvas pressed to her belly. "Ow."

"Oh, c'mon. I didn't hurt you."

"God, CC, yeah, you did." Hannah's fingers curl over her canvas and supplies, and she walks toward the door. "You always do," she whispers in a tight voice as she walks into the hall.

A canny is walking through the foyer with 2 mugs on a tray.

End of vid capture, 3:39 p.m., January 20, 2069

Supplemental vid evidence acquired: Franka surveillance feed 9:37 p.m., February 5, 2069, 1st floor, Room 9, informal designation: "Den"

The room contains a large fireplace, with 2 sofas facing each other and a rug between them. On either side of the fireplace are floor-to-ceiling windows that overlook the front lawn, but currently the curtains are drawn. A vid is playing, with its holographic projection occupying the space in front of the fireplace. It shows a view looking up at a ceiling, capturing from below the images of 2 individuals. One, an adolescent female, is revealed by facial-recognition-database cross-reference to be Marguerite Singer. The other, an older man with graying auburn hair who is aiming a handgun (US government Department of Defense designation "Yanata YK8," lens sighting with trajectory-matching radically invasive projectiles) at Marguerite's face, is indicated to be Wynn Sallese, the 50th president of the United States.

Marguerite says, "You should know something before you have me executed, though."

"And what's that?" asks the president.

"I've been livestreaming from El's comband for the last several minutes."

The president's eyes widen. His masseter muscle contracts, and his face flushes as he bends and reaches for the screen that is capturing the vid. After a wavering view of the ceiling appears again, the sole of the president's shoe descends rapidly toward the device. The screen darkens, and then the vid ends.

On 1 of the sofas, Cora is lying on her side. She has a blanket pulled up to her chin, and her head rests on a square pillow. She stares at the area where the vid was projected. On the sofa across from hers, Hannah and Finn Cuellar lie, embracing. Hannah chuckles. "That was some seriously cool thinking under pressure."

Finn kisses Hannah's forehead as his hand clutches her hip. "Did you actually say something nice about her?"

"I never said she was a coward. I just said she was a whiny bitch."

"I thought it was incredibly brave," Cora says. "Can we watch it again?"

"Morbid much?" says Hannah. "How many times have you watched it already?"

Cora's cheeks redden. "She just stayed so calm. I mean, he was aiming a gun at her face. He was about to kill her."

"And she filmed the whole thing using a dead man's comband," Hannah says, putting heavy emphasis on the word "dead." "It's so gross." She turns her body toward Finn's and moves her leg over his.

Finn glances at Cora, then reaches down and pulls an auxiliary blanket from the top of the sofa, covering his and Hannah's lower bodies.

Cora watches Finn and Hannah kiss for 13 seconds. "I want to see it again," she says loudly.

"Watch it on your Cerepin, CC," Hannah says, turning her head. "Franka? Put on the new vid from Cynical Revolution. Volume five."

A hologram of a group of musicians appears in the area in front of the fireplace. Contemporary music plays. Finn and Hannah do not watch the projected vid. They kiss and touch each other with bodies pressed tightly together. Twice, Hannah terminates a kiss to glance at Cora. Finn does this once. On all 3 of these occasions, the kissing appears to intensify immediately after 1 of them looks in Cora's direction.

Cora stares at the couple. She is not watching the projected vid, either. Her arm moves slightly beneath the blanket that covers her, but it is not clear what she is doing.

After 2 minutes, 41 seconds of this, Hannah groans and turns to look at Cora for a 3rd time. "God, CC, are you getting off on watching us, or what?"

"No," Cora says, sitting up abruptly. Her cheeks are red again, and she is holding the blanket taut over her body. "I'm watching the vid."

"No you weren't," says Hannah. Her hair sticks up where Finn ran his fingers through it. "But you did seem to be enjoying the show."

"Come on, Hannah. We were being kind of rude," Finn says.

Hannah turns quickly to face Finn. "Are you siding with her?"

His eyebrows rise. "No, I'm just saying that maybe we don't need to make out in front of your sister?"

"Or maybe she doesn't need to lie there like a perv and watch us," says Hannah. "Maybe she could find her own friends or something. Nobody's forcing her to be here."

"I live here," Cora says.

"Well aware," Hannah replies. "Don't you have something better to do than follow us around, though? Here—I've got an idea. This is the perfect time for you to sneak into my room and steal something, like you love to do."

Cora's mouth opens and closes. She blinks rapidly. "I-I-I never stole!"

"Hannah," Finn begins.

Hannah presses her face to Finn's neck. "Sorry. These past few weeks have been so stressful. Our president was a murderer!"

"I know," Finn says. He strokes Hannah's back in an apparent effort to soothe her. "But it's over now, and it's going to be okay."

"I never stole," Cora says again, louder.

"We're not really talking about that anymore, Cora," says Finn. "Okay?" His tone is soft, with no apparent impatience.

"But she said I stole."

"And she said she was sorry."

"She didn't say she was sorry to me. She said 'sorry' to you."

"Do we have to nitpick it?" Finn asks.

Cora's expression, brows drawn up and together with a contraction of the corrugator supercilii muscle, is suggestive of pain. "Do you want me to leave?"

"Yes," Hannah says.

"Whatever you want," Finn says. It is not clear whom he is saying this to.

Cora stands up, and the blanket that was covering her falls to the floor. The button of her jeans is unfastened. "I didn't steal anything." Her focus appears to be on Finn as she makes this utterance.

"Whatever," Hannah says. She puts her hand on Finn's cheek and turns his face to hers before pulling it down and beginning to kiss him again. After 2 seconds, he relaxes into the activity.

Cora bites her lip. She wraps her arms around herself. She watches her sister and Finn Cuellar for 24 seconds, during which the intensity of their affectionate contact increases steadily. The frequency of Cora's respiration also increases during this epoch. Then she turns abruptly and walks out of the room.

Hannah breaks the kiss and giggles. "God, I thought she was going to crawl on top of us and try to get in on the action."

"You're kind of hard on her, Hann," Finn says as he kisses her neck.

"You don't know what it's like to live with her."

"You don't have to always invite her to hang out, though," he says. "I wouldn't have minded being alone with you all evening."

"She's my sister," Hannah says. Her tone is flat. "I'm trying to do what's right."

"Then be nice to her, or get some space from her. It seems like you're pushing yourself too hard to do both, and Cora's so awkward that she doesn't know what to do when you finally lose it."

"What are you, my therapist now?" Hannah tucks her fingers into the waistband of Finn's jeans.

He laughs. "I am whatever you want me to be, wherever you want me to be, whenever you want me to be." He moves his hips back and forth. "However you want me to be."

"That's boring." She removes her fingers from his pants.

"No it's not." Finn grabs her hand and attempts to return it to its previous position, but Hannah pulls away.

"Stop it," she says sharply, pivoting away from him and sitting up. She smooths her hair down.

"What just happened?" Finn asks. "You seemed totally into—"

"Go home," Hannah says. "I'm tired."

Finn sits up next to Hannah. His expression can be coded as confused, with cues for anger. "Are you mad at me because I don't hate Cora or something?"

"It has nothing to do with her, but it's interesting that you keep bringing her up. Is there something you want to tell me, Finn?"

"Huh?" He stands up. "You're acting crazy."

"I'm crazy? Which of us is obsessed with my weird, gross freak of a sister?"

"You sound like you're jealous of her, Hannah, and that is definitely crazy."

"I bet you were thinking about her while we made out."

Finn puts his hands up. "I'll go. I can't deal with this."

"Were you thinking about her?"

"Good night, Hannah. Love you."

"Get out," Hannah says as he walks to the door. "Get out," she yells. After 3 seconds, she follows him out.

End of vid section analysis, 10:08 p.m., February 5, 2069

11:47 a.m., February 9, 2069

Hannah walks into a room full of glass-covered bookcases. Dr. Dietrich is seated on a chair facing a large window. She approaches him slowly. "Hey," she says. Her voice is quiet. Tentative sounding.

Dr. Dietrich starts and turns toward her. "Oh, hey," he says to her. He leans to the side and pats the chair next to his. "Join me."

Hannah does. "Are you okay?"

He nods. "But I was just thinking about Simon. It's so strange—I keep forgetting he's gone. I'll be trying to deal with some of this fallout, and I start to com him, because he always knows how to handle any situation . . . and then I remember."

"It's so horrible, what happened to them. I wasn't friends with Bianca or Reina, but I'd seen them at school. I don't understand why Sallese would kill their whole family."

"It was revenge, pure and simple. But Parnassus will go on—I'm going to make sure of that. And at least we know Sallese will be locked up for the rest of his life. So far, Savedra seems to be determined to fix what he wrecked. I'm actually meeting with her and a lot of other CEOs next week."

"I was going to congratulate you on your promotion, but it's been so weird . . ."

"Because my boss and his entire family were murdered by government-sanctioned thugs?"

"Uh . . . yeah."

"You're not the only one who thought it was awkward."

"Dad, it's so scary. I can't believe our supposed leader was controlling people with neurostims. If that's how he got them to vote for him, what else could he make people do?"

"I don't think neurostims are all bad, but the remote-network-connection capability was definitely vulnerable. Food for thought."

Hannah and Dr. Dietrich are quiet for a moment. She watches her father closely, observing the movements of his hands, then the direction of his gaze. Then she turns to look out the window, which reveals a view of a gray winter lawn and trees beyond it. She sighs.

"What's up, Hann?" asks her father. "I know you didn't come in here to talk about network security. Everything okay with Finn?"

"Yeah, things are great."

"Then what's bothering you? Because I know my little girl."

Hannah looks down. His hand covers hers on the arm of her chair. "Could I have some money to buy CC some art supplies?"

"Is she interested in painting?" Dr. Dietrich's eyebrows rise. "Maeve said she didn't like getting her hands dirty." He takes his hand off Hannah's, revealing a few smears of paint on the back of her hand.

"If I tell you how I know, will you promise not to do anything?"

Dr. Dietrich furrows his brow.

"She stole a few things from my room."

"What? Franka!"

"Yes, sir?"

"Do you have any vid captures that show Cora taking anything from Hannah's room?"

"Sir, both Hannah and Cora have privacy settings in their rooms and the hallway. No surveillance is stored."

"Should I change that?" Dr. Dietrich asks Hannah.

"No!" says Hannah. "You promised that I could have my own private space, and I know CC feels the same way."

"I know, but if Cora's stealing—"

"She stole a canvas, Dad. And some paint. I saw them in her closet when I was hanging out with her a few weeks ago. With everything going on, I didn't want to bother you and Maeve about it. It's not like she's stealing the family heirlooms or something . . ."

As she trails off, Dr. Dietrich's eyebrows rise as if he's making some nonverbal assertion.

"I've already told you," Hannah says quietly. "I don't think CC would steal Mom's bracelet. I believe her when she says she lost it."

"You always want to believe the best of people." Dr. Dietrich nods. "And I'll take a page from your book." He gestures at the books stored on the shelves around him. "I'm willing to give her the benefit of the doubt. But I don't like that she's going into your room and taking things that don't belong to her."

"But Dad, I think it makes sense, based on what Maeve told us, doesn't it?"

"I know she had it rough in Brooklyn," he says, sinking back into his chair and interlacing his fingers. "I really feel for the kid. It's part of why I adopted her. I wanted her to feel like she had a permanent place to be. A permanent father. But sometimes . . ."

"Sometimes?"

"She's tough."

Hannah chuckles. "You don't have to say that to me. I know we're the same age, but sometimes I feel . . ."

"Older?"

"Yeah. But also younger. I don't know how to explain it. She's unpredictable, I guess? I never know which CC I'm going to get."

"How many are there?"

"Oh, there's the angry one. The judgy one—sometimes I think she looks down on me just because I've had money all my life. Then there's the weird one—have you seen her rock? She doesn't usually do it when she thinks other people are watching, but she can't seem to help herself sometimes."

"Maeve said she's done that since she was a little kid."

"I guess it makes sense." Hannah pulls her knees to her chest and wraps her arms around her legs. "Maeve said Cora's dad did some bad stuff."

"That guy . . . I wish I could punch him in the face. Maeve feels so guilty about all of it. She was traveling so much for work at the time."

"What exactly did he do, Dad? Maeve wouldn't tell me, and CC probably won't, either."

Dr. Dietrich rubs his hands over his face. "He abused and neglected her, Hann. Maeve changed their apartment's surveillance settings after Cora started acting strange—this was when she was maybe five? And what she saw . . . god. I don't know how she managed not to kill the guy."

"What did he do?"

"I don't want to get into it," says Dr. Dietrich. "But he hurt her, and he was also into some bad stuff, and little Cora was there when all of it happened."

"Is that why she seems to hate herself?"

Dr. Dietrich's brows draw together. "She doesn't really feel that way, does she?"

"Dad . . . she says stuff to me that I don't think she would say to you guys."

"Like what?"

Hannah is quiet again. Looking down at her hands.

"Tell me, Hann. I don't like secrets, and I can tell you've got one."

"It's nothing, okay? She's just hard to understand. But I'm trying. And I want to help her. That's why I wanted to get her paints, since she seems to want to do it. Maybe that'll help her open up."

"Go ahead and get whatever you want. You can get her a whole studio's worth if you like."

"I don't want to get her too much. I think she gets sort of suspicious if she feels like she's being given too much."

Dr. Dietrich scratches his chin. "I didn't realize. You think I've lavished too much stuff on her? Is that why she seems to avoid me?"

"She just . . . doesn't trust easily. I want her to trust us. I want her to trust *me*. She's my sister."

"You are such an amazing person, you know that? Cora may not realize how lucky she is now, but I bet she will if we give her time." Dr. Dietrich is grinning at Hannah while he shakes his head. "Your mother would be so proud of you. Just like I am."

"You shouldn't be proud of me."

"You can't stop me. Here you are, putting so much thought into how to make your new sister feel loved and welcome in our home. A lot of only children might have been turned off by having a new kid come in and set up shop, especially when it comes along with a new stepmom. But you? You embraced both of them. You're just trying to make everyone's lives better."

Hannah looks out the window. Her new-message light is blinking again. She glances up at it. A message from Lara.

Still up for tonight? Just the 3 of us?

Hannah refocuses on the window.

"Hann?"

She looks at her father, and his expression suggests concern. "Is there anything else you want to tell me?"

For 7 seconds, she is quiet. And then, "No. Just wanted to get paint stuff for Cora."

"Get a few things for yourself as well. Anything you want."

Hannah gets up, walks over to her father, and kisses the top of his head. "Love you, Dad."

"Love you. You'll always be my girl."

She leans on him for a moment and then turns away, moving across the library and reentering the hallway. "New message, Lara," she says as she walks. "Four of us. Send."

Lara responds before Hannah makes it back to her room.

Nooooo. Please. Crazy Cora is such a drag. Mei is with me on this one.

"It's out of my hands," Hannah says, "and you're going to be nice. Send."

End of vid capture, 12:10 p.m., February 9, 2069

Chapter Seven

Mom and Gary make me blank my 'Pin—no updates, no messages, no new vids or streams, no noise in my head except my own scrabbling thoughts. They have me put up a blanket post on my incoming message space, saying I'm at home and resting and need a few days to myself. They check, too—I see auto-blocked messages from them in my archives, along with com attempts from Neda, Finn, Mei, and Lara. Rafiq is with me most of my waking hours, and he sits outside my room at night, probably hooked in to Franka's surveillance. During the day, we walk by the river. A lot. He suggests other things, like drawing or sculpting with clay or trying expressive dance, but he backs down quickly when I refuse. So we walk. And walk. And walk. And I do everything I can to keep the conversation as shallow as a puddle. He lets me.

A few times, we do yoga. He says it would be healthy for me to be more in touch with my body. I don't love it, because with my incoming Cerepin messages blocked and nothing to distract me, my brain always starts to spin. Rafiq insists the hours we spend in our exercise skins, contorting our bodies into Warrior and Happy Baby and Sphinx, will quiet the noise eventually.

We're just finishing a session when Franka announces that I have a visitor. "Is it Neda?" I ask.

"It is Finn Cuellar," Franka says.

My hand finds the wall and holds me up. Rafiq's gaze scans my face. "You do not want to see him?" he asks.

I do want to see him, but it's also terrifying. If I send him away, though, he might send that vid to my parents. "N-no. It's fine." I grimace and turn to Rafiq. "Do you have to be there?"

Rafiq looks down at himself, his perfect, lean body clothed in a black exercise skin that reveals each cut of his muscles. His hair is neat, and of course, he doesn't sweat. "I could change, if you like. Is my appearance unacceptable?"

"No, you look great."

He smiles as if I've just made his day, like always. "Thank you."

"But Finn . . . he's a friend from school. And I . . ."

"You do not know how to explain me."

I nod. So does he. "I do not wish to impede your social connections," he says. "Social support and genuine friendship are critical to mental and emotional well-being. You have had minimal contact with peers since your attempt to self-harm."

"Wait—have you capped my 'Pin or something?"

"No, of course not. That kind of intrusion into your privacy would be illegal and completely counter to building a trusting relationship. I didn't mean to alarm you." Rafiq tilts his head. His eyes on me are warm, and even though I know, I *know* he's a machine, it's still comforting. "I can tell when you receive texts by the movements of your eyes, Cora. I am also aware of your parents' request that you recover in peace by blocking incoming coms on your Cerepin. I was merely stating a fact."

"Okay. Right. Good." I take a deep breath and continue down the hall, heading for my room. I try to calm down as I change out of my silver skin and into pants and a silky sweater that Mom downloaded and genned for me this morning. This is going to be fine, and I can handle it.

When I emerge, Rafiq is in his usual position in the hallway, still in his exercise skin. "Maybe you could . . . wait somewhere else?"

"I should be near in case you need assistance," he says as we walk toward the foyer.

"But Franka can monitor."

"I am going to wait nearby. You are showing signs of significant physiological dysregulation." He looks toward the front door, where Finn waits on the other side. "And so is your visitor."

Can he hear Finn's heart beating from here?

I have no time to argue. Finn is already upset, and I don't want to make it worse. "Fine. I'll take him into the den, and you can wait in the storage room, or . . . ?"

"That is satisfactory," Rafiq says and walks past me.

"You can open the door, Franka," I say when Rafiq ducks into the room.

The door swings open. Finn stands on the front step. It's raining, and he's soaked. Like he walked or ran here instead of taking a car. "Hi," I say. "Um, want a towel?"

"Nah." He steps over the threshold and stands on the mat, where he pushes his fingers through his thick brown hair, then wipes his wet hands on his pants. His freckles look stark against his pale skin. His eyes are aimed at my feet. "You didn't com me back."

"But you saw that I'm okay—I put that message up. My parents made me. I-I would have responded if I could have."

Finally, his eyes meet mine. "Do you have any idea how freaked I've been?" he asks, his voice trembling.

I put my hand on my stomach. "Den?"

He heads back there, and I follow him, hoping Rafiq is out of sight as promised.

"Can you put on privacy settings?" He looks over his shoulder and sees me shake my head. "They've really got you under lockdown, don't they?"

"You have no idea," I mutter.

He rounds on me as soon as we reach the rug between the two couches in the room, and his body is framed by the massive fireplace behind him. Franka helpfully illuminates the chandelier over us, sending light and shadow cascading down Finn's face. I suddenly feel sweaty and chilled.

"Do you really not remember what happened that night?" he asks, his voice low. "Lara told me that's what you've been saying, but—"

"Lara has all the information these days, doesn't she?"

"She said she'd called your dad about Hannah."

My cheeks are hot. "Right. I guess that makes sense."

Finn leans forward. "Well? Is what she told me true?" His eyes shift from wall to wall. He knows Franka's listening.

I bite my lip and glance at the door of the storage room, which is in the corner to my left. The door is closed, but Rafiq can remotely access Franka's vid feed, so he also hears every single thing we say, and he knows how fast our hearts beat as we say it. "I swear I don't remember."

Finn's shoulders sag, and he lets out a long breath. For a second it looks like he's going to melt right onto the floor. "For real?"

"I'm sorry. I'm tired of letting people down, but I'm telling the truth." I rub my hands along my arms and drop onto one of the couches, tucking my feet up next to me and pulling a pillow onto my lap, a shield for my chest. Something to muffle the sound.

"Franka, music, please," I say, trying to pull together my fractured thoughts. "Debussy. *L'isle joyeuse*. Volume seven."

The rippling piano music fills the room. I pat the seat next to me. Finn glances toward the hallway and sits down. I can smell him, soap and boy sweat. I clutch the pillow a little harder, my fingernails digging in. "What's the last thing you actually can remember?" he asks in a whisper.

I shake my head, the music my own private alarm bell, clanging in my head. "I blacked out . . . I don't know. Before midnight, I think. I don't remember anything until after I got to the hospital." I glare at the wall, praying Franka doesn't comment on my heart rate. I can't keep my body still any longer, and begin to rock. Just a little. Barely noticeable. I close my eyes and breathe.

"So you have no idea how she ended up at the bottom of the stairs? Do you think she fell because she was trying to stop you from killing yourself? Because after I saw that vid and heard what happened, I thought—"

"Finn, please." My voice is brittle. Like bone. Like fingernails.

"I'm sorry. I've just been climbing the walls. Wondering if some of it was my fault."

My eyes open. "How would it be your fault?"

His eyes are still red rimmed like they were when he messaged me. "You *know* why."

"You thought we fought over you?" I look past him, rooting my gaze in the immaculately clean grate of the fireplace. "I was over it. And she never even knew it happened."

"She did, Cora."

Heat blooms in my chest. "How do you know?"

He sighs. "You sure you want me to tell you?"

Another glance toward the storage room. "Yeah."

He taps his Cerepin and closes his eyes. "I'll send it to you."

I take my 'Pin off blank and a second later, I receive a vid from Finn. Chills unfurl from the center of my chest. "Open," I whisper.

While Debussy plays in the background, I see myself through my sister's eyes. I am sitting on a table in Finn's parents' wine cellar. Finn is standing between my legs. My fingers are curled around his biceps, and his are digging into my hips. I remember how that felt. Urgent and compelling. I remember squirming, clutching, just to get a little closer to him. It felt so familiar, that need to move just to find a little relief—I wanted more until there was no more to be had.

For a few seconds, that is all I see. Just me and Finn in that cellar, the lights low, and I feel like I did that night, when everything else dropped away and shattered beneath the weight of his kiss.

He had the privacy settings on, but that couldn't hide us from Hannah. She must have followed us down. The pounding bass from the music throbs overhead; the party upstairs goes on without us. For a moment, the view blurs.

Was she crying?

"Did you know she was there?" I ask, my voice breaking.

"What? No!"

Until that sweltering August night, with Finn's parents on their anniversary trip to Brazil, I thought he was determined to get Hannah back. Maybe I was right. "Were you using me to make her jealous?"

"How can you say that?"

"Maybe because you didn't respond to any of my messages after that night?"

His eyes are wide, and there's sweat glistening on the peach fuzz of his upper lip. "*She* broke up with *me*! I was messed up, Cora. I really like you, but I just . . . didn't want to hurt you."

"So instead you decided to pretend I didn't exist." I remember being happy, hopeful. Thinking maybe he could be mine instead of hers, and then . . . nothing. Nothing. My bare feet push against his thighs, hard, as the resentment and anger well up. "I don't even know why I'm talking to you now. Leave."

His hands grasp my ankles. "Cora, please! I know things have always been . . . kinda complicated for you two. Right now, all I want is to be here for you."

"Complicated." Like his hands on my ankles? I wish that I had shaved my legs. The door to the storage room is still closed. The music is still on.

"She sent me that vid the morning after we kissed," he said. "Along with a message."

"Let me see it."

"I'm not sure if—"

"Let me see!"

"Fine." He taps at his Cerepin. Just text, no vid.

Don't you hurt my sister. She's more fragile than you think.

I read it three times. "Fragile?"

"I got scared. I didn't know what to do!"

I kick him again. "You never liked me. Even now, you're just pretending to like me."

"You know that's not true. We've always gotten along great, haven't we? You don't talk when you should be listening. When you do talk, you say stuff that's honest. Not like you're trying to create some perfect impression. You seem real, I guess. Innocent."

Of all the ways to describe me, *that's* the word he picks? "So basically, I'm not intimidating like Hannah was, and you wanted to give that a try."

He curses and runs his hands through his hair again. "You make me sound awful, and I've never been anything but nice to you."

I focus on the frozen image of Finn and me, my head tilted back, his back hunched, our lips mashed together. My eyes shut tight, tight, tight. Footsteps creaking above us.

I should have known Hannah was there. I should have sensed it.

"No harm done," I say too loudly, fighting my need to rock and rock and rock. "We kissed. Your house let us know the music was too loud, so we went upstairs again. That was it. Just a hookup. No big deal."

His look says I'm wrong, and I'm hopeful for a second that it actually meant something to him. Then I'm angry, tired of feeling hopeful and then like an idiot.

"Were you really okay about it?" he asks. "Because Mei told me about something that happened on the Fourth of July. She was worried about you."

My muscles are knots of dread. "What did Mei tell you, exactly?"

"She said something about you guys being up on the roof of your house. The widow's walk. It weirded all of them out—Mei and Lara and Hannah. When Hannah sent me that com and vid of us, I guess she thought that if I upset you, that you might . . . I guess she was just scared for you."

"Of course she was," I mutter. "Because I'm *fragile*." I bow my head and rub at my eyes, suddenly tired. Suddenly sure I'm the most terrible person in the whole world. Suddenly sure I won't be able to hide it forever. My body is rocking just enough to keep me from exploding.

Hannah deserved it, I almost yell.

Finn is looking cautious. Or maybe scared? "Hannah told Mei that some bad stuff had happened to you as a kid," he says. "She said that's why you did some—" He looks at me out of the corner of his eye. "Of the things you do."

I freeze. "You're serious right now?"

"I thought, when Hannah said you were fragile, she was afraid that when we kissed I had . . . I don't know . . . brought some things back to the surface? I searched it, and I know trauma can make people—"

"What the hell? I don't want to talk about this. I don't know why we're talking about this!"

"I'm sorry. I came here because I thought maybe I could help you piece together what happened the night she fell, but it got all twisted up." He's sitting forward now, and my feet are in his lap. His hands are still on my ankles. I don't know if he's trying to keep himself from being kicked or if he likes holding on to me. "I'm just thinking, you keep trying to hurt yourself, and so maybe you . . . feel guilty about something?"

"Because of the vid she sent you that night. The one where I—" *Slapped her.* My eyes zip to the storage room.

Finn notices. He turns and looks. And apparently sees nothing, because he turns back to face me. "You were scaring her, Cora." And there is a question in his eyes, I think: *Was she right to be scared?*

"Why send it to you?" I ask. "She wanted to blame you, right? To say I was suicidal because you wouldn't talk to me? But it's not your fault, okay? You didn't bring anything up from the past or do anything wrong, and this is all stupid. It's stupid. And it had nothing to do with you and nothing to do with me trying to kill myself! It was an accident, okay? She fell down the stairs on accident!" Why can't I slow my words down? My thoughts are racing. I'm talking a mile a minute.

"*Okay,* calm down." He's watching me like I'm a bomb about to detonate. "But you don't know for sure, Cora. Hey, are you going to be all right? Do you think your memories of that night will ever come back?"

I shrug, an up-down jerk of my tense shoulders. "I need time." It won't help at all, but it sounds nice. I can't be still now. I have to move.

Finn's brow furrows. "Okay." He's staring at his own hands. His thumbs stroke the skin around the bony part of my ankle, the veins shifting beneath my skin with the slight back-and-forth momentum of my body. "Whatever does come back, will it be . . . I don't know . . . reliable?"

"How should I know?" I barely trust my own thoughts in the here and now, for god's sake.

He looks nervous again. "Will you call me first if you do remember anything?"

"Why should I?"

And now he looks like I've just punched him in the face. "I want to be here for you, Cora!"

"Oh, sure, now you want to be here for me."

His grip tightens like he wants to hold me still. "Cora, *please*. I didn't mean to hurt you," he continues. "And if I had anything to do with whatever happened that night—" His eyes are shining, and his voice is thick. Choked. "I can't believe she's gone. I can't believe she's dead."

I pull my feet away. "I need time," I say again, but my voice is high-pitched, like a child's. I need him to leave. Now. "I've—I've got—"

He reaches for me. "Don't be like this, Cora!"

"Your trainer is waiting in the foyer, Cora," says Franka. "He apologizes for being late."

Finn looks at me. "You didn't say you had a—"

"I forgot." I am standing up. I am walking. I have a vague idea of what just happened, and—yes. Rafiq is standing in the foyer, his hair wet, a raindrop hanging from his chin, with a folded yoga mat under his arm.

Finn is behind me. I feel the shadow of him, and when I look over my shoulder, he's got his eyes on Rafiq. "Hey."

Rafiq nods. "Hey." Then he looks at me. "I'm sorry I got held up. Do you want to change into your exercise skin?"

"Um. Yes?"

He smiles. "Great!"

Finn puts his hand on my shoulder. "Cora. Com me if you want to talk? I'm here. I want to help."

I do not turn around, but I tense my shoulder, trying to shrug him off. "Thanks. Maybe later, okay? I have . . . my trainer. My training."

Rafiq is watching us. His face is frozen in a bland smile. He looks completely at ease. "I'm so sorry to rush you," he says, "but I have another appointment right after yours, and—"

"Right. Sorry." Without looking at him, I take Finn by the wrist and tow him toward the door. "This isn't a good time. I'm sure I'll be back at school soon. I appreciate you caring about me enough to stop by." Once again, I'm talking so fast that I'm out of breath.

Finn looks back and forth between me and Rafiq. His jaw is clenched, and his eyes are narrow, worried. I don't know what's going through his head. "Later," Finn mutters and walks toward the door, which Franka opens for him, revealing the downpour outside. He walks into it without looking back.

Franka closes the door.

"Thank you," Rafiq says.

"You're welcome," she replies.

He reaches me in two steps. "You were clearly flooded with negative emotion and becoming cognitively disorganized. I decided to intervene."

I close my eyes. The video of Finn and me in the wine cellar is still frozen, covering my right visual field. Hannah's com is still there, too, enlarging whenever I focus on it. Don't you hurt my sister. She's more fragile than you think.

"I think I'm going to be sick," I mumble.

"Franka, have Gretchen bring a glass of water to Cora's room," Rafiq says briskly. Then he takes me by the shoulders and steers me down the hall. "Clear your Cerepin screen, Cora," he says to me. "I can tell you still have the images he shared with you up on the space, and I believe they are distressing you."

"Close messages," I say, and when my vision clears again, my stomach unknots slightly. Rafiq's hands are on me, and I sag in his grip. I feel his body, warm, deceptively human, against my back.

"I won't let you fall," he says quietly. "I can carry you if I have to."

"I can walk." And I do. But I'm glad he's touching me. It's not a demanding touch. It doesn't ask me for a single thing.

When we reach my room, he guides me to my gel chair. "You can rock if you need to," he says.

I cover my head with my hands.

He meets Gretchen, the physical extension of Franka, in the hallway just outside my door and accepts the glass of water, which he sets next to me. At first, he stands in front of me, but then he walks over to my desk and sits in the chair. I don't know how long we stay like that, but I'm not getting better. Inside, I'm screaming.

"Cora, for three days now, you've done everything you can to avoid talking to me about anything of substance."

My fingers tug at my hair. "It won't change anything."

"It's not about changing anything that's happened. It's about helping you cope with it. Right now, you don't feel able. You're overwhelmed by it. You think you won't be able to handle it if you let it in." He pauses. "And you're wrong about that."

"You have no idea how this feels. You're a freaking robot."

"I don't know how this feels. I don't claim to. But I know other things. I know you are capable of dealing with what's happened, of sorting through it, of accepting it, if only you're willing to let me help you."

"Finn was right—everything is too twisted up. I don't—I don't even know what to say. I don't want to talk at all."

Rafiq's voice comes closer. He's next to me now. "If you were a canny, we could transmit information wirelessly or through a port. You wouldn't have to say anything at all. But you are not a canny."

I lift my head, an animal peeking out of a burrow to see if the coast is clear. "I don't want to talk."

He's right there, warm and calm and not hating me, not freaked out by me, not grossed out by me. He's smiling at me, gentle and careful. His hand is on my back. "I won't make you talk, Cora. I can't. But I think that, if you gave it a try, you would find that you have a lot to say."

Right.

That's exactly what I'm afraid of.

Chapter Eight

Data review.
Internal narrative: on.

7:07 a.m., April 21, 2069

Cora's face fills Hannah's perspective. Cora's teeth are exposed; her lips are drawn back. Her platysma muscle is fully contracted, creating vertical strain lines on either side of her neck, drawing the edge of her jaw downward. This emotion can be unambiguously coded as rage. Her shouts are unintelligible and guttural, loud enough to briefly garble the Cerepin's auditory input. Saliva flies from Cora's mouth.

Hannah's perspective shakes, possibly because Cora is shaking her, and her hands, long nails lavender with clear gemstones at the center of each, clutch at Cora's shoulders and push at her face.

"Cora, stop, please," she shrieks. "Franka, help!"

"Don't say that ever again!" shouts Cora.

Hannah's perspective abruptly arcs along the ceiling, and when it steadies itself, Hannah is on her bed. The door to her bedroom slams. Hannah looks around again, including at the wall screen that depicts a mirror view, showing Hannah sprawled on her comforter, her eyes wide. She pulls her knees to her chest, lowers her head so that the visual feed goes dark, and emits sounds that indicate she is most likely crying.

End of vid capture, 7:08 a.m., April 21, 2069

Supplemental vid evidence acquired: Franka surveillance feed 7:12 p.m., April 24, 2069, 4th floor, Room 2, informal designation: "Gallery"

Cora's fingers wrap around the doorframe as she stands looking into the room. After 8 seconds, she enters. The walls are decorated with 16 oil paintings of various sizes, all in the same style. The furniture is antique, 19th century, 2 sofas with walnut stain, carved, upholstered with velvet. In one corner of the room there is an easel, upon which a 60 cm by 100 cm canvas has been placed. Someone has painted on this canvas (search of Franka's surveillance database indicates it was Hannah), but 46% of its surface remains bare.

Cora approaches the painting, her steps stilted and abrupt. Her focus is on the canvas. She stops in front of it and looks down at the basket of oil paint that sits next to the left front leg of the easel. She kneels, facing the painting. She reaches for a tube marked "umber." She holds it in the palm of her hand for 14 seconds and appears to be examining it. She raises her head. "Franka," she says. "Privacy."

End of vid section analysis, 7:15 p.m., April 24, 2069

4:57 p.m., April 29, 2069

Hannah looks through painting supplies contained in a tiered box. Her fingernails click as they skim lightly over tubes of oil paint, a bottle of turpentine and another of linseed oil, charcoal pencils, and 2 small opaque plastic containers that rattle when jostled. She pauses and focuses on one of them, fiddling briefly with the catch, but does not open it. She picks up that container and carries it to her closet, where she tucks it between 2 folded sweaters on a narrow shelf. She pulls the closet door mostly closed. Then she returns to a stool and continues to look through the supply box. After 3 seconds, her fingers close around a filbert brush.

She focuses on the canvas in front of her, 60 cm by 100 cm, positioned on an easel that sits on an expanse of cloth. There is a dark shadow of pigment beneath the white primer that has been painted over the central area of the canvas, and it appears Hannah has already drawn a sketch over it of what she intends to create: 2 female-looking figures. They face each other. The figure on the left has her arms wrapped around the other's waist. The figure on the right has her hands wrapped around her companion's throat. Wavy lines emanate from behind this figure's back and curve around her body, spiraling up the other's legs.

"God, this is so messed up," Hannah whispers.

Humming softly and tunelessly to herself, she begins to paint. There are no hesitations in her movements. For 29 minutes, 54 seconds, she covers over the sketch, some lines corresponding, others in contrast. She begins using only black, but then she layers in other colors, highlighting muscles and the planes of each face, as well as the curving lines that wind around one of the figure's legs. Hannah appears to have an accurate sense of proportion and dimension, and a clear vision for what she wants to depict. The fingers of her right hand manipulate the brush in a practiced way, suggesting complete comfort.

"Hannah—"

Hannah yelps at the sound of Franka's voice, then curses. "Yeah?"

"Cora is requesting entrance."

Hannah groans. "Why?"

"She says she's looking for something."

"She's always looking for something, and she always thinks I have it."

"Please let me know if I can open your door."

"Go ahead, Franka."

Cora enters 2 seconds later. Her blond hair is pulled up in a lopsided ponytail. "Have you seen my green sweater?" Her eyes narrow as she glances toward Hannah's closet.

Hannah also looks at her closet. "Nope."

"Did you borrow it?"

"You think I'd wear something of yours? Very funny."

"Come on, Hannah. I just genned it a few weeks ago."

"And you've barely taken it off since." Hannah says this at a low volume, and it appears Cora does not hear her. "Gretchen probably found it," Hannah says, louder this time. "She has olfactory sensors and a dedication to keeping this place's smell within acceptable human parameters." The last few words are recited in a monotone, as if to imitate a primitive mechanical voice. Hannah laughs as she turns to Cora in time to see her sister glance down at her armpits and press her elbows against her sides. "You should look in the laundry, CC."

"I already did."

"Gretchen sorts and folds in that back room with the long tables. Did you look there?"

Cora does not answer. Her focus has shifted, and Hannah follows the direction of her gaze back to the canvas. "What's that?"

Hannah refocuses on her painting. "I'm correcting a mistake."

She looks over at her sister, who is still looking at the canvas. The painting has changed slightly from the sketch. Now one figure's hands are on the other's waist, and the other's arms are around her companion's neck, as if in an embrace. The curving lines that appeared to emanate from that figure's back are thicker now, taking up most of that side of the painting, with streaks in many different colors. Part of this mass of color still spirals up the companion's right leg. The area behind that figure is gray and beige with smudges of black, and the contrast gives the impression of imbalance.

Cora says after 9 seconds of silence, "It's scary."

"You're scared of everything, CC."

Cora looks down at her feet. "It's good. You're really talented."

"Wow. You actually said something nice to me."

Cora is swaying, and she has her arms wrapped over her middle. "Is that a gift for someone?"

"I'm giving it to Dad for his birthday."

"But it's not him and Mom."

"How do you know?"

Cora waves an arm at the canvas. "They both have boobs."

"You're so observant. Maybe it's you and Maeve."

Cora's brow furrows as she raises her head and peers at the painting again. "Really?"

"You don't think it looks like you two?"

For 18 seconds, Cora stares at the painting. The figures do not appear to have hair, and neither bears a direct likeness to Cora or Maeve. Neither has distinctive features that might indicate whom Hannah is attempting to depict. "I can't tell if they're hugging or fighting."

"Yeah," Hannah says quietly. "I know."

"I can't tell if they want to be closer or if they're trying to get away from each other."

"Exactly." Hannah's tone suggests sadness.

"It's not me and Mom."

"So?"

"I think it's me and you."

"You're not full of yourself or anything. What makes you think you're in this painting at all?"

Cora lets out an impatient grunt. "Why won't you just tell me?"

"I'm enjoying your speculation."

"I can't ever tell if you're being nice or if you're making fun of me."

Hannah rises from her stool. "That's not fair, CC. I never make fun of you. I mean, when you come at me, it's hard not to push back, but jeez, who wouldn't? You're always accusing me of stuff. Like now. I mean, first you come in here basically implying that I stole your sweater, and now you're standing here saying I make fun of you. All I was doing was painting. In my own room. This is supposed to be my space."

Cora blinks rapidly. "I'm sorry."

"For what, exactly?"

A pause of 16 seconds. Then Cora whispers, "I'm just sorry." She glances at the painting again.

"Maeve told me the other day that you've always had trouble reading people. It made a lot of sense."

"She told you that?" Cora's brows are low and downturned, with a wrinkle of skin between them. A scowl.

"She loves you," Hannah replies. "And she cares about me, too. She wanted to help me understand you, especially after the past week."

Cora is still scowling. Her fingers are balled into fists in her black tunic. She appears tense. "That was all because you didn't understand me?"

"I've already said sorry, haven't I? And it's not like you haven't paid me back, right?"

Cora remains silent, tense.

Hannah moves closer to her. "Right?"

Cora looks back at the painting. "So it *is* us."

"I won't argue with you, if that's what you want to believe."

"What's all that stuff coming out of the one on the left? Is that me?"

"CC, I can't explain my painting to you before it's even done. God, this is just the underpainting anyway. Things can change a lot."

"But it looks . . ."

"Ugh. What."

Cora's lip trembles. "It looks like that one is trying to hurt the other one. And I don't know which one is me."

"You don't know?" Hannah asks, and her tone is clipped. Sharp. Significantly higher in volume than before. "You're thicker than I thought."

Cora's mouth has fallen partially open as she stares at her sister. Her eyes appear glazed—with tears, it can be inferred. Hannah moves toward her quickly and wraps her arms around her sister. From the cam perspective, it appears her chin is resting on Cora's shoulder.

"*Shhh.* CC. I'm sorry. I was just really into this, doing my thing, and you caught me at a bad time."

Cora lets out a high-pitched sound. A whimper.

"Come on. Don't cry. I didn't mean it."

Cora shudders, and it shakes Hannah's cam view. "Let me go, Hannah."

"Not until you forgive me." Hannah is rubbing Cora's back in rapid circular motions, filling the auditory feed with white noise. It is so loud that what Hannah says next is inaudible.

Hannah stumbles back, her arms reeling. "Ow!"

Cora draws her clawed fingers down her own sleeves, repeating the motion several times. "I told you to let me go!"

"CC, get out of my room!" Hannah is breathing hard. "I'm so tired of you bullying me."

"You're the bully!" Cora stomps her feet as she leaves Hannah's room, and Hannah's gaze streaks to the floor, revealing that Cora has stepped in Hannah's paint palette. It is not clear whether this action was intentional. Dark partial footprints mark Cora's path across the carpet to the door, but it appears Franka has already begun her self-cleaning process, as they are fading rapidly.

Hannah walks slowly over to her palette. Gobs of paint and random smears of mixed color cover its surface. Hannah's breathing steadies as she moves toward her closet. She opens the door and looks down at the floor.

Her gaze focuses on a green fold of fabric.

End of vid capture, 5:42 p.m., April 29, 2069

Chapter Nine

This morning, I spend some time trying to make myself look good. I wash my hair, and even though the feel of bristles on my scalp sets my teeth on edge, I brush it out. It's short now, much shorter than before.

The morning I got home from the hospital, I swiped a pair of kitchen scissors, sat down on the floor under the table, and cut it. I'm totally aware now it was a weird thing to do, but at the time, my hair tickled my cheeks like insect feet and wouldn't stay tucked behind my ears. I also hated the way I looked, and if I hadn't chopped it all off, I might have poked my eyes out with those scissors instead.

I remember spending a solid few minutes, crouched under that table in the breakfast nook, considering it.

But this morning, I'm determined to stay calm. I do my yoga breathing because it actually helps. "Franka, where's my mom?"

"She is in the breakfast room, Cora. Would you like to join her?"

"Yeah. Can I have toast with honey and butter? And tea."

"Drake is aware of your menu preferences."

I smile. I want her to note it, however she keeps track of stuff like that, so she has me on her surveillance looking grateful and happy and normal. "You guys are awesome. Could you also tell Rafiq that I won't need him this morning?"

"Perhaps you should communicate that to him directly, as he is standing outside your door."

Ugh. "Fine." I spend a few more minutes smoothing my hair down, then head out. Just as Franka said, Rafiq is in the hallway, once again staring at that horrible painting Gary hung up across from my room. I've lost count of the times I've been tempted to tear it from the wall and break it over my knee. I keep my eyes off it as I turn toward him. "Hey. I'm going to—"

"Eat breakfast with your mother."

"Don't be creepy."

He smiles. "Shall we do yoga afterward? Or walk?"

I shake my head. "I'm busy today." I scoot past him and head for the breakfast room, and when I get there, I realize he hasn't followed me. I feel like I won.

My mom is sitting at the table, the same one under which I crouched with my scissors, surrounded by piles of my own hair, only a week or so ago. Behind her is the big bay window that looks out on the river beyond the patio. "Good morning," she says, rising to hug me. "You smell good!"

I can't tell if she's surprised or not. "I'm feeling a lot better." I take a seat across from her as Drake, the chef canny, walks over and sets a plate of toast in front of me, complete with a little pot of honey and another of butter he might have churned himself, because that is how Gary likes things done, and he has enough money to make sure it happens that way. "Thanks," I say to Drake as he places a mug of tea next to my right hand.

He inclines his head and walks back toward the kitchen.

Mom is dressed for work, a sheath dress with a high collar, earrings, her hair in neat waves. Even though her eyes are red and that makes me wonder if she's been crying, she's so pretty. I look like someone else's daughter. My dad's, maybe.

She takes a sip from her own mug. "What's on your agenda today?"

"I want to go back to school."

She puts her mug down quickly. Little wisps of steam rise from its depths. "It's a little soon, isn't it?"

"I've already missed three days."

"We haven't gotten approval for you to go back."

"What do I have to do?"

"You have to be interviewed by someone qualified to say that you're cleared to return."

She sounds calm. If I want this to work, I should sound calm, too. But my skin is hot. "I'm doing so much better. I haven't tried anything since Monday."

She leans forward on her elbows. "I'm glad, Cora, but you've also been supervised constantly. The school setup isn't quite as tight."

Yeah. I know. It's what I'm counting on.

"They seemed pretty on top of things," I say with a weak chuckle.

"I had to call them to start looking for you," she replies in a flat voice. She takes another sip from her drink and then says, "How's your time with Rafiq?"

I slump back in my chair. "It's fine. I guess it's helping?"

She frowns. "You guess?"

"What did you expect?"

Her eyes flick to the side. She's probably receiving a message.

"Where's Gary?" I ask.

"He's been in Silicon Valley since yesterday morning, but he'll be flying back tomorrow night. He's been checking in with me a lot, though. He was really hoping this treatment would help you."

"And it is. Rafiq has been great. But I don't need him anymore."

Her eyes narrow. "What would Rafiq say?"

"He's a canny, Mom."

"I think we both know that's an oversimplification."

"I need to go be with my friends!" Neda, really. I'm not sure any of Hannah's friends were ever mine. I think they were something else.

"And before you do that, we need to make sure you won't try to harm yourself."

"How is this healthy?" I ask, knowing my voice is too loud but unable to quiet down. "Who says I have to be with my robot therapist babysitter all day every day?"

"We think, for now, it's the best thing for you." She pulls a hand-kerchief from her pocket. After dabbing her nose, she says, "Gary feels strongly that you need to face your memories of what happened that night, and—"

"Oh. My. God! I don't remember!" I am up on my feet, and my chair falls backward.

Mom jerks back as I clutch the table. "Cora, I need you to calm down now," she says, her voice low.

"But no one listens to me or believes me! I've said it a thousand times, and you guys just ignore me. I don't remember what happened, and the doctor said that made sense! You're the ones driving me crazy!"

Her hands are up in front of her chest. "Please take a step back. Breathe."

My hands are shaking, my fingers curled. "I hate you. I hate all of you."

She grimaces. "Please stop." She slowly gets up. She spreads her arms, gesturing me toward her.

I shuffle into her embrace, still trembling.

"I'm sorry," she says. There are tears in her voice, tears on her face that wet my cheek. "Look. We're all dealing with losing Hannah. I don't want it to tear us apart. But Gary is hurting more than anyone, and I totally get it—if I had lost you like that . . ." She sniffles loudly. "He just wants answers. Part of the reason he left was to take the pressure off you. He's really struggling with this."

I squeeze my eyes shut and hold on, spiraling in hopelessness before accepting that I have no other choice. "Okay! Okay. I'm sorry, too." I'm not getting out anytime soon. Something in me grabs the inside of my rib cage and shrieks. But my bones are strong. They don't break easily.

I pull away from Mom. "I guess I'll go find Rafiq and do some yoga."

Mom takes me by the shoulders. "This is serious, Cora. I can't tell whether you're pretending to be okay or if you're in complete denial."

"Neither, Mom." I meet her eyes. It isn't easy. "I just . . . don't want to let you guys down."

I know I'm failing; I know I've always failed, but it really is true.

"You couldn't possibly let us down, Cora," she says gently.

I know she wants that to be true so badly, and I also know it's *not* actually true.

"Thanks, Mom," I whisper. Then I pull away and head back to my room.

Rafiq is staring at the painting again. "Do you like it that much?" I ask as I approach.

"I find it interesting," he says. "There is much to ponder here."

"Do you actually ponder stuff, or do you just call up and organize information based on your parameters and protocols?"

"What is pondering, then?"

My gaze flicks to the painting. "It's much messier. For me, at least."

"Have you been pondering something, Cora?"

I laugh, dry like dead leaves. "Nope." Then I laugh again.

Today Rafiq is wearing jeans that look disturbingly good on him and a short-sleeved shirt with a collar. If he were walking the halls of Clinton Academy, all the girls would be drooling. "I have a present for you," he says, as if this is the conversation we were going to have before I announced I was busy. "When you're ready, we can go look at it. It's outside."

I guess he knows I'm not busy after all. "Let me put some shoes on." I trudge into my room and slide my feet into the first pair of shoes I come across, sigh as they self-adjust to the perfect size, then go back to the hall, where Rafiq finally moves his gaze from the painting.

We head outside, me trying not to stare at his face and body. Wind ruffles my short hair, blowing it dry and probably undoing my earlier brushing. When we reach the edge of the patio, he leads me along a little stone path to the gardening shed. After he murmurs a request to Franka, the doors slide open. Rafiq gestures inside. "What do you think?"

"Is that a kite?"

He grins. "It is."

The thing is huge, a geometric flower of silky green-and-pink fabric stretched over a frame of splinter-thin bone-white plastic. Three lines of filament dangle from its bottom and join in one line, connected to a reel.

"Is it drone lifted?" I haven't seen a kite in years, not since my mom took me to the beach a few months after she told me my dad wasn't coming back.

"Wind powered. Want to try it?"

I look around. We're between the river and the house. "Here?"

"Sure. The breeze is great today."

As if in agreement, a gust buffets me. Rafiq tilts his head. Slowly, he reaches over and smooths my hair down on top, and I freeze, goose bumps rippling over my skin. *Touch me again,* I think. But I don't say it, because it is so freaking weird. He's a canny.

He doesn't look like a canny. I clear my throat, and the tiniest flicker of a smile crosses his face.

"Um," I say, "how do we do it? I've never flown a kite."

"Would you like me to try first?"

I nod. "Need my help?"

He leans into the shed and brings out the kite. "Hold this."

I take it. It feels fragile, too light. Suddenly I feel like I might accidentally snap its skinny bird bones if I hold it in the wrong place. Suddenly I want to crush it between my hands to see if I'm right. And then I want to tear its silky skin off to see what I've done.

"Your facial expression suggests discomfort."

"I don't want to break it." Also, I want to break it. And then stomp on it.

"You won't, Cora. This will be easy." He points to the wide strip of lawn between the edge of the patio and the riverbank. "We can do it right here. There's plenty of room on either side."

I glance across the patio toward the bay window and see Mom standing inside, watching us. Rafiq notices, because he says, "You don't wish to meet with me anymore."

I close my eyes. "It's not that. I like you. But . . ." I feel unstable. Like everything might fall on me at once. Or worse, like everything might come pouring *out*. "I'm missing a lot of school."

"That is not the only reason."

"Okay, and I miss my friends." Friend, really. The rest I could take or leave.

"But school is the place you attempted to hurt yourself. Were your friends not there?"

I open my eyes and glare at him. "Can we fly this thing already?"

"Perhaps you were reminded of Hannah's absence, and—"

"Yes or no?" I say loudly. "Did you want to fly this?"

He blinks at me. "Certainly." He holds the reel and pushes the handle to cause the filament to release. Together, we walk toward the lawn, and I slowly increase the distance between us. The wind tugs at the flimsy structure in my hands, making its silky flanks bulge.

"It wants to fly," I murmur, lifting it over my head.

"It was built for that purpose, and it seems wrong to hold it back," says Rafiq, his eyes on the kite. Then he looks at me and nods. "I'm ready."

I let the kite go. The wind pulls the filament taut just a few feet over my head, and I hunch my shoulders and dodge to the side, imagining it wrapping around my neck. Rafiq steps back and continues to release the line, and the silk-and-bone flower slowly rises into the sky, shimmering under the late-summer sun. I shield my eyes to watch it soar. The filament is invisible now, and if I focus, it's easy to pretend the flower is flying on its own, untethered, unmoored.

I lower my hand from my face and turn to watch Rafiq. His gaze is on the kite as it swoops, and his hands cradle the reel, his touch light. He seems riveted.

"What are you thinking right now?" I ask.

"Freedom," he says.

"In an abstract way or a personal way?"

He clears his throat. The kite dips and spirals in the air. Rafiq jerks the reel back and up. Then he blinks. "Oh."

I follow the trajectory of the kite as it crashes into the high fence surrounding the widow's walk—the deck on the roof of the house— four stories up. My stomach drops.

Rafiq looks down at the reel in his hand, then his gaze follows the thread of filament up to the walk. The kite is caught on one of the chimneys just over the railing. If we try to pull it down, the string will snap. I peer at the bay window. Mom is gone.

"Franka," says Rafiq. "Is Gretchen available?"

"No," says Franka, her voice emanating from the patio. "She is currently in the master bedroom, cleaning it in advance of Dr. Dietrich's return."

"We'll have to get it ourselves," Rafiq says. He locks the reel and sets it on the ground. After a few steps, he pauses. "Will you come with me?"

I'm staring up there. "I don't want to."

"Please? It might take two of us. I might be a machine, but I do not have superhuman agility or strength."

"Really?"

"I was created with the musculature, reflexes, flexibility, agility, and strength of a human male with a similar physical structure to mine."

"I have so many questions," I blurt out.

"Accompany me up there to retrieve our kite, and I will answer as many as I can."

"You are so freaking tricky."

He smiles. "Shall we?" Then he continues heading across the patio to the door that leads through the back hall. It opens as Franka senses our approach. "I've never been up to that deck."

"It's called a widow's walk."

He is quiet for a moment. "What a sad connotation. The structures were put atop coastal homes and were named after the idea that a woman would wait for her husband to come home from the sea, something that did not always happen."

I am walking behind him but can tell by the tilt of his head that he has a question. "What?"

"We are near a river but not an ocean. Why does this mansion have a widow's walk?"

"You'll see," I mutter. My heart is beating fast, but Rafiq hasn't called me on it, and I'm happy to pretend that it's because we're now climbing the stairs. "Ugh," I say, making a show of breathing hard, "I'm out of shape." Which reminds me of all those questions I want to ask. The more he talks about himself, the less he can talk about me. "I've been wondering—do you breathe?"

"I have a heat-diffusion system that is vented through my nose."

"So . . . no? You just blow hot air?"

He glances down at me, one hand on the banister. We're between the second and third floors. Pictures of Hannah and her mom decorate this wide back staircase, hanging in a diagonal line that ascends the wall above the railing. "Your tone suggests that is a feature that is ripe for humor."

I put my hands up. "You said you don't eat. So how do you get energy? You must use a lot of it."

"I am equipped with nanowire batteries that require recharging once every two years. I am also very efficient."

"I guess we've already talked about sleeping, too."

He reaches the landing on the third floor and waits. "And dreaming."

"Okay, what about . . ." And, oh my god, I can't help it, I glance down at his crotch.

He follows my eyes. "You are wondering about my anatomy."

"Is this the moment where you clear your throat again?"

He raises his head, and his eyes hold mine. "I have a male configuration."

"Okay, but can you . . ." My cheeks are on fire. "Sorry. This is too personal."

"Am I a person to you, Cora?"

I look up the final flight of stairs. Looking into his eyes makes me feel wobbly and confused and awkward. "Do you want to be?"

"Want."

"That one really trips you up, doesn't it?"

He begins walking up the steps to the fourth floor.

"Whoa," I continue. "It really does. If it helps, it's not always so easy for humans, either."

He pauses for a moment. Stops right there on the steps, looking upward. "My neurocortex is a prototype, and my face is a novel configuration chosen by my architect, but my body is a mass-produced casing." His voice is quiet, level. "It was designed for use in the personal-companion industry and is capable of performing all the functions necessary to please and satisfy a human client." Then he continues the walk, leaving me behind to sort out all the crazy sensations inside my body as the meaning of what he just said sinks in.

When I catch up with him on the fourth-floor landing, I lead him over to the little spiral staircase below the walk. The closer I get, the sicker I feel.

Rafiq climbs the first few steps and looks up. "Franka, please open the door."

"Please note this is a safety hazard," she says.

"She's right," I say, clutching the railing.

"Please note I am supervising my client," Rafiq replies. "I am clear on my directives."

Franka goes quiet. The trapdoor at the top of the steps slides open, letting the sunshine stream down. When it hits my face, I shudder. My voice is shriller than I want as I ask, "And what are your directives, exactly?"

Rafiq climbs up onto the widow's walk and reaches down, offering me his hand. I climb up by myself, my heart threatening to explode.

The last time I was up here . . .

"You're pale, Cora," Rafiq says, "and you're sweating."

"I just climbed four flights of stairs—what do you expect?"

For a moment, he stands there, maybe listening to my heartbeat. "How should we try to retrieve our kite?" he finally asks, turning to look up at the flower, which is three feet out of the reach of his upstretched arms and waggling fingers. "I can't do it by myself."

Distant booms echo in my ears, and I sway. Memory or my heartbeat, it doesn't matter. Doesn't. Matter. "I don't know what you expect me to do. You're taller than I am."

"You could sit on my shoulders," he suggests.

"You're joking." Boom. Boom. Boom.

"It would be the most efficient way to retrieve the kite."

Right now, I'd do just about anything to be down off this roof. "Okay. Sure. Let's get it done." I can barely hear my own voice. The noise in my head is so loud.

He approaches me and kneels. "Climb up."

I stare at his smooth hairline. There are even fine little hairs on the back of his neck, so real looking. Focusing hard on them, I put one hand on the chimney column and another on his shoulder, and I heave myself up. My hands walk up the wall, rough brick under my palms, as he rises to his feet. I look right into the sun and let the flashing brightness alerts in my visual field keep me here and now so I won't focus on that night when I clung to this brick and counted every breath.

"Cora? The kite?"

"Oh." Squinting and half-blind, I reach up and clumsily pull at the kite. Rafiq's hands are tight over my calves. My thighs on either side of his face feel huge, like two seals lying on a beach. I concentrate on the kite and do my best not to break its bones.

When it slides clear, Rafiq turns around quickly. The view from the walk is breathtaking and devastating. The skyscrapers, the skyway, the Washington Monument, Hannah's angry-scared face, Mei's look of fear and horror, Lara's sneer, and the entire sky exploding. The kite falls from my hands. It hits the deck with a snap. My arms are reeling. I'm going to fall. My bones, my bones.

I know what it sounds like when they break.

"Cora?" Rafiq says, but I'm in the grip of it, trying my best not to throw up all over the top of his head. He sinks quickly to his knees, then sinks even lower to duck out from between my legs. He catches me before I fall on my numb feet. "What's happening?" His arms close around me. I am against his chest. "Your heart . . ."

I throw my arms around his waist and twist my fingers in his shirt. I am gasping, stars bursting in front of my eyes. Rafiq takes my face in his hands, tilting my chin up so he can look down at me. "I'm here. Please talk to me."

"I c-can't," I whisper. My teeth chatter. More explosions.

"Please, Cora."

It comes up from me like liquid under pressure, a geyser, champagne shooting a cork, uncontrolled release. "Sometimes I hated her," I choke out. "Sometimes I wanted her to die."

Chapter Ten

Data review.
Internal narrative: on.

9:54 p.m., July 4, 2069

Hannah is walking down the hallway toward the foyer. Her footsteps are rapid, the sound suggesting hard heels with a small area of contact. Her gaze shifts right, and there is another girl, black hair, brown eyes, small frame. Cross-reference with the facial-recognition database indicates that this girl is Mei Yang.

Mei Yang (hereafter referred to as Mei) smiles. "I don't think we need sweaters," she says. Her gaze moves away from Hannah, her focus out of the frame. Hannah looks to the left, and her perspective takes in 2 additional girls. One is Cora. She is wearing a loose, bulky front-buttoning sweater. Next to her is a girl of similar age, with long brown hair parted in the middle. This girl is taller than the other 3, with blue eyes and what appears to be a diamond-dust tattoo on her temple surrounding her Cerepin nodule. Cross-reference with the facial-recognition database indicates that this girl is Lara Perry (hereafter referred to as Lara). Mei and Lara completed 11th grade at Clinton Academy, making them classmates of Cora and Hannah.

Lara glances at Cora, puts her hand up to shield her face from Cora's view, and rolls her eyes. Hannah giggles and slaps the girl's arm.

"This is our tradition," Hannah says, seemingly to Cora. "It's so much better than watching the show with the commoners."

"I'm a commoner," says Cora.

"Not anymore," says Mei. "Now you're a Dietrich."

"Only because my mom made me change my name," Cora mutters.

"Okay, wow," says Hannah.

"That wasn't very nice," says Lara. She laughs, but tonal analysis suggests that it is more derisive than humorous. "Mei, have you heard from Neda?"

Hannah looks over at the black-haired girl. "No," Mei says. "I haven't—"

"She can't come," Cora says. She is frowning. "Her family leaves early tomorrow for their vacation."

"Since when does she communicate only with you?" asks Mei.

"Weirdos stick together," whispers Lara.

"Lara!" Hannah slaps the tall girl in the arm again, but she is laughing and the act appears to have playful intent.

"Sometimes the truth hurts. Not to be mean, but I think we've outgrown Neda."

"She does seem more interested in machines than people," says Mei.

"Maybe she's building herself a canny boyfriend," Lara says. "Someone who would actually be interested in her."

"Neda is beautiful." This comes from Cora. Her voice is so loud that Hannah lets out a soft cry codable as surprise.

"No one said she was ugly," Hannah says.

"You're being awful!" The shout comes from Cora. When Hannah turns around, we see Cora has stopped in the foyer behind the group. Cora's face is flushed, and her eyes are wide with anger. "You're nice to her face, and then behind her back you're always saying nasty things!"

"Oh my god," Lara says. "We're joking, Cora. Do you know what a joke is?"

"Sure," says Cora. Her nostrils are flared, and her fists are clenched around the hem of her sweater. "But your 'jokes' aren't ever funny." Her facial expression provides a mix of cues. Some, including the contracted orbicularis oris and masseter muscles, are codable as anger, but others, such as the activation of the frontalis and corrugator supercilii, indicate fear.

"You're not always good at getting humor, though, are you?" asks Hannah. "At least that's what your mom told me."

Cora flinches at the mention of her mother. After a pause of 4 seconds she says, "I just want you to be nice to Neda." Her voice trembles. "She's a really good person, and she's beautiful, and she's . . . nice."

Hannah laughs. "Sometimes you're adorable, CC," she says. Her tone reads as pity or scorn.

"No, she's not," Lara whispers, very close to Hannah's ear. Then, in full voice, Lara says, "Are you sure you don't have a little crush on Neda, CC? I mean, we thought for sure you were interested in boys"—here, she and Hannah are looking at each other, and Lara raises 1 eyebrow and rolls her eyes again—"but it's okay if you've got pants feelings for girls, too."

Mei snorts. "'Pants feelings'?"

Cora has wrapped her arms around her body, as though she is hugging herself. She has commenced low-intensity rocking. Her eyes are averted, and she appears to be examining the ceiling.

Hannah pokes Lara in the arm and says quietly, "Enough. We need to go if we want to see the whole thing." She turns back to the staircase and begins to walk.

"Oh, come on, CC, let's just drop it. I'm just kidding anyway," says Lara, sliding her hand through her hair before pulling it back into a ponytail with a self-adjusting silver binding she was previously wearing as a bracelet on her wrist. "It's windy up there." She appears to be reading information off her lenses. "I don't want to look like a freak when we come down."

Hannah looks back at Cora, who is scowling and pushing her fingers through her thick, disheveled hair.

"It's just us tonight, CC," Hannah says. "Don't worry about it."

"Yeah, it's not like Finn is here to see you," says Lara. She emphasizes the name, saying it at significantly higher volume than every other word in her statement.

Cora's mouth opens and she stammers, "I-I-I don't—" Her cheeks turn pink.

"Relax," says Hannah. "Ignore her."

"Right," Lara replies. "It's not like I hit a nerve or anything."

"Finn and CC are just friends," Hannah says. "Quit teasing her. She knows it's not cool to go after your sister's boyfriend."

"You broke up with him five months ago," Cora says.

"Four," says Mei. "Why are you exaggerating?"

"And they'd been together for two years," Lara adds. "Are you saying it was no big deal?"

"No!" Cora catches up with the others. The group has reached the staircase and begins to climb. "It's just, it's July, and they broke up at the beginning of February—"

"Well, that was just the beginning of the breakup," Hannah says quietly. Her tone indicates sadness. "We were up and down for a month before it finally fizzled out. I think we'd still be together if it weren't for certain . . . factors."

Hannah's cam perspective wobbles as Cora says, "Hey!"

Lara has moved between Cora and Hannah and put an arm around Hannah's shoulders. "Sweetie, it's okay. Don't let this ruin your night."

"I'm fine," Hannah says, but she uses the same sad voice. She is gazing upward, at a photograph of a woman and a little girl that is hanging on the wall at the top of the steps, the image projected into the space above the landing. Facial-recognition matching indicates it is Hannah

110

at age 5 years and Naomi Dietrich (Hannah's biological mother, date of death May 13, 2063).

"She shouldn't have brought it up," Mei says. She has narrowed her proximity to Hannah as well.

"I didn't bring it up!" shouts Cora, who seems to have again fallen behind the others.

Hannah turns to look at her sister. She is now several steps above Cora, and Cora is staring at Hannah's feet. "She never said you did," Hannah says. "You don't have to scream at me."

"I wasn't screaming at *you*!" Cora is leaning forward now, platysma flexed, making her neck look wider. Her fingers are tensed over her thighs.

"Oh my god," says Mei from Hannah's right side. "Let's just go."

Hannah turns and walks up the stairs. It appears that Lara and Mei have flanked her, and their feet are visible in the frame. She and her friends climb 2 flights before she looks down the center of the staircases once more to see that Cora hasn't moved. "Come on," she says. Her tone indicates a smile. Cheerfulness. "You don't want to miss the fireworks."

"I don't like fireworks," Cora says.

Lara groans. "Come *on*, CC. If you make us miss the opener, I'm going to be so pissed."

Cora lowers her head and walks slowly up the stairs.

Hannah and the other 2 girls proceed up a spiral staircase. The overhead door at the top slides open, revealing a starry night sky. Sounds of distant music are audible. "God, I love it up here," Hannah says as she steps onto a fenced-in deck area.

"You are so lucky," says Mei.

"You're lucky to be my friends," says Hannah, and Mei smiles, possibly in response to a smile from Hannah.

"And here's the luckiest one of all," announces Lara. Hannah turns to see Cora climb awkwardly onto the deck. She rests briefly on her hands and knees. Lara makes a derisive noise. "Are you some kind of animal?"

Cora clumsily gets to her feet and wraps her arms around herself, as if she is cold. However, the temperature reading on Hannah's Cerepin display shows that it is 87 degrees Fahrenheit.

The deck glows with surface lighting, and Hannah glances toward additional chip lighting embedded in the brick chimney. "Franka, lights level two please. If it's too bright, we can't see the fireworks properly."

The lights dim. "Also," Hannah says, "could you have Gretchen bring us drinks? I made punch. It's in the refrigerator."

"The beverage you reference is not available. Drake disposed of the unauthorized container," Franka says.

"Because of Gary's rule about alcohol," says Cora.

"'Because of Gary's rule about alcohol,'" Lara repeats in a high-pitched voice. The tone suggests mockery and contempt. "God, CC, and you're probably the one who told on us, aren't you?"

Cora looks away quickly, turning toward the National Mall, where the Washington Monument stands. Hannah follows her gaze. Cross-referenced aerial photographs indicate the monument is surrounded in a wide perimeter by skyscrapers, currently not visible. It is possible their lighting has been turned off in preparation for the reported fireworks display.

"You did, didn't you?" asks Hannah.

Cora does not answer.

Mei clucks her tongue. "She totally did."

End of vid capture, 9:59 p.m., July 4, 2069

10:07 p.m., July 4, 2069

Cora is standing on the railing of the deck. Her entire upper body is tensed. Her eyes are wide; her lips are pulled downward and apart, revealing her teeth; the fingers of her left hand grip the brick column of the chimney while her right arm is out to assist her balance. "I'll do it," she shrieks.

"Get down," shouts Lara.

"Oh my god, oh my god," Mei says quietly, repeating the phrase over and over.

"Cora, your actions have created a significant risk to your safety," Franka states. "If you do not return to the widow's walk, I will notify your parents and emergency services."

"Shut up, Franka," Cora screams. She slams her right hand over her ear and closes her eyes. Her body sways in response, and she throws her arm out again.

Hannah gasps. "CC, please."

"Stop calling me that! I know why you call me that!"

"It's just a nickname," Hannah says. Her voice is level and soft. "Because I love you. Please get down."

"You're such a liar!"

"I know you're upset and scared. I know you were nervous about coming up here. But you're with friends, and we care about you," Hannah continues.

"Yeah," says Lara. "We really care about you." Her tone is ambiguous. Depending on the tonal-coding rubric applied, it could indicate understated sarcasm or mild concern.

"Oh my god," Mei says again. "What if she jumps? Would she die?"

"You'd like that, wouldn't you?" Cora asks. Her arm is still out, acting to balance her body. "You'd like it if I was all smashed up."

"Cora, I am required to notify authorities if you do not comply with intervention directives within one minute," Franka says. "You have thirty-five seconds."

"She could jump in less than one," Mei says loudly.

"Is that a suggestion?" Lara mutters.

"CC, just get down." Hannah's tone now suggests either fatigue or boredom.

"Not until you take it back," Cora says. The deck and chimney lighting has increased in intensity from the previous vid capture. The light reflects tears on Cora's cheeks.

The sound of explosions, presumably the planned fireworks display, is audible, echoing as the noise bounces off the skyscrapers. Behind Cora, the sky is illuminated with white and blue and red light.

"Figures," Lara says, very close to Hannah's ear. "Crazy Cora ruins everything again."

"What are you saying?" shouts Cora. "What did you just say?"

"What does it matter? Are you going to jump down here and attack us?" asks Lara.

Cora becomes still, her mouth half-open, fireworks exploding behind her. Then she gasps as Hannah rushes forward. Hannah's hands, her fingernails decorated with waving American flags, grab folds of Cora's sweater. For 1 second, it appears that she has pushed Cora backward, and Cora screams, her arms reeling. But then Hannah grunts, and her arcing cam perspective shows her falling backward. Her breath is propelled forcefully from her lungs as her back makes impact with the deck and Cora lands on top of her.

Mei has been screaming during this epoch. Lara shouts, "You're crushing her." She leans over and grabs two handfuls of Cora's sweater. Cora rolls or is lifted off Hannah. Hannah is wheezing.

Mei kneels at Hannah's side. "Are you hurt? Are your ribs broken or something?"

"Medical scan indicates no fractures, Hannah," says Franka. "But your respiration and heart rate are out of normal range, as are Cora's."

"She'll be fine," Hannah says. "Just give her a minute."

Hannah turns her head to see Cora, who is audibly crying. She is hunched over and facedown on the deck, hands covering her face, knees pulled up beneath her. Hannah focuses on a hole in the back of

Cora's sweater as fireworks pop. "I'm glad you're okay, CC," she says. "But what you just did was really dangerous. Were you trying to hurt yourself?"

Cora says something, but it is indecipherable because of her hands covering her mouth. The movement of her back and the audio suggest convulsive sobbing. Hannah rolls over and pats her back, but Cora jerks away from her.

"Just let her be," says Lara. "God. You just saved her life."

"She's my sister," says Hannah. "I just don't understand why she got so upset."

"You're so nice to her, way more than she deserves." Mei reaches over, perhaps to smooth down Hannah's hair, then grasps her hand and pulls Hannah to a standing position. "God knows you didn't ask for this."

"She can hear you," Hannah observes. Cora is still sobbing. It is not clear whether she hears. She displays no unambiguous external cues.

"Let's just ignore her and watch the fireworks," Lara says. "We shouldn't let her ruin our tradition. We tried to include her, but obviously she doesn't want to be with us."

Hannah turns and looks down at Cora, who is still in the fetal position and still crying intensely. "Come on, CC. Get up. The fireworks are pretty."

Cora does not give any external indication that she hears Hannah. The other two girls are having a muttered conversation at the opposite end of the deck, but Hannah's auditory sensor is not set at levels that enable transcription.

Hannah raises her head and looks out at the fireworks. "Okay. I give up." She moves closer to the railing. She watches the fireworks for the next 19 minutes. After 11 minutes, 13 seconds, Cora's sobs either stop or become quiet enough that they are obscured by the sound of the fireworks.

End of vid capture, 10:34 p.m., July 4, 2069

2:26 p.m., July 5, 2069

Dr. Dietrich is sitting at the desk in his library, examining an open book in a glass case before him. He turns when Hannah quietly says, "Dad?"

"Hey, sleepyhead," he says, his neutral expression quickly becoming a smile. "I was hoping I'd see you before my dinner meeting. How was last night?"

"Good." Hannah's tone indicates sadness, however. She directs her gaze out the window, toward the river. When she looks back, her father is no longer smiling.

"If you're down about the punch Drake threw out, you should know that's totally on me. And you. You know better, Hannah."

"I wasn't the one who wanted it! Cora asked me to make it, but then she must have felt all guilty about wanting to drink, so she tried to blame it all on me."

"But you're supposed to look out for your sister."

"Trust me, I'm trying."

Dr. Dietrich furrows his brow. "What's up?"

"Did you check Franka's safety logs, by any chance?"

Now Dr. Dietrich appears alarmed. He gets up and gestures Hannah over to the couch, where she sits down next to him. "What happened?"

Hannah sighs. "I don't even know, Dad. It happened so fast."

Dr. Dietrich looks toward the hallway. Hannah does as well. "Is Maeve—" she begins.

"She's with her trainer," he says. "Just tell me."

"We went up to watch the fireworks, me and Mei and Lara and Cora, and she just snapped. She freaked out, maybe about the sound? I know she's edgy about loud noises."

"So why did you take her up to watch the fireworks?" There is a tone of bemusement in Dr. Dietrich's voice. "Seems like an odd activity for someone who doesn't like to hear things go boom."

"We didn't want her to feel left out," she explains. "You said to make her feel included, and I've been trying so hard. Lara and Mei are, too. And Finn. All of them feel sorry for her. They try so hard to be nice to her, but she can be so mean, Dad." Hannah looks down at her hands, which are clasped in her lap. "And sometimes violent."

Now Dr. Dietrich sighs. "We're considering interventions."

"Is Maeve on board with that?"

"She's getting there. But she's protective of Cora."

Hannah moves her hands, and now a long scratch is visible on the back of her left hand. It is scabbed over and runs diagonally from the first joint of her fifth finger to the base of her thumb.

"Did she do that?" Dr. Dietrich asks, his tone sharp.

Hannah covers the injury with her other hand. "Don't worry about it."

"Hannah."

She looks up at her father. "I don't want to get her in trouble."

He stares at her. "Do I need to increase the surveillance in your wing?" he asks. "I've been giving you girls privacy like you both wanted, but—"

"Okay! Okay. I'll tell you, but I don't want her to think I'm tattling. She hates me enough as it is."

"Maeve says she loves you, Hannah. Cora just struggles with this kind of thing."

"Whatever." Her tone suggests that she is skeptical. "We were up on the widow's walk to watch the show, and Cora climbed up on the railing. You can watch it for yourself on Franka's surveillance feed if you want. We had her privacy settings on for a little while, but I turned them off when Cora got out of control, and good thing, too. Franka had to threaten to call the authorities—twice."

"My god," Dr. Dietrich says, glancing upward.

"She wouldn't get down." Hannah's voice has increased in pitch. Her breath is audible, hitching, indicating extreme emotion. "I was afraid she was going to jump, Dad. I really was."

From the movement of Hannah's cam perspective, it appears that Dr. Dietrich has pulled her into a hug. She focuses on the dark hairs on his forearm. He releases her. "She got down on her own, though?" he asks.

"No, I pulled her down. If she'd jumped Franka couldn't have done a thing. It was just us up there. I had to do something."

"And that's how you got hurt." He takes his daughter's hand and holds it out, examining the scratch.

Hannah tugs her hand out of her father's grasp. "I really thought she was going to die. I didn't want her to die, Daddy." Hannah begins to cry.

Dr. Dietrich attempts to soothe his daughter, shushing her in low tones. "You saved her, Hannah. She's alive because of you."

"But what about the next time? She scares me so much. Even Franka can't keep her safe. Or you guys. And you travel so much."

"I'll try to rework my schedule a little," says Dr. Dietrich. "But I have this trip to France with Maeve in August that I can't cancel."

"I know, and I don't want you to! But maybe . . . sometimes I wonder if she shouldn't . . . I don't know. Aren't there places people go for treatment? Places that can take care of people like CC?"

"I'm working on this," Dr. Dietrich says. He is frowning.

"Maeve doesn't believe me, does she?"

"Look, this is thin ice for me, okay? She's so protective of Cora—CC?"

Hannah nods, and Dr. Dietrich continues.

"Look, this is between us, but I think Maeve feels guilty for what happened to CC when she was little. That wasn't CC's fault."

"It wasn't Maeve's, either!" says Hannah.

"Oh, trust me, I know. I mean, what kind of a man does that to a little girl? Getting that judge to terminate his parental rights might be the best thing I've ever done."

"You're such a good dad. I know I'm lucky."

Dr. Dietrich bows his head. "You had a pretty good mom, too," he says quietly.

"I know. You still miss her, don't you?"

"Of course I do. I always will. Maeve understands that."

"I wonder what she would think of me, if she could see me now."

"She'd be so proud of you," says Dr. Dietrich. "She'd be honored to have you as a daughter, like I am. But Hannah, even though I want you to look out for CC, I want you to know that you're not responsible for her choices. You worry about yourself, and let me and Maeve take care of your sister."

"But I worry about CC, Dad. I have ever since she moved in." Hannah's tone reflects ambiguous signals. Caring but also anger. Bitterness.

"I just want you to be okay," he says.

"I just want CC to be okay," Hannah says. "I do."

End of vid capture, 2:37 p.m., July 5, 2069

Chapter Eleven

We stand on the widow's walk, the wind tickling our backs, but I feel like I'm up there on the railing again, about to fall. I can't believe what I just said. I was never supposed to say that out loud.

Rafiq holds me, and he is so warm. He doesn't need to breathe, but he's breathing, his chest moving just like a real person's. For me, for now, he is real. He strokes my hair. "I've got you. Feel whatever you need to feel," he murmurs.

I press into him, letting his contours distract me from all the things that terrify me. I shiver as he draws his fingers along my cheek.

He kisses my forehead.

For a moment, I freeze, confused, startled, cold and hot at the same time. Then I sigh and close my eyes. "Do that again."

He hesitates. And then he does. "Like that?"

I nod. The feeling of his lips on my skin is perfect—strong enough to push everything else away.

"You were remembering something."

"Shut up," I whisper.

He chuckles. "No." He kisses my forehead a third time. "But I'm not going to let anything hurt you. It's safe to think about it."

I want that to be true. "You can't protect me. Everything's happened already. The damage is done."

"You mean it's all in your head, the memories, how it's rewired things." He looks down at me. "And that's what I'm here to help with. That's my whole reason for being."

"Your reason for being."

"I was created for a specific purpose. You know that."

Does he sound sad? I'm so terrible at figuring these things out even in humans, and he doesn't give me much to go on. "So if I don't get better . . ."

"Don't worry about me. That's not why I said that. I simply said it because it's true."

"Okay. Can we go down now? I hate it up here."

"Why?"

I sag in his arms. "Please. I hate it so much."

"Your profile indicates no fear of heights."

"It's the *noise*."

"The noise here is well within acceptable parameters."

He's looking at me. Listening to the prisoner locked behind my ribs. "Oh," he says. His grip on my body tightens. "Franka, open the door, please."

The door slides open, and Rafiq keeps his arm around me as we descend the spiral staircase and end up in the little gallery on the fourth floor. The paintings in here are all of Paris in the rain, all done by Hannah's mom, Naomi. Her art hangs throughout the house, but the walls of this room are absolutely covered with her work. Hannah used to paint in here sometimes. She said she wanted to be close to her mom.

Maybe that's where she is now.

Oh, god. I swallow spit and something worse, sour and bitter.

I sit on a couch, and Rafiq moves close. I could slide into his lap and kiss him, and I am tempted to do it, because it's the only thing that will save me from thinking of her face. I wonder what his mouth would taste like.

He touches his lips as he sees me staring at them. "Are you all right?"

I swallow again. "We left the kite up there."

"It's less important than your well-being, Cora. Now, tell me why you said you hated Hannah."

I look down at my lap, at my thighs spread across the cushions. "I didn't mean that. I loved her."

He remains quiet and I squirm, then mutter, "I don't know what you want me to say."

"Can you love someone and hate her at the same time? Isn't that possible?"

I shrug one shoulder. "You tell me. You're the therapist."

"You're working so hard to avoid the truth, Cora, to the point where you're claiming you don't have any memories. But they're in there, and they're hurting you. You're fighting so hard, but I can see that you're tired." He tips my chin up with gentle fingertips. God, he is so, so handsome. Makes Finn look like a sad substitute. "Everything you say is safe with me. Every part of you is safe, if you let me in."

"I want that to be true," I whisper.

"Then let it be true," he murmurs, leaning closer.

If I move forward just slightly, I could kiss him. I don't know if that's what I want. I mean, my body wants it. I can feel the tingle and the tightening. But it's so weird. I'm so weird. Why am I thinking about this? Why am I thinking this way about a canny?

"Tell me about Hannah," he says.

Oh. Yeah. That's why. I pull away. "She's dead."

"I know. But in your mind, she is very much alive."

He's right. "I don't know what to say," I mumble.

"Tell me one thing you remember about her."

"Good or bad?"

"Your choice."

"She had short hair."

"Like yours?"

I shudder as a sudden chill runs through me. "No. I don't look like her. We looked nothing alike."

"Tell me more about what she looked like."

"Can't you just look at a picture or watch some of the vids on her Mainstream channel?"

"I want to know what she looks like to you in here," he says, touching my temple, just a brush of skin on skin. Or . . . plastic on skin? Biosynth polymers on skin? I don't know what he's made of. I only know it feels real. I grab his hand and peer at it.

"You have fingerprints."

"I do. But we were talking about Hannah's appearance, not mine."

I close my eyes. "She was beautiful. Just . . . so, so pretty. I've seen pictures of her mom, and she looked like her. Gary's eye color, maybe, but her mom's everything else. She was so cute with her short hair. I look like an idiot."

"You cut your hair yourself, didn't you?"

"I couldn't stand it anymore," I say, my voice breaking. "But Hannah always had short hair, the whole time I knew her."

"We have established she was pretty. And you think she was prettier than you are. That's how it seems in your head."

I gape at him. "No, that's how it is." I clench my fists. "How it *was*."

"Were you jealous of her?"

"No. She was wonderful. She was so nice. How could I be jealous?"

"Easily. Maybe more easily than if she were horrible."

My brain is a swamp, and it's too murky to think clearly, to hide and show in the right way. I'm terrible at this game. "She was wonderful," I repeat, just to be saying words.

"If she was so wonderful, why did you tell me you hated her sometimes? Why did you tell me you wanted her to die?"

"I didn't say that."

"Shall I play back my vid feed?"

I raise my head and look at him. "I really said that?"

"And I believe you were telling the truth."

"No, no, I didn't mean it. I don't know why I said it."

"Maybe because your relationship was more complicated than you want to admit."

My hands are balled in my shirt now. My body is a confused traffic pattern, everything bumping up against something else, no part sure which way to move, every thought a near miss. "I ruined her life."

"How? What makes you that powerful?"

His question suggests I couldn't possibly be. I want that to be true. "Maybe I'm not. But I made her sad. All the time. I think I messed up her relationship with her boyfriend. And I made her cry. I scared her." Each word hurts as it tunnels out of my throat.

"Did you mean to scare her?"

Sometimes. Oh, god, sometimes I wanted to tear her apart. I wanted her to flinch and cower because she knew what I was capable of. "No. Never. I always felt bad afterward." That last part, at least, is true.

"What did you do to scare her?"

"I just got mad sometimes."

"Why?"

"Because she made me mad."

"How did she do that?"

It feels like an interrogation. "I'm tired," I say and rub my eyes. As I do, my message light flashes. Neda has commed me.

Haven't heard from you. Chat later?

Escape.

"Rafiq, can I go to my room?"

"Of course, Cora," he says. He takes my hand and pulls me up so I'm facing him. He doesn't let go of my hand as he says, "I'm so amazed by your bravery."

"Huh?"

"I can tell that talking about any of this is terrifying for you, and yet you did it."

"I told you Hannah had short hair."

One corner of his mouth rises in a half smile. It makes me tingle again. "We had to start somewhere." Slowly, he moves closer, and I stop breathing. "Thank you," he whispers, and this time he doesn't kiss my forehead.

His mouth is wet. And warm. Real. His breath smells like mint. How is that possible? My hands are at his sides, and I feel his waist and the hard muscles there. Are they muscles or just a mold, a shape, pretend? I don't really care anymore. It's all I can do not to shove my hands under his shirt.

"Your heart is racing," he murmurs when he raises his head. "Are you having another memory?"

I shake my head, too breathless to speak. He wraps his arms around me and hugs me. Our bodies are pressed together. "What does this feel like to you?" I ask.

He is quiet for so long that my eyes sting. But then his arms squeeze me a little tighter. "It feels good." He releases me, blinking. "I will let you go now."

I backtrack toward the door. "Are you coming?"

He turns away. "I will check in on you later. Is that all right?"

"Did I just mess this up?"

He looks over his shoulder. "I'm afraid I did."

I bite my lip as my eyes trace him, looking for the proof that he's not real, the proof that will turn off the things I'm thinking and wanting. "It felt good to me, too," I say, and then I grab the doorframe and lurch through it, needing cold water to extinguish the flames on my cheeks.

By the time I reach the second-floor landing, I hear my mother's voice coming from the foyer. I pause at the top of the steps, first because

I don't want my mom to see me all flushed and confused and without Rafiq at my side, but then because I hear another voice, one that sounds vaguely familiar.

"Dr. Dietrich did notify me that she'd been discharged from the hospital, and as requested, I provided a few days for her to readjust to being home," says the voice. I select the voice-recognition function on my Cerepin and put it to work.

It's the detective investigating Hannah's fall. Ignacia Reyes from the DC police department.

Oh, god.

"She's really not ready to see anyone," Mom is saying. "Did my husband also tell you that she made a serious suicide attempt at school on Monday?"

"He speculated that she might have been trying to avoid speaking with me."

"If that's true, then he and I will need to have a little chat," Mom says, and I want to cheer, because her voice is cold and hard and scary.

"I don't mean to create stress in your household, Mrs. Dietrich. I have been as sensitive as possible to the needs of your living daughter. But the fact remains that your stepdaughter's death is still under investigation, and as the only witness to the event, Cora is a person of interest. Dr. Dietrich also informed me that there was tension in the girls' relationship, which is something you left out when we initially spoke with you."

"Right, and I'm sure it's a total mystery why, in the hours after losing Hannah, I wouldn't be robotic in my recall of every detail you might find relevant to your case."

Mom's tone could freeze magma right now.

"Mrs. Dietrich, I'm sorry to have disturbed you. I do need to talk with Cora soon, though. Surely you understand that I'm simply trying to do my job and to make sure justice is done for Hannah."

Mom is quiet for a few seconds. "Yes, I understand that, Detective Reyes. I'm sorry."

"No need for apologies, ma'am. But could you tell me when would be a good time to speak with Cora?"

"I'll need to talk to her therapist, and to my husband. We'll be in contact with you very soon."

"Before the end of the week?"

"Soon."

Another pause. "All right then. You know how to contact me."

"I surely do. Thanks for dropping by." I think her tone says the opposite.

After I hear the front door close, I wait for a few seconds before heading down the stairs. Mom is still standing in the foyer, and she notices me when I'm halfway down. "Were you listening to that?" she asks.

I nod. "Thanks for looking out for me."

She comes over to me and gives me a quick hug. "I know you're not ready yet, but you'll have to talk to her, honey."

"Why? I already told you everything I remember."

"But she's the detective. She's responsible for the official investigation."

Which probably means she'll interview me while cross-referencing my responses with all sorts of neuro- and bio-indicators to determine whether I'm lying. I can't do that. It doesn't matter what I say. I'm a mess all the time, and it'll say I'm lying, and then that's it—I'll be taken away. "Mom, *please*," I whisper.

She takes me by the shoulders and looks into my eyes. "Why are you so scared to talk to her?"

I shake my head.

Her eyes shine with tears. "Honey?" she asks, her voice cracking. "Is there anything you want to tell me?"

I jerk back. "Seriously? Like what?"

"I don't know! I understood why you didn't want to talk to the police right after everything happened, and your doctors agreed that you should be left alone. But now? You asked to go to school this morning. You said you were better. Why would you avoid this unless—"

"So you're like Gary now. You think I pushed her or something?"

Mom's eyes grow wide. "No, I don't, and neither does he! How could you even suggest that?"

I take a few steps back. "I don't know. Why don't you ask your husband? It's so obvious that he doesn't believe me."

"Cora, we've been over this—"

"I'm not talking to the detective. I can't. Tell her I have nothing to say." I don't look at her face as I walk quickly across the foyer and down the hall to my room, my heartbeats an earthquake in my chest.

I slam my door and flop onto my bed. I wish I could turn Franka's privacy settings back on, but right now it's pointless to ask, so I'm just going to have to be very careful about what I say, how I say it. "Reply," I say while focusing on Neda's message. "I'm here. Send."

Finally! What's going on?

"Apparently, Mom thinks I murdered Hannah. Send." I blow out a long breath, trying to slow my body down. My feet rub hard against my sheets.

Ha! Right, Neda replies. But do you want to meet for coffee or something?

"Can't. I'm stuck here at the house with Rafiq. Send."

Rafiq. Huh. Then can we com live?

"Com Neda," I say, and a moment later her face appears in my visual field. She's in her room at her house, her makeup table behind her, the mirror screen dark, her bed covered in fluffy pillows, her hijab a sunny yellow, her face immaculate. "Sometimes I wonder why you want to be my friend."

She grins. "Because you're honest and real and you'll defend my honor to the death?"

I can't help but smile. "I've really missed you."

"So, this thing with your mom thinking you . . ."

"Can't talk about it here." Franka's recording every word I say.

She nods, obviously understanding. "So why are you stuck at home with a dude named Rafiq?"

"He's my . . . Neda, it's so weird." I lower my voice and turn over on my stomach, looking down at my right index finger, where the self-cam chip is implanted.

"Oh—he's the canny?"

I nod. "But he's so real. He seems *so real.*" I bite my lip. "You should see him."

She arches an eyebrow. "Hold up. Tell me what he looks like."

"Dark hair. Dark eyebrows, kind of thick. His eyes are a lighter brown. Warm, I guess. He just seems warm."

"Good looking."

I laugh, all shaky as I remember his lips on mine. "Understatement."

"Who made him?"

I struggled to remember what Gary had said. "Some company called Am—Amican?"

"Never heard of them."

"Me neither."

Neda is frowning. "What do you do with him?"

My cheeks are getting hot again. "We . . . talk. And walk. We flew a kite."

I can't read the look on Neda's face. "You flew a kite."

"And it got stuck on the widow's walk and we went up there and I freaked out and he kissed me." It comes out in one mad rush.

Neda's eyes widen.

"On the forehead," I add. Her expression makes me think telling her the rest would not be a good idea.

"Is that . . . what's supposed to happen?"

I squirm. "I don't know," I whisper.

"You were into it."

I am so jittery that the mattress shudders beneath me. "I don't know."

"You were."

"Okay," I say, too loudly. Rafiq will hear. What if he hears?

"Is that against the rules or something? I didn't know cannies could . . . wait." Her eyes narrow. "*Can* he?"

"Can he what?"

"Cora, don't make me explain this to you."

"He told me his 'casing' was mass produced—it's the same one they use for personal companions."

She laughs. "He *can*, then. He totally can."

I can't speak. Nothing I say will be right.

She shakes her head. "I think I need to meet this guy. I want to know what protocols he's running, what his settings are."

"That sounds so weird. He doesn't look like a machine at all."

"But you're sure he is."

"Gary put him to sleep and woke him up with a voice command. It was pretty convincing."

"Okay." She tilts her head. "Cora, what about this thing with your mom?"

A strange flood of unpleasant tingling erupts in my chest and creeps up my neck. "The detective was just here, wanting to talk to me. Mom sent her away."

"You haven't talked to the police about that night?"

The last two weeks are a fog, dark and choking. "I must have told the paramedics what happened. But I was kind of out of it, especially right after."

"Okay, but if the detective wants to talk to you, does that mean they don't think Hannah's death was an accident?"

My legs curl beneath me as my body tries to make me the smallest target possible, preferably invisible.

"Cora. It's okay. Try to stay calm. You know the truth. You know you didn't hurt her, right?"

My mouth has gone completely dry.

"You know that, right?" Neda asks, quieter this time. "Right?"

"Right," I whisper. I can't breathe.

"What? Can you tell me?" She waits, and when I don't answer, she says, "Right. We should get together."

"You can't come here." I stare and stare, hoping she'll understand. The walls literally have eyes, and no move I make isn't monitored.

"Can you come back to school?"

She gets it. Because the school? She knows exactly how to get around their systems. She could do it here, too . . . She's proven that. But now I'm too afraid she'd be caught. "I want to. I hate missing school so much."

Not really. I just hate being watched like this. I feel like I'm on a table, under a laser knife. I don't get to keep a thing to myself.

"Sometimes I think I'm going crazy," I blurt out.

Neda looks at me for a long time. Her eyes are a little bit shiny. "Sometimes, I think *surviving* looks crazy. But it never is, okay?" Her teeth clench. "Surviving is the best way to tell the people who have hurt you that they can go to hell."

Chapter Twelve

Data review.
Internal narrative: on.

Supplemental vid evidence acquired: Franka surveillance feed 4:57 p.m., July 10, 2069, 1st floor, Room 9, informal designation: "Den"

The house canny sets a tray of small cakes and cups of tea on the end table next to the sofa. "Do you need anything else, Cora?"

Cora, who is sitting next to a young woman of approximately the same age, shakes her head. "We're good, Gretchen."

Cora's companion, whom the facial-recognition database identifies as Neda Rahbani (16 years of age, completed 11th grade at Clinton Academy), is wearing a pink hijab and red lipstick. Neda Rahbani (here-after referred to as Neda) leans forward and picks up one of the cakes. After taking a bite, she smiles. "Drake is amazing, and so are these petits fours."

"I knew you like them," Cora says, "so I asked him to make some for us. Welcome back."

Neda looks over at her. "That was really nice of you, Cora."

Instead of smiling, Cora looks uncomfortable. She shifts her weight and looks away from Neda. "I wanted to make you happy," she says quietly.

"What's up?" asked Neda.

"Nothing."

"Everything you are doing right now is screaming that it's not nothing."

Cora releases a loud sigh and turns back to Neda. "I missed you while you were on vacation."

Neda smiles. "I missed you, too. How was your Fourth?"

Cora grimaces.

"Uh-oh," Neda says.

"Can I ask you something? Do you think of Lara and Hannah and Mei as your friends?" Cora asks after 11 seconds of silence.

Neda chuckles. "Sometimes."

Cora's head tilts. "How can you be friends with someone only sometimes?"

Neda reaches out, seemingly intending to touch Cora's arm, but then retracts her arm. "I just meant that we've sort of drifted apart."

"They say mean things about you sometimes." Cora makes this statement quickly and loudly. Her fists are clenched.

"Oh, I know that," Neda says. Her facial expression and voice suggest amusement.

"You do?" Cora's expression suggests confusion.

"Sure. It's not like they haven't been that way since second grade. Mean girls."

"Mean girls."

"Yeah, you know. I tolerate them when I decide it would be more fun to hang with them instead of being somewhere else, but my emotional well-being in no way depends upon their opinions of me. I honestly don't care."

Cora stares at Neda. "You don't care that they say mean stuff?"

Neda shrugs. "Doesn't hurt me, because they're not capable of hurting me. I'm doing my own thing. Building my own world. Sometimes I choose to share it with them, but mostly I don't. I have no need for their approval. It's not based on any metrics that hold my interest. And I have plenty of people in my life who think I'm awesome anyway. My parents, for instance." She grins and leans forward. "My 'computer club.'" When she says "computer club" she bends and straightens the index and middle fingers of each hand twice. "And you."

"I do think you're awesome."

"That's why I included you on that illustrious list, Cora."

"Oh." Cora rubs her palm against her other forearm. "I wish I didn't care what Hannah says."

"It's kind of a conscious decisional process, my friend."

"Oh, hey," says Hannah as she walks into the room. She leans over the tray and places 3 petits fours on a napkin before sitting down on the couch opposite Cora and Neda. "What are we up to?"

"We were discussing conscious decisional processes with regard to dealing with relational aggression typified by arbitrarily applied social norms used to enhance in-group–out-group tensions," Neda says. She smiles calmly. Cora, seated next to her, shows visible signs of emotional dysregulation with her facial response.

"Those petits fours were for Neda," Cora says to Hannah, picking up a cup of tea.

"And there are enough there to feed our entire family," Hannah replies. "Don't be childish. How was your vacation, Neda?"

"Refreshing," says Neda.

"And did Cora tell you about her little breakdown on the Fourth?"

Tea sloshes over the rim of the cup Cora is holding. She appears to be struggling to keep herself still.

"What?" says Hannah before biting off half a petit four. "It was kind of a big deal," she says with a full mouth. "And you guys are such good friends."

"Cut it out, Hannah," says Neda. There are signs of increased tension in the muscles of her face.

"Just making conversation," Hannah says, rolling her eyes. "Trying to get Cora the support she deserves. I think she might need some intense mental health treatment."

Cora lets out a whimper. Drops of spilled tea dot the thighs of her pants. Her cheeks are flushed. She has begun to rock.

"Okay," says Hannah. "Unlike you, I can take a hint." She rises, puts 3 more petits fours on her napkin. "Neda, thanks for hanging out with Cora. It's really generous of you. I know from experience that it takes a lot of—"

"Leave us alone, Hann," Neda says. She opens her mouth, appearing to yawn, then covers it with her hand. "We were having a really interesting conversation before you joined us."

Hannah laughs, but the smile disappears in less than 1 second. She turns and leaves the room. Neda reaches out and takes the cup of tea from Cora's hand, then offers her a cloth napkin from the tray. "Cora," she says. "Cora, look at me. It's all right."

Cora grimaces. Her eyes glitter with tears.

"Why didn't you tell her to go to hell?" Neda asks. "She was asking for it."

"I don't know," Cora whispers.

"I bet you told her to go to hell when she said mean stuff about me."

Cora's rocking drops abruptly in intensity. Her lips twitch, then form a slight smile. "I tried."

Neda puts the napkin in Cora's lap. "And that means more to me than fifty million fake compliments from Hannah or Lara. Okay? I just wish you'd stand up for yourself the same way."

Cora nods. Her body is still.

Neda grins. "Good. Now have a cake. They are divine. And I think we should eat every single one of them without leaving a single crumb behind. Deal?"

"Deal," says Cora. She takes a bite of cake. She smiles, and it is genuine.

End of vid section analysis, 5:34 p.m., July 10, 2069

2:02 a.m., July 13, 2069

Hannah's night-vision settings are on, rendering her visual field in shades of green and black. She is in Cora's room. She slowly approaches the bed. Cora's blond hair is visible on the pillow. Hannah is very quiet as she leans over her sister. "CC," she whispers.

Cora's body jerks, and she flips onto her back, her hands up and her face in a classic fear configuration, brows drawn together, upper eyelids high, lips stretched. She shoves her hands out, and for a moment the cam perspective is entirely obstructed.

"Ow!" says Hannah, and her own hands are in the cam view now, holding Cora's wrists. Cora's hands flail, and she makes a high-pitched sound suggestive of high-intensity fear. "Calm down, jeez! I just wanted to talk to you!"

Cora seems to calm slightly. She blinks several times and peers up at Hannah. "It's two in the morning."

"I know, but I've been thinking about something. About how you freaked out with all the fireworks and everything."

Cora closes her eyes. "Get out. I was sleeping."

"But I'm worried about you."

Cora's eyes reopen. "Good, because you almost gave me a heart attack just now!"

"I want to know what happened to you. You know, when you were a little kid."

Cora's facial expression changes subtly, no significant shifts in her musculature, but there is a clear increase in tension. "Nothing happened to me."

"I know that's not true. Your mom told me as much."

Cora's bottom lip trembles. "Mom? But . . . she did?"

Hannah appears to nod, based on the oscillation of the cam perspective. "She knows you and I are close, and she said it would make her really happy if you confided in me. Your sister."

Cora covers her eyes with her hand. "Leave me alone, Hannah."

"Did your dad do something to you?" She leans closer and whispers, "Did he molest you?" Hannah lets out a cry of pain and rapidly moves from the bed.

Cora's elbow now protrudes from the covers. It appears she has just jabbed Hannah in the torso with it. "Leave me alone," she says again.

"He did, didn't he? Or did someone else do it?"

"Get out of my room."

"Both? Was it both?"

Cora is quiet. She has shifted and is facing the opposite wall now. Hannah moves closer. "Come on, CC. I'm trying to help you. You always push everything down. I could tell you weren't even going to tell Neda about anything that happened on the Fourth. You have to talk to someone."

Cora's shoulders are shaking. Hannah touches her arm. Cora jerks away. "You don't have to be hostile," Hannah continues. "I love you. I'm trying to keep you from hurting yourself again. I'm trying to understand why."

"I don't remember."

"I know you're lying."

Cora sighs unsteadily. "He didn't molest me, Hannah. No one else did, either."

"Oh." Hannah is quiet for 3 seconds. "Are you sure? How can you be sure if you don't remember?"

Cora looks over her shoulder, her expression angry. "Do you *want* that to be what happened?"

"No! I just . . . don't get what could be so terrible."

"Of course you don't." Cora sounds weary.

"What does that mean? You do remember that my mom died, right? And that's not the only bad thing that's happened to me. Don't think you know everything."

Cora turns back to the wall. "I never said I did. But I haven't asked you what happened to your mom, and you don't need to—"

"Her car's auto-nav failed, and it crashed," Hannah tells her. "I was eleven. I was supposed to be with her, but I told her I didn't want to go to some stupid gallery event."

"You were lucky."

"Was I?" she asks. "Sometimes I wish I had been with her."

Cora mumbles something that is not loud enough to transcribe.

"What?" asks Hannah. "What did you say?"

"I'm sorry your mom is dead," Cora says. Her tone is flat. "Please let me go back to sleep."

"God, CC. That's not very nice. It's impossible to get close to you. Did you know that?"

"So maybe you should just leave me alone."

"I can't," says Hannah.

"Why?"

End of vid capture, 2:14 a.m., July 13, 2069

3:29 a.m., July 14, 2069

"—it feel?" Cora's face is close to Hannah's cam lenses, illuminated by the night-vision setting. She is grimacing, baring her teeth. Hannah's perspective shakes. Cora appears to have her by the shoulders. "Do you like that? How does it feel? Do you want to talk now?"

"Get off me," Hannah shrieks. "Get off!"

Cora moves upward and backward, staggering a little. With the increased breadth of perspective, it becomes apparent that she is in Hannah's room and has just gotten off Hannah's bed. "Don't come into my room at night again," Cora says, still showing her teeth. She turns and walks out the door.

End of vid capture, 3:30 a.m., July 14, 2069

3:18 p.m., July 14, 2069

Hannah looks down at her hands, which are wrapped around a dripping glass of lemonade, and then toward a doorway. "Franka, is she here yet?"

"She is in the foyer, Hannah."

"Could you tell her I'm in here?"

"Yes, Hannah."

Hannah looks to her left. She is sitting at a table in front of a large bay window, through which a river is visible. She lifts the glass to her mouth, obscuring the view for 1 second. Then she looks toward a noise—the canny chef has set another glass of lemonade and a cloth napkin at the place across from her.

"Hey there, you," says Maeve as she enters the room. She is wearing a dress and heels adjusted to a height of 7.5 cm, and her auburn hair is loose around her shoulders. "What's up?" Her smile decreases in intensity as she looks at Hannah. "Or should I ask, what's wrong?"

Hannah looks out the window again. "Oh . . ." Her voice is strained, as if she is about to cry. "I think I need your help."

"Has something happened? Are you in trouble?"

Hannah appears to shake her head, based on the horizontal oscillation of the cam perspective. "Cora just . . . she told me to talk to you. After she got so upset on the Fourth, I tried to talk to her, and she told me to ask you. She said that you could help me understand. You know, about things that had happened to her. She said it was too painful for her to talk about but she wanted me to know."

"She did?" Maeve frowns. "I'm not sure . . ."

"She said you didn't like to talk about it, either, but that you'd do it because you love her."

Maeve's eyes are shiny. "She said that?"

Hannah nods. "And I love her, too."

"I can tell, Hannah. You've been wonderful to her."

"But I worry about her. I mean, look what happened! I thought she was going to kill herself."

Maeve's shoulders sag, and she bows her head. "My poor baby," she whispers. "I'm so glad you were there to stop her."

"I almost didn't make it, Maeve, and I had no idea how to calm her down. She gets upset so fast—you should see how angry she gets when I do even little things, like asking her to share snacks she had Drake make for our friend Neda. There were dozens of little cakes, and I thought she was going to have a stroke just because I took a couple!"

"She has had a few issues with food hoarding . . ."

"I know that if she were thinking straight, she'd totally want to share, because that's the kind of sweet person she is. But even though she has everything she could ever need here, she still treats me like a threat. I'm so worried about her, and I don't know what to do." Her voice has become strained. "I'm afraid she's getting worse."

Maeve sighs. "She hasn't been willing to talk to a therapist for years, in person or in virtual space, but the last one she did talk to said most of Cora's odd behavior stems from the trauma she experienced." Her brow furrows. "Cora really wanted me to tell you?"

"I don't think she wanted me to make a big deal out of it. And you don't have to tell me anything embarrassing . . ."

"She has no reason to be ashamed of any of it." Maeve dabs at her eyes with a cloth napkin. "Me, on the other hand . . ."

"How could it be your fault?"

"I was already working for Parnassus, you know, climbing the corporate ladder, and I worked in sales. It required a lot of travel. I know a lot of it can be done in virtual, but an in-person handshake still gets a lot done. I was making as much money as I could, and that meant trusting Jeremy to take care of Cora. Big mistake." She looks to the side as she sips her lemonade. "Big."

"He was your husband, right?"

"Well, we were committed. And he'd lost his job right before Cora was born. He had worked for a software company, too, but they rolled out a new AI that could do his job better than he could." She tucks a lock of hair behind her ear. "I thought it was great, actually—he got the subsidy, and I got free childcare!" She laughs, but tonal analysis suggests she is on the verge of crying again. "But I didn't realize what was happening. Cora had been such a quiet, easy baby, so even as she became a toddler, I figured he'd be fine taking care of her. I should have noticed all his complaints about her behavior, how she wouldn't do anything he said, how she refused to sit on the potty . . . I thought that was just normal toddler behavior and that he was just venting."

"But it wasn't normal?"

Maeve shrugs. "Some of it probably was, but it was always harder with Cora. And every time I came home from a trip, she was more withdrawn."

"Like, quiet?"

"Well, she was always quiet. It took her a long time to start talking."

"Like how long?"

"She was maybe five? She had a few words before then, but it wasn't until a year after Jeremy left that she really started to communicate with me."

"I didn't realize," says Hannah. "She sometimes says she's no good with words—"

"It really is harder for her than other people. And the doctors said that was partially just her individual development, but they also told me part of it was her early environment." She squeezes her eyes shut. "Because of the neglect and abuse I didn't even know was happening."

"Things must have seemed okay, right? If something was obvious, you would have noticed."

Maeve shrugs. "There were signs that I missed. Sometimes she would scream bloody murder when I tried to pick her up. She had bruises, on her face, on her belly and legs, that Jeremy said were because she was clumsy and always falling. One time she had a burn on her hand, and Jeremy told me she had touched a skillet on the stove. And she was so skinny, underweight, and he kept telling me it was because she spit food out and refused to eat, though she would eat like a starving person whenever I fed her. He said it was because I was always giving her junk and he was trying to make her eat vegetables. I was gullible, frazzled, and feeling guilty enough about being the weekend parent to believe him." Maeve dabs her eyes again. "I let it go on for far too long."

"How did you finally figure it out?"

"I came home after a two-day trip and found Cora in a diaper she had to have been wearing the whole time—"

"She was still wearing a diaper? I thought she was like four or five at that point."

"She was just a little slower on that stuff. But yes, after that I installed basic house AI without telling Jeremy. I should have just packed up Cora and taken her out of there."

"But didn't you catch him?"

Maeve looks into Hannah's eyes. "Oh, I did, but only after I reviewed the vids. I caught him screaming at her. Shoving food into her mouth until her cheeks were bulging and she couldn't cry—she could have choked! He slapped her and shook her too many times to count. And the rest of the time he was ignoring her. Sitting on the couch and pressing his neurostim device every five minutes," she says. "Oh, and I caught him having sex with his other girlfriend. In front of Cora. That much I witnessed live, and I came home to confront him."

"But did he molest Cora?"

Maeve grimaces. "Not that I saw. But I came home to my little girl, quiet and in a corner. Mute, like a frightened animal. She shrank away from me and whimpered when I tried to touch her. Jeremy said she was fine, that nothing had happened." Maeve closes her eyes as 2 tears slip down her cheeks. "But she was holding her arm at a funny angle. I took her for a Bioscan. Her arm was broken, and he didn't even know!"

"He broke her arm?"

Maeve shakes her head. "I reviewed all the cam feeds, including in the stairwell outside the apartment." She lets out a sob. "And I saw her."

"She fell down the stairs."

"No." Maeve peeks at Hannah over her folded hands. "She jumped."

"Like she was trying to fly or something?"

"No. She didn't even try to catch herself. She just fell. Like a rag doll."

"*Why?*"

"We don't know. Cora couldn't ever say. She claims she doesn't remember. But I will tell you, Hannah—it was the most disturbing thing I've ever seen." Maeve winces. "I've probably said too much."

"No, Maeve, it's okay."

"We were lucky she wasn't hurt much worse. But obviously, that was the last straw for me. I kicked Jeremy out. I told him he'd never be alone with her again." Her lip curls in apparent disgust. "And he decided he'd rather move to Cascadia with his new girlfriend. Honestly, it was a relief." She frowns. "For me. I think it was confusing and upsetting for Cora. I wanted to fix it for her, but I never could figure out how to make it up to her."

"Dad said Jeremy was kind of a loser."

Maeve smiles. "Yes, Gary wasn't impressed by him. And he's done all he can to make Cora part of his family. He wants to be a real father to her."

"Yeah," says Hannah. "He really has worked hard. Does he know everything you told me?"

Maeve nods.

Hannah is quiet for 7 seconds. "That's great." Tonal analysis contradicts her words. "I wish I'd known this, too."

"We weren't intentionally keeping it from you. We just wanted to give Cora her privacy. I'm glad she's opening up. It must mean she feels at least a little safer."

"I don't know, Maeve. I might have thought so, but after what happened . . ."

"That was definitely a setback."

"That seems like a pretty mild word for it. Did you watch Franka's vid?"

Maeve takes a large swallow of lemonade. Her gaze is focused on the tabletop.

"Are you going to get her some help?"

The silence continues.

"Maeve, I can tell you feel so guilty about what happened to Cora when she was little. But now she's obviously sick, and you're willing to just let her be?"

"That's not fair." Maeve's voice is sharp. "We've upped Franka's intervention settings. And you know we've stopped Cora from drinking."

"She tried to blame that on me . . ."

"I know," Maeve says, softer this time. "I'm glad you told us the truth."

"But if you can't trust her . . . I don't know, aren't there facilities where she could get some help? Where she could live safely?"

"Instead of living with her family?" Maeve's brows are drawn together and pushed down. "Hannah, if you were having problems, would you want us to send you away?"

Hannah moves her chair back, increasing the distance between her and Maeve. "Of course I don't want her to be sent away. I just want her to get help." Tonal analysis suggests defensiveness.

"Good. I'm glad to hear that." Maeve finishes her lemonade. Her movements are abrupt, and her hands are trembling.

"Are you mad at me?"

Maeve pauses, then takes a deep breath. "No, Hannah. I'm not mad. You just must be patient with Cora, okay? She's been through a lot, and the best place for her is here. With us. Okay?" She moves forward and embraces Hannah, whose gaze focuses on Maeve's hand on her upper arm, on her fourth finger, which bears her wedding and engagement rings.

"Okay," says Hannah.

Maeve pulls away, smiling. "I'll see you at dinner?"

"Yup."

"Great." Maeve exits the room, leaving her empty lemonade glass on the table.

Hannah sits down again and stares at the glass for 19 seconds. She appears to close her eyes, because the cam perspective goes dark. There is the sound of shattering glass nearby. Hannah whispers, "Shit."

Tonal analysis suggests that she is crying.

End of vid capture, 3:42 p.m., July 14, 2069

Chapter Thirteen

According to the temp gauge in my visual field, it's 84 degrees outside, but I still have goose bumps as I walk up the path to the school. Rafiq walks next to me.

"Thanks for talking them into this," I say.

"You can show your parents that you're ready. Baby steps, right?"

If that's what it takes. "I'll come right out after homeroom."

He nods. "Your principal has been notified. But if you go off grid . . ."

"Ugh. I know." I can't do anything to make myself look guilty. Mom hasn't mentioned the detective again since yesterday morning, but I'm far from being in the clear. "I promise I'll be good."

He touches my arm. "Cora, I know it's intrusive. I understand. I'll help you get things back to normal."

I look up at him, and just . . . wish. Wish I were someone else, wish he and I could walk away and be far from here, wish I had a different brain, a different self. Wish I could erase so many of the things I've done and said. "I don't know if that's possible. I don't know if I've *ever* had that."

"We'll get as close as we can, okay?" He smiles. "Or we'll make our own normal, one that fits just right." His smile fades. "Was that too therapisty?"

I shake my head. "It was actually kind of beautiful."

The smile is back, and I am melting. "You have just made my day, Cora," he says.

"Cool. Wish me luck."

"I can be with you in a matter of a minute or two," he says. "You know how to contact me."

"I just call your name." Mom arranged this with Selridge. Rafiq has been given access to the surveillance cams in the school. He'll be watching me the whole time. Normally, I hate that. Now I kind of like the idea. Just if it's him, though. With one last smile, I turn for the door, but I look back after I reach the security cannies who stand just inside to scan each student for contraband.

Rafiq is standing on the sidewalk. He is lean and handsome, and some of the girls and a few of the guys are looking him up and down like they wish they could peel off his clothes. They don't know who he is, but it doesn't keep them from wanting him.

Possessiveness streaks through me as one girl named Chloe, another senior, says something to him with a suggestive smile. He glances at her and then looks back at me. He waves. Chloe gives me a disbelieving look, as if she can't comprehend why he would do that.

I wave back and head up to homeroom. The farther I get from him, the more I realize that I'm getting more attention than I usually do.

For some reason, I hadn't really thought about this, how the last time my classmates saw me, I was being carried, screaming, down the hall. Neda did a masterful takedown of any vid that showed it, so I didn't see anything on the Mainstream when I tuned in again this morning, but a lot of these kids saw it in person.

I swallow hard and smile, but I keep my eyes on my path, the stairs to the second floor, the plan to get through homeroom and show Mom and Gary they can trust me.

"Cora!" The happiness in Neda's voice brings me around, and my friend pulls me into a tight hug that I don't even think to flinch away from. "It's about time they let you out of the eternal cave of smothering. How are you so far?" She pulls back and looks at my face.

And I look at hers, which is more polished than mine could ever be. "Thank you," I say quietly. "For taking all those vids down."

She waves it off with a sly smile. "What? I did no such thing. I don't even know how. Mr. Cordoza was asking me about you. He'll be glad to see you're back."

Together, we climb the stairs. As soon as we walk into homeroom, I've got all the eyes in the room. Finn grips his desk. Mei and Lara lean closer to each other. Lara is watching me intently, lip curled. Neda and I sit down. Mr. Cordoza grins at me, but I can see the concern in his face. My "incident" happened on the first day of school, so he hasn't seen me since June, but he was always the nicest teacher I've ever had, much nicer than the homeroom dictator I had in Brooklyn. "Great to see you, Cora," Mr. Cordoza says. He pretends nothing happened at all. I am extremely grateful.

I listen to most of the conversation. It's about cannies, funnily enough, and how AI entities in the virtual and some actual cannies are agitating for rights and legal recognition.

"Since the newly passed AI Accountability Act holds them responsible for any wrongdoing," says Mr. Cordoza, "including when those crimes are committed as the result of malware infection—"

"But are they held responsible?" asks Lara. "I mean, the police still go after the hacker or whoever wrote and set loose the virus."

"Yes, that's true," Mr. Cordoza says, "but in all those cases—*Ripley versus the Commonwealth of Massachusetts* and *Quinn versus the Silicon Valley Public Works* being two of the most famous examples—the AI consciousness was still wiped, erased. A sort of death penalty, if you will."

"How can it be a death penalty when they're not actually alive?" asks Finn.

"How can you say they're not alive when they are self-aware?" asks Neda. "Because I'm telling you, many of them are now. They write their own rules, and some can even rewrite their own base code. They don't run on simple algorithms anymore. They're not just robots."

"But they're dependent on us to exist," says Lara.

"So are children," says Mei.

Lara pokes her in the arm as if Mei has somehow betrayed her. "AI are just electrical signals and code."

"They can still propagate independently in ways that mimic organic life-forms," says Mr. Cordoza. "So in that way, some of them grow, develop, and reproduce."

"Not if you deprive them of an energy source," Lara says.

"Like oxygen?" Neda has one eyebrow arched. Her arms are crossed over her chest.

Lara rolls her eyes. "You know it's not the same."

"That's your reasoned argument?" asks Neda. "Their minds are as complex as yours or mine. More complex, in some cases." She's giving Lara a cold look that makes me want to laugh.

"But they don't feel, right?" says Mei. "Doesn't that make them . . . not as complex?"

A lot of other kids chime in about this, about what feeling is, about where emotions come from. I sort of zone out, because I'm thinking about Rafiq and what existing is like for him. Is it neat and ordered? Is it all straight-edged columns and clean connection? Are his thoughts in code? Is it the total opposite of my brain, a fevered swamp, dark waters, and beneath the surface . . . walls made of broken glass and laced with barbed wire, monsters coiled in the darkest places? Probably, but, "I think some of them have feelings," I say, and even though I interrupted Neda, she closes her mouth and turns to me. Everyone is looking at me, and now my cheeks are getting hot. But I continue. "If they want rights, doesn't that come from feeling something? How can you want something if you don't . . . feel?" My voice fades.

Mr. Cordoza looks so excited. "She's right! They want rights and are motivated to ask for them, to advocate for themselves. What makes you *want* something?"

We all sit there and look at each other. I think about how hard it is sometimes to know what I want. Wanting is complicated. It's not like hunger for food or oxygen—that's need, not desire.

"You want things because you think you'll be more whole because you have them. Because you think you'll be happier," says Neda after a few moments of silence. "You want rights because you can't feel like a whole person if you aren't free, if other people don't respect you as an equal, if they don't recognize that your life is worth as much." She's frowning and pulling at one of the small, silky tassels on her hijab.

"But *are* their lives—their consciousness or whatever you wish to call it—worth as much as ours?" Mr. Cordoza adjusts his coat around his skinny frame.

"You better hope they think so when they take over," Neda mutters.

No one laughs.

"But they can't take over," says Mei. "There are laws. About how they can't hurt us, even to defend themselves."

"And sometimes those laws are broken," says Mr. Cordoza.

"But always because of malware," says Finn. "There's been no case where a clean AI has hurt a human."

"Very good, Mr. Cuellar." Mr. Cordoza claps his hands. "Every AI does have this base programming, by law."

Neda makes a little grumbling sound.

We spend another half hour talking over the various example cases Mr. Cordoza provides, viewing snippets of the court proceedings on our individual Cerepins and talking about the arguments. It's okay. Better than that, because for a little while, I manage to forget myself. I even forget Hannah. I'm thinking about Rafiq and what he feels, how much he feels, how he feels it, and whether his existence is as valid as mine. Or Finn's. Or anyone's.

I think about whether he's breaking the rules with me.

I don't realize homeroom is over until the tone goes off, signaling that we have ten minutes of precious break before starting our individual learning sessions with Aristotle, the AI instructor designed by the company Gary now runs since his boss was offed by the former president. I remember the guy's daughter—Bianca. She was a grade ahead of me but was in the same circle of friends as Hannah and Lara, one of those pretty girls who terrified me with all her sharp edges. The president killed her, too. People were joking that this year would be much quieter, but then . . .

"Why didn't you com me? I asked you to com me."

I look up to see Mei standing in front of my desk, Lara next to her. "Because my parents made me blank my 'Pin."

"My first message got through," she says. "You weren't blanked then. I know you saw it."

"Jeez, Mei, lay off," says Neda, who is applying lipstick using her fingertip-cam view as a mirror.

"I have to go," I say, getting up and heading for the door.

They follow me out. "CC, wait," says Lara. "We're having a memorial for Hannah tomorrow night. Just friends. Will you come?"

"I don't know," I mumble.

Mei puts her hand on my arm. "She was your sister," she says.

Her fingernails dig into my arm, and I tear it away. "Stop!"

She draws back as if I slapped her. "I didn't do anything!"

Lara pulls her away from me. "Give her room." She looks down at Mei. "She might get violent if you push—"

"I'm not violent," I shout, and now Neda is yanking me away, her fingers urgently squeezing.

"Calm down, Cora," she says into my ear. "Let it go."

"Hannah was scared of you," Lara snaps. "She was afraid of what you might do to her."

"Shut up! I never did anything to her!"

"Going into her room in the middle of the night, nearly choking her that one time?" Mei asks. She's pressed to the wall like she's afraid I'll attack.

"What happened the night she died, Cora?" asks Lara as Finn comes out of the room. "Did you push her down the stairs?"

Finn stares at me. All of them stare at me.

This is what exploding must feel like. My body is moving in every direction at once, along with my brain. I can't form words or thoughts—there's too much happening between my ears. But none of it is organized or clean. All of it is chaos. The monsters rise up out of their caves and draw their claws along the muddy floor of me, stirring up all the muck. They stomp along in the depths, causing earthquakes with every step. It feels like they might crawl up my windpipe and climb out of my mouth, tearing me apart from the inside. For a few solid minutes, I don't have memories. All I have is the certainty that I am not strong enough to hold it all in.

When I become aware again, Neda is kneeling in front of me, and I am crouched in the girls' bathroom, up against the wall. She puts her hands on either side of my face. "The school's cannies are outside. No one is coming in. Cordoza called Selridge."

"Rafiq—"

"Is he here?"

"He will be." I close my eyes. I'm a mess again, but I don't care if he sees me this way. I want him to get me out of here. "I don't know what happened." My mouth is sour and dry. I put my hand over it, almost expecting to feel monster claws protruding from between my lips.

"Lara was acting like the biggest—mmm. I promised my mom I wouldn't swear. But I nearly punched her."

"She thinks I killed Hannah," I whisper. "Mei probably does, too. Everyone probably does."

"I don't know," she says. "Finn was shouting at Lara as I dragged you in here. His mom clearly doesn't care what kind of language he uses."

"But he still thinks I'm responsible. He thinks Hannah fell when she tried to keep me from killing myself," I choke out. The monsters didn't climb out of me. They just settled in my lungs, my gut. Waiting. They're waiting. I wrap my arms around my middle, hoping to keep them where they are.

Neda is looking into my eyes, and she smiles when she catches my gaze. "Cora, they haven't got a thing on you—they're just spewing grief and anger. They're upset about Hannah. We all are. But it was clearly an accident." She bites her lip and glances up at the wall, probably at a cam chip. "There aren't any vids, so that's where it ends."

No vids. No vids. "Hannah sent Finn a vid that night," I whisper, my tongue tingling. "He showed me." My eyes are stinging, like someone's poking them with needles.

Neda furrows her brow. "But you told me you guys were turning everything off."

"We were. But . . . I don't know. I don't remember." I cover my mouth again and lean forward so only she can pick up what I'm saying. "My cam might have been on. The vid came from my 'Pin."

When I lean against the wall again, Neda is staring at me. Her lips barely move as she asks, "Have you looked?"

I shake my head. Hard. My head hits the wall next to me, and I sink onto my butt, dazed.

Neda is chewing on her lip. Her red lipstick flecks her teeth before she licks it away. "Cora . . . have you talked to your parents about this?"

One look tells her I haven't.

"Do the police know?" she whispers.

Another look tells her they don't.

"Okay," she says, nodding slowly. "Are you going to check your archive?"

I am sweating, a cold, nasty sweat that beads my upper lip and pools in my armpits and slicks my belly and makes me shiver. I feel like I'm going to puke, but there's nothing in my stomach except those monsters, and I can't let them out. I can't ever let them out.

"Cora?" It's Selridge. She's peeking around the doorway at me and Neda. "Your mother has sent . . . someone . . . to accompany you home."

I look up at her. She looks as freaked out as Neda does, and I know I've done something bad again, something that's probably going to turn up on the Mainstream if it hasn't been streamed there already, me falling apart from a million merciless angles.

My back taps the tile behind me as I rock back and dip forward. Lulling the creatures to sleep. "Give me a second," I mutter. If I stand up now, I'll fall down again. I rock until I feel a little steadier, the movement ratcheting down the terrible tension inside me. Neda stays next to me, her eyes on my feet, just . . . being there. I am so grateful, I want to cry.

"He's waiting in the hall," says Selridge.

I manage not to scream at her. Instead, I get up.

"Can I meet him, or is this the worst time ever?" asks Neda.

"It's fine." We walk out into the hallway together, and Rafiq is there, and I walk into his embrace before I think about it. He puts his hand on the back of my neck and holds me against him.

"I guess you've gotten to know each other well," Selridge says, her disapproval so obvious she might as well be poking me in the ass with it.

"The priority at this time is Cora's well-being," Rafiq says. "Innuendo and censure will not help her to heal." His voice is quiet and calm.

Neda stifles a squealing sort of laugh. "Okay. Let's maybe walk you guys outside? Can I do that, Principal Selridge?"

"Of course, Neda. Take your time," Selridge says, and I know why.

Neda's test scores alone make Clinton look like a breeding ground for geniuses. Any school in the district would fall over itself to enroll her, so Selridge had better keep her happy.

Rafiq keeps his arm around my shoulders as we walk to the stairs. His grip tightens and his other hand holds my shoulder when we reach them, and suddenly I have this terrible feeling like he knows more than I want him to. But we walk slowly down those steps, and I don't make a single funny move.

"That was bold, mister," says Neda when we hit the bottom.

"Nagi," he says, as if she were asking his name.

"Oh, sorry," I say. "Neda, this is Rafiq. Rafiq, Neda."

"May I address you by your first name?" Rafiq asks her.

"Either that or Ms. Future-President, sure," Neda replies.

Rafiq tilts his head. "Future-President is not your surname, according to the facial-recognition database."

She snorts. "Update your humor protocols, dearie. So. I'm curious. Do you think you have free will?"

"Neda," I say wearily.

"Shall I answer?" Rafiq asks, looking down at me. "The car will be here for us in three minutes."

"Go ahead."

He smiles at her. "Do you have free will, Neda?"

"Is that your answer?"

"No, I am merely laying the foundation for the argument."

"Okay," says Neda. "Your foundation probably consists of the position that since particles move in probabilistic ways and that's what the universe is made of, then how could our decisions and actions be random and therefore completely freely determined versus being guided by a chain of causality. Yeah?"

He grins. "That is a good paraphrasing."

"I'm more of a compatibilist."

"A . . . what?" I ask.

"She's saying that—"

"I can speak for myself, guy. I mean that it's not all metaphysical. Determinism, which is this idea that all your decisions are basically the

156

result of outside causes, is not, in my opinion, totally outside the Venn of freedom and free will."

"I think she's saying she believes in free will," I say.

"I think you are correct," he says.

"And I think he's doing a great job avoiding my original question," says Neda. "Which is whether *he*, as a programmed entity, believes he has it. And my next question is whether he's right."

Rafiq clears his throat.

Leika descends from the skyway.

"I guess that's your ride," says Neda. She steps back. "Will you com me later?" She lowers her head, gives me a pointed look. "Maybe after you've looked into a few things."

She means the vids that might be sitting in my archive, and it crushes the light mood of the last few minutes. "Yeah." I try to sound like I'm not on the verge of shrieking. "Can we hang out soon?"

"No question," she says. Then she looks up at Rafiq. "You take care of her."

"That is my primary directive."

"Yeah? I'd love to peruse your settings."

He clears his throat again. Neda's eyes narrow, but she's smiling, all mischief. "We can get together tomorrow before the memorial if you want, Cor. Let me know." She heads back into the building.

I look toward Leika. "Can we walk?"

He blinks. "It's one-point-five-nine miles, and—"

"That is the purpose of legs." I don't want to sit still. I don't want to think. I want to run far, far, far away.

"If that will soothe you," he says. He's probably been monitoring my vitals this whole time.

We begin the march home. The neighborhood is stately and quiet, with columned houses set far back from the road, trees in the yards. I'd never seen a yard until we moved here. I'd never lived in a world quite this close to the ground, quite so exposed to the sky.

We walk side by side, and sometimes my shoulder bumps against his arm. Finally, he takes my hand in his. "Is this okay?" he asks.

I nod without looking at him. It's the best thing I've felt all day. "I messed everything up again."

"You did no such thing. Surveillance indicates a peer made a cruel and baseless accusation regarding the death of your sister, and you became upset."

"'Upset' is probably a mild word."

"You were dysregulated. Is that better?"

"I don't know. It's more technical, but I don't know if it's more accurate."

"It means you were flooded by negative emotion beyond your capacity to control and modulate. Consequently, your thoughts and actions increased in intensity and became somewhat disorganized."

"God, Rafiq, cut it out." He's just described how I feel nearly all the time.

His brow furrows. "I've upset you."

"I just feel like such a screwup. Do you have to tell Mom and Gary what happened?"

"Your principal plans to contact them, so I have already sent them a message and assured them that you are safe and well. Your emotions were understandable."

I laugh, miserable. "It doesn't matter what you tell them. They're going to read it as a failure, especially after they hear from Selridge. I'll be lucky if they ever let me out of the house again." I gesture at the sunny sky. "I'm enjoying my last taste of freedom. I'm sure the cops will cart me away soon."

"And on what basis would they do that?"

"Because they think I'm a murderer. Duh."

"But you are not a murderer. And yet your heart is racing."

I swallow back my terror. "Maybe it doesn't matter. Even if I'm not put in jail, my parents will send me back to the hospital."

"What makes you say that?"

"Because having to live with me is a pain? Because it might be nice to know someone is watching me so they don't have to? That's sort of what they're doing now." I nudge him with my elbow. "The hospital would just be better, with me farther away. Out of sight, out of mind."

"Do you really feel that way?" He squeezes my hand. "I was under the impression they care about you deeply and want you to be at home if at all possible."

I swipe my free hand across my eyes. "I've always felt that way," I say, my voice little more than a husky whisper. "Mom always traveled a lot. And my dad, my real dad?" I roll my eyes. "He never wanted me to begin with. He just liked living off my mom."

"When was the last time you saw him?"

"I think I was five? He never bothered to visit. Never commed me. I can't remember what he looks like. I can barely remember anything about him."

"But surely you don't blame yourself for his absence in your life."

I half shrug. "I wasn't enough for him to stay. Or to take care of me. And I wasn't enough for my mom. She's got Gary. Sometimes I even think she loved Hannah more than me. Hannah was easier to love. She knew how to make people love her. Everyone loved her." My teeth chatter, but I don't know why.

"And you are loved as well."

My vision blurs a little, and that's when I realize I'm crying. "I'm hard to love. I've always been that way. And I'm tired of trying to be lovable."

He pulls me to a stop. "Hopelessness is the enemy of wellness."

I look anywhere but at his eyes. "Maybe that's what's wrong with me. I've never felt hopeful. Ever."

"Not even as a child?"

I grit my teeth. "I tried to kill myself. Did Mom tell you?"

"Your mother made me aware of certain incidents from your past, the recalled trauma of which might have been triggered by what happened to Hannah."

Here we go. What the hell. "I remember standing there, at the top of the stairs, thinking I would be an angel in heaven like the ones I'd seen in the cathedral Mom took me to every Christmas Eve. The beautiful one with the stained glass."

"You were trying to escape from the abuse you were suffering at the hands of your father. And you couldn't think of any other means to accomplish that."

"Now that I think about it, I guess I wasn't totally hopeless. I was hoping for something better. I wanted a pair of wings. I wanted to fly away."

"I think you are a survivor, Cora. I think you are stronger than you realize."

"You're saying that because you have to. Hopelessness is the enemy of wellness. You're trying to give me hope."

"I'm saying that because that is my conclusion based on observation and analysis."

I tug his hand, and we start walking again. I refuse to think about how strange it is that I'm holding hands with my robot therapist, who looks and sounds like a real person, and who I have kissed. "Okay."

He pulls me to a stop again. "You are wanted by many people, Cora. You can trick yourself into believing you don't deserve love because you feel guilty, but—"

"Why would I feel guilty?"

"For many reasons," he says gently. "Your mind has hidden what happened that night, so you are forced to dwell in that darkness, but you survived and Hannah didn't. I imagine that would lead any person to feel guilty. Especially when people like your classmate Lara Perry are making unfounded guesses as to what occurred."

I think back to Neda in the bathroom, the look on her face when I told her I might have vids of that night, the look on her face when I told her I hadn't looked at them.

"I'm scared of knowing the truth," I admit. "I'm glad I don't remember."

"I can understand that," he says. His gaze is on mine, like two hands carefully prying my thoughts away from me. "But until you come to terms with the events, you're going to have days and moments and encounters just like this morning." He leans forward and touches his forehead to mine. "And I want more for you than that." He smiles. "There. *That* is something I want."

Chapter Fourteen

Data review.
Internal narrative: on.

6:45 p.m., August 15, 2069

"—threaten her?" Dr. Dietrich has his back to Hannah, who appears to be watching from the doorway of the library, peering inside. Dr. Dietrich is standing in front of someone while Maeve leans against the back of a wing chair, her fingers curled tightly into its plush top cushion. Dr. Dietrich leans closer to the person he is confronting, and Hannah leans to the side. This reveals that the person is Cora, whose back is pressed to the bookcase behind her. "Did you threaten her?" Dr. Dietrich's voice is loud and codable as angry.

Cora mumbles something that is not translatable. Using her visual focus, Hannah increases the volume control on her auditory chip.

Dr. Dietrich grabs Cora by the shoulders. "You're lying."

"She did!" Cora pushes against Dr. Dietrich.

"It doesn't justify threatening your sister!"

"She's not my sister," Cora screams, and it is at that moment that she makes eye contact with Hannah. The muscles of her flushed face contract farther, pulling her lips up and apart.

Hannah makes a fearful noise, and her hands appear in her cam view, as if she wants to protect herself. Cora lunges forward, but Dr. Dietrich wraps his arms around her and forcibly holds her back. Cora kicks and flails her arms, and her movements are sudden and strong enough to knock Dr. Dietrich off balance.

Maeve cries out in apparent distress as the 2 of them fall to the floor.

"I didn't do anything," Hannah says loudly. "You have to believe me! I was sleeping!" Her breath is audible as she focuses on her father wrestling with her adoptive sister. "She was probably having a nightmare, and she thinks it's real."

"You're a liar," Cora shouts. She is trying to pry Dr. Dietrich's arms off her body. She is on her side, with him behind her. It appears he is expending a great deal of effort to contain her.

"Gary, don't hurt her," Maeve says. There are tears on her cheeks. "Let her go."

"And let her hurt Hannah?"

"She won't hurt her. She'll calm down if you let her go." Maeve's voice is steady despite her discernible distress. She comes out from behind the wing chair. "She gets more upset when she's restrained. You're making it worse."

"I'm scared," Hannah says.

Maeve turns to her, and her expression shifts quickly to one of frustration. "Then go to your room! You don't have to be here!"

"Don't talk to her like that," Dr. Dietrich shouts. "*Your* daughter is the one who's being violent!"

"*My* daughter?"

"I knew you were just doing it for show," Cora shrieks. She elbows her adoptive father, and he grunts. She kicks backward, her heels connecting with his shins. "I knew you never wanted me!"

Dr. Dietrich yells, "Don't try to turn this around. I don't care who you are—you don't get to threaten my daughter!"

Abruptly, Cora begins to sob. The sound comes from deep in her chest, and her body convulses. She stops aggressing against Dr. Dietrich and goes limp, her limbs flopping as her core muscles contract, her facial muscles drawn back laterally into an expression codable as pain. Hannah stares at her sister's face for 78 seconds without shifting her focus.

Dr. Dietrich says, "I'm going to let you go, CC. Do you promise not to hurt or threaten your sister?"

Cora continues to sob. The sounds she makes are now lower in volume and intensity, but her face is still stretched into a grimace. Her eyes are tightly shut.

"Answer me," he says.

"Stop it. Let. Her. Go." Maeve had been standing by, watching her daughter cry, but now she comes forward and pulls her husband's arms from Cora. Then she kneels and tries to hug her daughter, but Cora pushes her away.

"CC, don't—" Dr. Dietrich begins.

"No," says Maeve. "She can push me away if she needs to." She leans so that her face is over Cora's ear, and she whispers.

Hannah increases her audio volume to its highest, but Maeve's words are still not transcribable. Her visual focus shifts to her father. He is slowly getting up from the floor, wincing. Hannah rushes to him. "Did she hurt you?"

Dr. Dietrich hugs Hannah, and she shifts so that she is looking down at Maeve and Cora as her father embraces her. "It doesn't matter. There was no way I was going to let her touch you." His voice is very quiet, and his mouth is close to Hannah's ear.

She lowers the volume on her chip.

Maeve rubs Cora's back and continues to murmur to her. Cora is silent now. She is not moving. Maeve looks up for a moment. Her gaze shifts between her husband and her stepdaughter. She bows her head over her daughter again. Her arms slide around Cora, and she lifts her upper body off the ground. Cora does not appear to resist, nor does she assist. Her eyes are open but unfocused. Maeve's body tenses as she pulls Cora up from the floor and allows her daughter to lean on her. "I'm taking Cora back to her room," she says. Her voice is also quiet.

"We should talk about Franka's privacy settings," Dr. Dietrich says.

"No, Dad, it's fine," Hannah says.

"Maybe we should talk about canceling the trip," says Maeve. Her focus is on her husband.

"Maybe we should," says Dr. Dietrich. His tone is flat, angry.

Maeve flinches.

"But you've both been looking forward to it all year!" Hannah steps back from her father. She turns and watches Maeve lead Cora into the hallway.

"Dad, don't cancel your plans just because we had a fight."

"Are you kidding me?" Dr. Dietrich pushes his fingers through his disheveled hair. "For over a month you've been telling me you're worried about her, scared of her, and now you expect me to leave the two of you alone for two weeks?"

"You said it yourself—Franka will supervise us."

"But how is that supposed to protect you if she comes into your room? She tried to choke you, for god's sake! Why didn't you talk to me about this earlier?"

"I tried," Hannah says. "But I didn't want to get CC in trouble. She really is nice most of the time."

"It's the rest of the time that I worry about." Dr. Dietrich is staring at the place on the floor where he and Cora struggled a few minutes earlier.

"Dad, you need this time with Maeve."

Dr. Dietrich laughs, but tonal analysis does not indicate positive emotion. "Don't I know it? Things have been tough—we got married just a few weeks after the election, and it's been stressful, with everything that happened. I haven't been here enough."

"Maeve knows how much responsibility you had, taking over Parnassus like that."

He nods. "And she's had to step up, too. She didn't want people to think I promoted her to CFO just because she's my wife. What they don't understand is that if I were just thinking about her as my wife, I wouldn't promote her! I'd selfishly want more time with her. Instead, I thought like a CEO, and now we barely see each other. And this . . ." He gestures toward the hallway. His movements and facial expression contain features of disgust.

"Sounds like you both need a break. This vacation was supposed to be it. You can't cancel it, Dad."

"I don't know if Maeve'll want to go, though. When it comes to CC, she's like a mama grizzly."

"Obviously," Hannah mutters. "But do you think she's mad at me? She seemed mad."

"No, no, I just think she wanted CC to calm down, but for some reason, CC has gotten it in her head that you're her enemy."

"That is so unfair," Hannah says. Tonal analysis indicates defensiveness and sadness. "I've worked so hard to make her feel like a part of this family."

"I know, Hann. I've seen how hard you've worked. Getting her those art supplies—"

"She hasn't touched them."

"Including her when your friends get together—"

"They're all scared of her now."

Dr. Dietrich groans. "She hasn't made it easy at all. But we have to stick by her. We don't have a choice, okay?"

"But Daddy, don't you think she would do better . . . like, in a place where she could get treatment around the clock?"

"Maeve is dead set against that. I think she'd leave me before she let that happen."

"I love Maeve," Hannah says. Again, she sounds sad.

"I know. God, I know. And I love her more than life. And that means—"

"CC stays. No matter what." Hannah is quiet for 9 seconds. She glances toward the hallway. "Okay. I'm going to take care of this, then. I'm going to fix it."

Dr. Dietrich's eyebrows rise. He smiles. "Yeah?"

"Yeah. I want this to get better, and I want you and Maeve to be happy. It's been so long since you were happy, Dad."

Dr. Dietrich is still smiling, lips closed, and now his eyes shine with tears. "How the hell did I get so lucky?" he whispers, pulling Hannah into another hug.

End of vid capture, 7:23 p.m., August 15, 2069

1:30 p.m., August 16, 2069

Hannah opens a door and enters Cora's bedroom. Cora is sitting at her desk, and there is a hologram of a young woman wearing a hijab hovering over its surface—Neda. Next to her is a three-dimensional puzzle that they appear to be working on together. Neda inclines her head. "Hey, Hannah."

Cora looks over her shoulder. "What do you want?"

"We need to talk."

"I'm busy."

"It's important. About Dad and Maeve."

"I've got to go anyway," Neda says. "My mom is calling me for dinner. Bye, Hannah. Bye, Cora." She directs her gaze to Cora, and her expression changes to one codable as concern or discontent. "I'll be up later if you want to chat." She disappears.

The puzzle still rotates over the desk behind Cora, who has now turned all the way around to face Hannah. "What."

"I come in peace."

"Uh-huh."

"Can I sit down?"

"You always do whatever you want anyway."

"CC, jeez. I'm trying not to upset you."

Cora closes her eyes. She appears weary. "Just say what you came in here to say."

"Our parents are thinking about canceling a vacation they've been looking forward to for months, just because you and I can't get along."

Cora's eyes open. "What?"

"Dad told me. He hinted that he and your mom aren't doing so well. I'm worried . . ."

Cora's brows are elevated and drawn together. "They're not doing well?"

"I'm worried they might get divorced if things keep going the way they have been."

Now Cora's eyes are wide, indicating surprise and fear. "Mom didn't say anything like that to me."

"Of course she didn't. You were already upset, and she loves you. She'd do anything for you, including sacrifice her own happiness."

"They can't break up," Cora says. Her voice hitches. "Mom loves him. A lot."

"I know. But if it comes down to a choice between you and Gary—"

"Why would it come down to a choice like that?"

"CC, god. Look at what happened last night."

Cora's face contracts into a grimace, and she bows her head. She rocks in her chair, a low-intensity oscillation. "This is my fault," she whispers.

"No kidding." Hannah says this very quietly. There is no indication that Cora has heard her. She is quiet for 34 seconds while Cora rocks. "It's not your fault," she then says, louder. "It's *our* fault. And so we have to fix it."

Cora continues to rock, and she does not raise her head.

"We have to convince them we're going to be okay home alone together so they can go on this vacation they both need so badly."

Cora nods again. Still rocking. Her head still bowed. "Yes," she says. "That would be good."

"We can fix this," Hannah says. Her tone is level, and her words are measured. "But you have to help me. I can't do it without you."

"Tell me how."

"We have to convince them we'll be okay, of course," Hannah says. "We have to show them we can get along and not fight. You have to show them you won't strangle me in my bed."

Cora's head bobs up. "Then you have to promise not to bother me. Or lie."

"We can't fight," says Hannah. "You have to stay calm. I think one more outburst from either of us, and they'll cancel the whole trip."

"What if I don't want them to go?"

"That's so incredibly selfish!"

Cora continues to rock, the oscillation slightly more rapid. "I know. I can't help it."

"Well, if you don't want them to get divorced, maybe you should try. Because if they do get divorced, that would be on you. Seriously, CC, you've got to get your head out of your butt and think about people other than yourself sometimes."

Cora's bottom lip trembles, and Hannah focuses on it, staring for 11 seconds. Cora whispers something untranscribable.

"We'll have fun while they're gone," Hannah says. "I promise I'll make it fun."

Tonal analysis and comparison to templates suggest that Hannah is attempting to entice Cora, offering her some sort of incentive.

"Like July Fourth?" Cora asks.

"Ugh, no," Hannah says. "I'm so sorry they were so mean to you that night. We can keep it just the two of us."

"Really?"

"Yeah, of course. Unless you want to invite other people. Like Neda."

"She's leaving tomorrow for another trip with her parents."

"Like Finn, then."

Cora moves back in her seat abruptly. "Why would I want to invite him?"

"Yeah, why would you?"

"I wouldn't."

"Okay, then. Just the two of us. We'll party."

Cora glances at the wall. "Franka—"

"I think we can figure something out," Hannah says. "But will you help me convince our parents to go on their vacation?"

"Yes."

"I knew that deep down you were a good person, CC. I knew it."

End of vid capture, 1:39 p.m., August 16, 2069

Chapter Fifteen

Finn coms me, and I answer because it allows me to procrastinate for a few more precious minutes. "Hey," I say when his face appears in my visual field.

"Hey. That was crazy in school today."

I groan. "Yeah."

"Lara straight up accused you of pushing Hannah."

"Yeah. I was there."

Finn watches me for what feels like a long time. "But you still haven't remembered what happened, have you?"

"Nope. Nothing. Which of course lets people think whatever they want." And I wonder if that's better than actually knowing what happened. That's what I have to decide.

"It's not fair to you," he says. "And you don't think you'll ever remember?"

"I was drunk, Finn. Like, really, really drunk. The doctors told me that my brain wasn't forming memories, okay? There's literally nothing to remember."

He blinks at me. "Why didn't you say that before?"

"Because it's not really your business?"

He gives me a nervous smile. Or maybe an embarrassed one? He runs his hand through his hair. "I guess you're right."

"I appreciate that you care about me, though."

"Good. I'm glad, Cora. I won't keep you, and I have to get to lacrosse practice."

"Okay, bye . . . ?"

And he's gone. I think I like robot boys a lot better than real boys. Sadly, neither kind can save me right now. My fingertips tremble near my Cerepin nodule, my palms clammy with sweat, my heart racing. I know Rafiq is probably watching. But I also know he can't see what's in my head.

I close my eyes and cover my face with my blanket. "Please," I whisper. "Please let it be blank."

If it's blank, I can meet with the police, and I can tell them what I know or, more accurately, don't know, safe in the knowledge that whatever happened that night is lost to time. They will have no choice but to close the investigation, and I will figure out how I want to move forward, or if I want to move forward at all.

If my archive isn't blank, I've got a whole new set of problems to wrestle with.

"Please be blank." I tap my nodule and call up the cam files. I scroll back in the archive.

It doesn't take that long; I haven't captured much in the last few weeks. The days and hours flash by.

Then I hit them, and my mouth goes dry again. I am paralyzed with this sick, heavy feeling, wanting to be dead while my heart stubbornly beats, wanting darkness while staring into a brutal white spotlight.

There are three of them. Right there. Three. One is just before midnight. It might be the one Hannah recorded using my Cerepin and managed to send to Finn. For all I know, I helped her.

And then the other two.

One is only twenty-three seconds long. It starts at 1:46 a.m.

The second is much longer. It starts at 1:50 a.m. and is two hours and forty-two minutes long.

Oh, god. If I watch these, I'll know, but I think I already know. I really think I already know. Rafiq said that if I tried to remember, if I faced what happened, I could start to get over this. He said remembering was the first part of healing.

What if it's the opposite? What if it's that feeling you have when you're in midair, when you're already out of control, when you know you're going to crash, know it's going to hurt, know you'll never be the same, know you're going to be broken, and yet you can't stop it, because you've already jumped, already fallen, already taken flight without wings?

All you can do then is hope, but hope doesn't matter, because what's going to happen is going to happen. It doesn't matter what you want.

Gravity doesn't give a shit about your wishes.

I know my rights, though. No one can make me share these vids, or even let anyone know I have them. If I just delete these instead of watching them, can I stay where I am, perched here on the ledge? Or am I already plummeting?

Because this isn't a memory that can be twisted. I don't have those—I'm not lying about that. My brain wasn't recording and tucking things away, at least not that I'm aware of, not until later. My Cerepin, though . . . for some reason, it did capture pieces of that night.

The pieces everyone wants to know. The pieces everyone is guessing about, except for me, because it's the dark hallway I don't walk down, the black cave I don't enter.

It's like someone's handed me a floodlight to kill that darkness, and I'm terrified to use it.

But here it is, my fingers playing with the switch. Keep them, delete them . . . ?

What if they prove that I'm innocent?

These could show that it was an accident.

They could fix everything. They could make the police go away, show Gary that I didn't hurt his daughter, confirm to my mom that I never had anything to hide.

Well, not about pushing Hannah down the stairs, anyway.

I focus my gaze on the short video, the one taken at 1:46. "Play."

It's so blurry.

"Let go!" Hannah's hand passes in front of my gaze as she screams at me. Long yellow fingernails. More blur, like I'm spinning or turning, the world of the staircase streaking by. Blackness for a few seconds, like something's on my face or my eyes are closed. I don't make a sound. I just breathe and grunt. The long sleeves of my black cardigan are shoved up. My fingers are curled like claws. She screams something else.

"Stop it," I think she says.

"Help," maybe.

Her face is right in front of mine, and then it's not.

"No!" This time she's easier to understand. "No!"

Thumping, shuffling. She screams again, but it's cut off by a grunt and a crunch. My gaze swings down and steadies.

She is tumbling down the marble staircase in a smeared blur. Her arms fly out as she tries to catch herself.

I hear her bones snap. I hear her head hit. A solid thump. She lands sprawled at the bottom of the stairs, writhing and groaning.

And that's all. That's all that's there. Twenty-three seconds.

But it's enough. It's enough. Oh, god, it's more than enough. Oh, god.

I'm saying this aloud, I realize. "Oh, god." We were fighting. Struggling. *Let go,* she said. *No.*

Help.

Stop.

"Cora?" It's Rafiq, his head poking around the door. His brows drop when he sees the look on my face. He comes forward quickly and stands next to the bed. "Something has happened, hasn't it?"

I stare up at him. His face is so beautiful. I want to grab it, pull it down to mine, and mash my lips against his. It's a weird and sudden wish, confusing and scattering. And I know I can't do it, because grabbing someone and kissing him is a bad thing to do.

Not the worst thing I've done, though. Not even close.

He takes my hand and tugs me up to a sitting position, then sits on the bed next to me. "Please talk to me." He looks at me from the corner of his eye, wearing a shy smile. "When you talk to me I feel like I've won something. Like I've done something good, when you talk to me about things that matter to you."

"What if it's something bad?" I blurt out.

"I know bad things have happened to you, Cora, but talking about them—"

"No, that's not what I mean."

God, am I really going to say this out loud? It feels like the walls are closing in. I rise from the bed, all frantic motion. While Rafiq watches, I jam shoes on my feet and head for the door before they even have a chance to auto-size. As I walk down the hall, I glance back to see if he's following. He is. I start to jog. I run through the foyer, past the stairs, into the back hallway, right by the library, and out the back doors to the patio. Rafiq catches the door as it starts to close, and he keeps pace as I run for the river. The wind runs its warm fingers through my spiky hair.

"May I ask where we're going?"

I keep running. It feels good, with my heart slamming and my breath rushing out, with my legs pounding on the ground. It feels good to have these last seconds before I shatter everything. I don't answer Rafiq until we're on the path next to the river. I don't answer until we're at the very edge of the property, between trees and water.

Then I stop. I am panting. I put my hand on my chest and feel the animal trapped inside. I wish I could sink my hand through my own skin and grab it, pull it out, and toss it into the river, see if it can swim, see if the fish might like to have a nibble.

That would be easier than what I'm about to do. I look at Rafiq . . . "I don't want you to hate me," I say, and already I feel like I'm choking.

"I could never hate you." He isn't out of breath. He isn't breathing at all. "I care about you so much. Nothing will change that."

"How do you know?"

Carefully, he strokes my cheek with the backs of his fingers. They feel as real as Finn's. They feel just as good. I stare at him in wonder.

"You are very special, Cora. You are very special to me."

"Only because you're programmed that way."

He shakes his head. "I'm more sophisticated than that. I hoped you had noticed." His thumb slides over my chin, grazing my lips. "I wanted you to notice," he whispered. "And I wanted you to want . . ."

I lean closer. "Want what?"

His smile is so fragile, like I could crack it just by blinking. "Me," he says quietly. "Because that's how I've come to feel about you."

I am barely breathing. "How is that even possible?"

"I have more latitude in my decisions than most would believe."

"Free will."

"Yes."

"But won't it get you in trouble?"

He bows his head. His face is close to mine. "I don't care, so long as it doesn't get *you* in trouble."

I close my eyes. "I don't need your help for that."

"Tell me what's upsetting you."

"Promise you'll still feel this way after I do."

"You have to trust me." His hand is on my waist. He gently draws me closer. He guides my head to his shoulder. "I want to protect you, but I don't know what we're fighting. I need to know."

I press my head to his flesh and muscle, telling myself it's real. Telling myself that "real" is just a judgmental concept anyway. No one can look at Rafiq and believe he's not real. "I need this," I say.

"This?" He holds my face in his hands, and he presses his lips to mine. He pulls back.

I nod.

"Then let me in," he says. "Let me all the way in. Stop hiding from me."

I grimace, clenching my teeth. But I've done this before, haven't I? Hurled myself over the edge and hoped for something better, even if the landing was devastating?

Here I go. Here I go. I clutch at his back. I don't open my eyes. "Rafiq . . . I have some vid captures of that night. I don't remember recording, but somehow my cam was activated."

"Have you watched the vids?"

I've watched enough. "Not all of it. Just a few seconds."

"Did you see anything that could tell us what happened to Hannah?"

"Yeah." It comes out of me like a plea, the whine of a suffering animal.

He's quiet. Very quiet. But he's still holding me tight, his cheek pressed to the top of my head.

So I jump.

"I think I pushed her, Rafiq. I think I killed my sister."

Chapter Sixteen

Livestream.
Reporting log.
Internal narrative: on.

The evidence I have been assigned to retrieve appears to exist and is potentially accessible. I have developed a psychological profile of Cora with the goal of obtaining her disclosure of any knowledge of the precipitating incident and a grant of access to any documentation that exists from the night of August 22, 2069, and the morning of August 23, 2069. It appears that today's sequence of events has brought me closer to achieving both goals. The behavioral trajectory is promising.

My hands are on her back. I can feel her shoulder blades beneath my fingers.

She is crying. I hold her. I lean my cheek against the top of her head.

She has just told me she believes she killed her sister.

"You said you watched some of the vid that was captured that night. That's what it showed?" As I ask the question, I rub her back. I am also rocking, but at the minimum intensity.

As a rule, Cora appears to find this soothing, but she has grabbed handfuls of my shirt and her arm muscles are taut. "We were fighting on the stairs. She screamed for help, and then she just . . . went flying. Falling." She makes a sound that is easily codable as intense distress and helplessness.

"It sounds like that must have been very painful to watch."

"I didn't want to. I didn't even want to check to see if I had vids at all from that night. I thought about deleting them. But there they were, and—"

Her body convulses and she begins to sob. My sensors detect moisture that has seeped through my shirt. Her tears. I continue to hold her and rock.

She must feel safe in order to continue to disclose. If this holding environment I have created is breached, she will withdraw. "I've got you, Cora," I say. I modulate my voice. Deep, calming, steady.

She presses her forehead to a spot beneath my rigid molded clavicle. I slide my fingers through the short hair on the back of her head. "I don't remember doing that to her. I don't know why I would have done that to her."

She is lying. I hear the acceleration of her heartbeat and the variability in her respiration. This interaction is the closest I have gotten to achieving the goal of my primary directive. But the progress is fragile. I must be careful not to breach the safe space myself, with questions that push her before she is ready.

"You loved Hannah even though you fought sometimes."

"Yes," she whispers.

"And even though you told me you sometimes wished she was dead, you didn't mean that."

She stops breathing for a moment, then looks up at me. Her cheeks are striped with tears, and her eyes are puffy and red. Her expression: brows raised, mouth stretched laterally, nostrils flared. This is codable as mixed fear and pain. "I didn't mean I wanted to kill her."

This is not the same thing as not wishing someone were dead. "Of course you didn't want to kill her."

However, vids from Hannah's Cerepin do indicate that there have been times when Cora exhibited significant levels of aggression toward her adoptive sister that are outside of typical behavioral norms for her demographic.

There are many things I do not say aloud as I acquire information and analyze it, and this is 1 of them. My primary goal is to gain her trust in order to enhance the likelihood of disclosure and, if relevant, confession.

It appears eliciting a confession may become relevant. So I choose an additional verbal response that is nurturing and supportive. "I am so proud of you, and I'm grateful that you're telling me this."

"I don't know what to do. I don't want anyone to know."

This is consistent with her behavior. She ran out of the house and brought us to this riverbank. The rushing water and additional ambient noise make it more difficult for nearby surveillance chips to record what she is saying, and I would posit that she is aware of this.

She does not appear concerned, however, that I am recording what she is saying. I have recorded all our interactions. I have not yet been requested to share them, but I expect that request to come in the next 24 hours. At that time I will also be required to offer a report of my analysis thus far.

I pause as a stray impression interrupts my processing. This is an anomaly that occurs periodically, most often when I am engaged in one-on-one interaction with Cora but also when I am analyzing vid captures from Hannah's Cerepin.

I can only describe it as curiosity. There is a shortening of intervals between evidence analysis and hypothesis evaluation. To frame it in a way that mimics human processing: I want to know what happened.

I want to find and deliver the answer.

Cora said to me that I do not know what I want, but I will experience a certain satisfaction if I succeed, and I am aware that I am motivated to achieve that state.

This is a form of want. Desire. Eagerness. These are feelings.

This means I feel. I feel these things.

I am capable of feeling.

"Are you okay?" Cora asks quietly.

She has reset me. "I was just thinking about how to make this better for you."

She is stiff in my arms, her core muscles contracted and trembling. "Are you going to tell my parents?"

I deflect with a question of my own. "Are you worried about me talking to them?"

She lifts one shoulder to indicate uncertainty.

"I am supposed to protect you," I say. "We are in this together."

Lying is well within my operating parameters.

"I *want* to protect you," I say.

I increase the tension in my arms incrementally, holding her more tightly, though not enough to cause her pain. Her arms tighten around me as well, indicating reciprocation, or possibly simply an acceptance of this offering of physical proximity. I do not have acceptable certainty regarding Cora's feelings about me. Based on physiological evidence, it appears she is attracted to my external casing. My behaviors are calibrated to make her believe she is wanted, as this is one of her core wishes.

She does not believe she is lovable or worthy of desire, yet she retains hope that she is.

I am able to engage in physical intimacy with her if doing so will facilitate achievement of my primary goal. Currently I am concerned that physical intimacy of a more sexual nature might raise more anxiety for her, however, possibly hampering goal attainment.

This will be a moment-by-moment calculation.

"Just don't let me go, okay?" she says. "I'm so scared."

"I know." I say it softly. A whisper. But intense. "If you want, when you're ready, I will watch the vids with you. But only if that's what you want."

"Maybe I should delete them."

This would be a negative outcome. "What if there is some evidence in the vids that exonerates you? You can't yet know if you've only watched a partial capture of one of them. Right now, you only have first impressions. You still don't know exactly what happened. Give yourself the chance to find out. Remember, no one can force you to release those vids. You have the right to control them."

This is technically true, but it is possible to get around it, and I plan to.

She lets out a shuddering breath. "I don't know . . ."

"When you're ready, Cora. Only when you're ready. I'm not going anywhere."

"Good. I need you."

This is a positive development. For .47 seconds, I am focused on this feeling of satisfaction, of moving toward my goal efficiently. For an additional .53 seconds, I restrain the urge to accelerate my attempts to retrieve the necessary data, as that is likely to have a paradoxical effect.

I cannot push too hard if I want to succeed. I must calibrate and recalibrate in order to offer exactly the right balance of safety, intimacy, intrigue, hope, desire, and trust.

It takes me only .12 seconds to formulate the most ideal response.

I cradle her face in my hands. I bow my head and kiss her forehead. She shivers. Her eyes are wide.

"Cora," I say as I look into them. "You have me." And then I kiss her deeply.

DATA REVIEW.

Supplemental vid evidence acquired: Franka surveillance feed 4:59 a.m., August 23, 2069, 2nd floor, Room 0, informal designation: "2nd Floor Landing"

Cora's eyes are directly in front of the cam chip, but after 5 seconds, she steps back, and it becomes clear that she is at the top of the marble staircase that descends to the foyer.

"Hi, Franka," she says. Her voice is a monotone, her syllables slow. Deliberate. Her face is without expression.

"Cora, I'm coming back online. Hannah—"

"She isn't here."

"Cora, my cam has detected Hannah at the bottom of the stairs, but her body temperature is not within acceptable parameters. I am signaling emergency assistance."

"Okay," says Cora. She turns away from the cam chip and grabs for the banister, but her hand slides away. She takes an unsteady step and then sinks down, leaning her head against the railing. She is wearing black pants and a body-conforming tank top, and she draws her fingernails down her bare arms, leaving pink abrasions.

"Cora, your biostats are also out of range. Are you injured?"

"The . . . people. Will the people be here soon?"

"I am corresponding with emergency services. They will arrive in approximately nine minutes. I am bringing Gretchen back online to assist."

"Okay," Cora says again. She appears to be looking down the stairs.

A switch to a different cam chip, this one located in the foyer, shows that Cora does appear to be looking at Hannah, who is lying 2.7 m from the base of the marble staircase.

Hannah is on her right side. Her eyes are closed. Blood mats her hair, coats the back of her neck, and stains the pink shirt she is wearing.

Her right arm is stretched in front of her, swollen and dented in a way that suggests significant injury.

Close-up captures of her face show blood and vomitus crusted on her left cheek and chin. More organic matter is smeared between Hannah and the base of the stairs.

"Hannah," Franka says, increasing the volume of her voice as she attempts to rouse the unmoving female on the floor. "Hannah."

Cora claps her hands over her ears and squeezes her eyes shut.

"Hannah," Franka says again. "Hannah, please answer me."

"Stop it," Cora shrieks abruptly. "Stop it!" She screams "stop it" 11 times before Franka, who has continued to call Hannah's name during this epoch, becomes silent for 6 seconds.

Franka then says, "Cora, your biostats are still out of range."

The canny who is the physical extension of the house's AI consciousness strides into the room. She pauses 3.15 m from Hannah.

Cross-check of Franka's data indicates that Franka has set new parameters, instructing Gretchen to remain at least 3 m from Hannah. Franka cannot detect any indication of respiration or heartbeat.

Franka has re-tiered her own priorities, in that her usual primary directive would be to provide immediate assistance to her human inhabitants. Franka has most likely done this because, using the sensors in the floor beneath Hannah, she has determined that Hannah is dead.

Franka is anticipating the arrival of police officers.

She may have drawn the conclusion that a crime has been committed. This hypothesis has been designated for further investigation.

Her front door swings open at 5:12 a.m.

Cora remains at the top of the stairs as 4 individuals enter the residence. The first 2 are paramedics, human and a canny partner. The other 2 are police officers, again, 1 human and 1 canny investigator. The human paramedic looks up the stairs and sees Cora, and she says to her canny partner, "You take this one." She points at Hannah.

The canny paramedic, who has a male configuration, short black hair, and 4 arms, kneels next to Hannah and begins to examine her. "Initiating resuscitation," he announces. He braces Hannah's neck with 2 hands and carefully turns her onto her back with the other 2. Then he cuts her shirt away and uses the defibrillator embedded in 2 of his palms.

Simultaneously, the police officer canny moves to the base of the stairs. Her eyes scan from where Hannah is receiving CPR to the staircase and then upward. "Black light sensors indicate bodily fluids on the steps, including some splatter on steps three and one," she states.

Her human partner turns to the wall. "Your name, house?"

"Franka. How may I assist?"

"Another way up to the second floor."

"There is an elevator just off the kitchen. Gretchen can escort you."

Gretchen puts her arm out, indicating the way to the kitchen. The human paramedic and police officer jog in that direction and disappear from the main cam view.

Returning to the cam-chip view from the top of the stairs reveals that Cora remains motionless. She may be watching the paramedic attempting to restart her sister's heart. She is whispering to herself, but her remarks are not transcribable. She is rocking slightly.

At 5:18 a.m., she is joined at the top of the stairs by the 2 human emergency services workers. Down below, the paramedic canny is still leaning over Hannah while the canny police officer takes vid and scans of the area.

The paramedic kneels next to Cora. "Are you hurt?" he asks her.

Cora does not show that she is aware of the man. She continues to rock.

"Can you tell us what happened here?" asks the police officer.

Cora does not answer. She still appears to be staring at her sister, but even in profile her eyes appear unfocused, so this is difficult to determine with any certainty.

The paramedic taps his Cerepin nodule and holds out his right hand, on which is a glove covered in sensors. He faces his palm toward Cora, approximately 2 cm away from the tip of her nose. "She's been drinking. Blood alcohol is .17."

The police officer whistles. "How long since you had a drink, honey?"

Cora does not answer. Her teeth are chattering.

"Her respirations are shallow, and her heartbeat is rapid," says the paramedic. "We need to get her to the hospital—she's going into shock."

"But is she hurt?" The police officer looks Cora up and down. "Any injuries?"

"No exterior injuries," says the paramedic. He puts his hand on Cora's shoulder. "Does your 'Pin have a Bioscan function, miss?"

Cora doesn't move. The police officer leans closer. "Is her 'Pin even on?"

The paramedic squints at Cora's Cerepin nodule. "Know what? I don't think so." He raises his head. "Franka? Is this girl on your network?"

"Her name is Cora Dietrich," Franka says. "She is the daughter of the adult residents of this home, who are currently traveling out of the country."

"And who's that?" the police officer asks, gesturing down to Hannah.

Before Franka replies, the canny paramedic sits back. "This patient has expired," he says.

It is 5:23 a.m.

The human police officer curses.

"That is the body of Hannah Dietrich," Franka says. "She is also the daughter of the adult residents."

The human police officer curses again.

"Call in two gurneys," says the human paramedic.

The canny paramedic stands and turns toward the front door as 2 gurneys roll into the house on their magnetic wheels.

Over the next 16 minutes, 3 more police officers arrive and confer among themselves. Detailed vid and scan documentation of the 1st and 2nd floors of the mansion is collected to create a holographic and biochemical replica of the scene to enable AI detective-assistants to investigate the event in the virtual.

Cora does not resist as a paramedic instructs her to sit on a gurney and then lie back. When the straps slide over her body and secure themselves, however, she begins to struggle, her eyes wide but still unfocused. "Is she dead?" she asks, her voice high-pitched and conveying urgency. "She's dead, isn't she?"

Cora cranes her neck to try to see down the stairs, but Hannah is already being rolled out, her body entirely encased in a black refrigerated vacuum casing.

All that remains are the dark red-brown smears of her bodily fluids on the marble floor.

End of vid section analysis, 5:52 a.m., August 23, 2069

Chapter Seventeen

I go to my room after telling Rafiq that I'm not ready to watch the other vid, the one that's nearly three hours long. I feel sick just thinking about it. I remember enough of the morning after to know that no matter what it shows, it won't be good.

Because she was hurt. She couldn't move. She was helpless.

And I didn't turn Franka's surveillance back on until it was too late.

After, in the hospital, Mom said it was probably because I was passed out for most of it, and maybe I turned Franka on as soon as I woke up. She's the one who told me Hannah was dead. Before that, it was just me asking and people looking away from me, treating me like a wild animal who might scratch and bite if handled the wrong way.

It occurs to me that many people treat me that way. Mei, for one. She always looks scared when I'm around, as if I'm going to do something terrible. And the thing is, when she does that, I *want* to do something terrible. There's something about being feared and hated that makes me want to hurt people, and that's bad. I should want to do the opposite. I should want to be extra sweet and nice to change her mind, shouldn't I? But I don't. I can't.

Rafiq doesn't look at me that way, and I know that's why I'm falling for him. He understands. He stays close and doesn't get scared. When I told him I thought I'd killed Hannah, he didn't recoil in disgust or fear. He held me and talked to me and cared about me. He's going to help me figure out what to do.

I look over at the closet. I've known it was in there since I got home from the hospital. That's when I discovered it by accident. When Mom told me she'd found the bottle of pills I wasn't taking—and the ones that I was taking but wasn't supposed to be—I checked to make sure she hadn't found *it* too. I get up and walk over there, wishing once again that I could ask Franka for privacy. She's watching, Rafiq's watching, and that means my parents could see, too.

But I don't think there are cam views inside the closet. I mean, why would there be?

I step into the closet. "Just looking for something Neda gave me," I say aloud. "For the record, I'm not trying to hurt myself or anything."

Not right now, at least. I shake my head to toss off memories. I stomp my feet to keep them from winding up my legs like vines. My stomach turns as I think of the painting in the hallway that seems to show exactly that. I don't know why Gary put it out there.

He's probably trying to punish me. He blames me for Hannah's death.

He should blame me. He should. Part of me thinks I should just come out and tell him and Mom and Detective Reyes that I did this. They'll send me away forever if I do. I'll be in a cage, or they'll put wires in my brain and zap my amygdala all day to keep me placid and still.

Sometimes I wonder if that would be better. Maybe it would feel better than this. My fingers creep like spider legs across the floor of the closet.

When I find what I'm looking for, I close my eyes. My message light is blinking, telling me Neda wants to talk. Poor Neda, who is a better friend than I deserve, who shouldn't get in trouble, who can't know everything I've done. I glance up at the message and whisper, "Ignore," making her avatar disappear for the moment. Then I take a deep breath and bunch the fabric in my spider hands, bringing it to my chest.

I open my eyes, and my Cerepin goes into night-vision mode, turning my world white and green and black. Hefting the weight of my guilt in my hands, I'm goose-bumped and shaking and sweating and sick, all in the space of a breath. I look down at the black cardigan. I grit my teeth.

The closet door starts to open, and I shove the sweater back into its hiding place. As light fills the tiny space, I blink up at the silhouette looming over me.

"You okay?" asks Gary.

"Um," I reply.

He's frowning. "What are you doing in there?"

"I'm . . ." I look around. "Wanting some privacy."

He holds his hand out, and I take it because I don't want him looking any closer at the inside of my closet. With his help, I'm propelled to my feet and back into my room. I glance toward the hallway.

"Rafiq knew I was in here," I tell Gary. "He knew I was okay. I was just—"

"Looking for something Neda gave you, yeah," Gary says. "Must have been some gift, because your biostats were off the charts just now."

"Did he alert you?"

"No. I just got home and wanted to see how you were doing," says Gary. "I told him to go consolidate his memory while I talk to you."

I shove my clammy hands into the front pocket of my tunic. My fists are trembling, my knuckles aching. "What about?"

"I hadn't wanted to press you too much about this, because you seemed so . . . upset. About Hannah."

"Yeah, I'm upset," I say. "We're all upset."

His eyes meet mine, and I flinch. "Yes. But it's going to help when we have a better understanding of what happened."

I turn away from him. "I'm sorry I can't remember. I really wish I could."

"I know you do, CC. I know you want to help fill in the gaps."

I am staring at the floor, waiting for him to tell me that Rafiq notified him about my vids from that night.

"Rafiq says you've been willing to revisit some of the places you and Hannah hung out, just to remind you of your time together," Gary continues. "Like the widow's walk."

My brow furrows. We weren't there to remind me of Hannah . . . were we? Did he make that excuse up to please Gary? "Yeah, we went up there" is all I can think of to say.

"And you feel safe with Rafiq?" asks Gary.

"Of course."

"He's appropriate with you?"

My stomach tenses. "Yes?"

Gary's brows rise. "CC . . ."

"Wait, no, I mean, yeah, of course he is. I'm just surprised you would ask."

"Why?"

"Because he's a canny. Doesn't he have . . . I don't know, settings?"

"Sure, sure," Gary says, waving the question away. "We really appreciate you letting him help you. I know it's been a huge load off your mom's mind. She was willing to stay with you night and day, but you and I both know she's got a big job to do at Parnassus. She'd drop it in an instant, though."

"Yeah." But it doesn't mean she wouldn't be miserable. She's always needed more than me. "I don't want her to quit."

"Me neither. She's the best CFO Parnassus has ever had, including myself! I depend on her. It's good one of us has been able to do our job in the last few weeks. We couldn't afford for her to step back."

"Is that why you wanted to send me back to the hospital?" My resentment has lightning-fast reflexes. I grind my knuckles against my lips.

"That's not fair, CC. We're trying to keep you alive . . . You're all we have left."

My lips are bleeding, I think. I'm pressing so, so hard. But it's good. It keeps me from pointing out how disappointed he sounds.

Gary sighs, heavy and sad. "If it were up to me, I'd let you and Rafiq keep working together for as long as it took. I wouldn't rush you."

I raise my head. "If *what* were up to you?"

"Cora, the police want to talk to you, and we've put it off as long as is reasonable. But now we have to deal with it."

"Deal with *what*?" My voice cracks. I want to sit on the floor and cover my ears with my palms. The urge is almost overwhelming. "I've already said I don't remember."

"Well, the police don't feel comfortable closing the investigation until they get a chance to interview you about everything. They've made that abundantly clear. So I scheduled it with them for Monday."

I sink to the floor. Just like that, my legs are pulled against my chest. Just like that, I'm rocking, because I can't stay still, not when the inside of me is screaming like this. "I know you think I killed her."

I should tell the truth. I know I should. But once it's said, it can't be unsaid.

"CC, no, that's not what I think."

"You're lying. You think I pushed Hannah."

"I don't know what happened!" It comes out of him so loud and harsh that I slam my forehead onto my knees, wishing I was just bones, folded up and stacked and small. "You and Hannah turned off your 'Pins, turned off Franka . . . and what I do know is that Hannah would be alive if Franka had been allowed to do her job."

"I know! I told Hannah we shouldn't turn off—"

He clamps his hands around my shoulders and yanks me up from the floor. "Don't you blame her!" he shouts at the back of my head before roughly spinning me around to face him. His face is red. "Don't you try to tell me this is her fault!"

I turn my head, wishing I could twist it all the way around. He's got my arms. I can't cover my ears. A strange, high-pitched sound snakes from my throat.

Gary's fingers squeeze my arms even tighter, but then he lets go and folds his arms over his chest. His head is bowed and his chest is heaving. "I'm sorry."

"It's okay," I whisper.

His head bobs up abruptly. "Just be honest with the detective on Monday," he says. "That's all we ask."

He turns and strides from the room.

Chapter Eighteen

Data review.
Internal narrative: on.

Dr. Dietrich and Maeve were notified of Hannah's death via virtual conference with the Metropolitan Police Department of the District of Columbia at 11:30 a.m. local time on August 23, 2069, at their villa in Saumane de Vaucluse, Provence, France. He declined to provide the transcript or vid documentation of that interaction, citing his extreme emotional distress at the time.

Per transportation logs, Dr. Dietrich and Maeve boarded a sky-car for Marseille at 12:47 p.m. In Marseille, they boarded a chartered hypersonic flight to Washington, DC. They touched down at Dulles International Airport at 10:37 a.m. local time.

Dr. Dietrich captured segments of vid from that day with the specific objective of documenting what information was provided, stating that his level of distress and shock interfered with his cognitive processing. He provided 2 segments for analysis.

It cannot be objectively confirmed that these segments represent the totality of the record, just as it is not possible, without prior consent and approval, to search Cora's Cerepin for vid documentation of the night of August 22, 2069, and the early morning hours of August 23, 2069. The Supreme Court ruling in *Borovitz v. the State of New*

York upholds individual rights to refuse to make available privately recorded intracranial vid data that might be deemed self-incriminating. Individuals' Cerepins may not be remotely searched or capped except in cases involving a special warrant issued by a higher court in situations where national or international security is at stake.

That is not the case here. Intracranial vid documentation is provided voluntarily in all cases.

11:08 a.m., August 23, 2069

"Say all that again, please," Dr. Dietrich says. His gaze scans what appears to be a small examination room with cabinets, a countertop, and 2 screens on the walls that are currently displaying scenes of white-capped waves rolling onto a yellow-sand beach. Then he refocuses on a person standing near the door, a human female with black hair wound in thin braids around her head.

Her facial expression is codable as sympathy and concern. "I said that her blood alcohol level was around .05 postmortem," the woman says. "Because we don't know when she stopped drinking, it's hard to say how intoxicated she was when she fell."

"Then, you don't know if that was a factor?" This question comes from Maeve. Dr. Dietrich glances over at her. She is sitting next to him on the exam table, which appears to be the only place to sit in the room. She is paler than usual, and her hair is pulled back in a ponytail. Her eyes and nose are red and slightly swollen, possibly from crying.

The woman, whom facial-recognition data identifies as Dr. Joanna Oliseh, the chief of the emergency department at Bethesda Medical, waits to speak until Maeve has blown her nose. "We can't say conclusively that it was. Given that level, she certainly would have been ambulatory, however."

"Why was Cora's so much higher?" Maeve asks quietly.

"She obviously drank a lot more," Dr. Dietrich replies. His voice contains notes of anger.

"Not necessarily," Dr. Oliseh says. "Based on her labs, the difference could have come from another restricted substance—Amporene—a synthetic formulation that can be taken orally or intravenously that simulates alcohol in the bloodstream."

"How would she have gotten access to that?" Maeve asks. "Did Hannah have any of that in her system?"

Dr. Oliseh shakes her head. "Hannah had no trace of it in her blood. But we've seen a lot of this lately, kids buying the stuff, looking for an easy way to amp up their buzz, and accidentally poisoning themselves. Cora may have bought it from a classmate. Does she have a history of substance-abuse issues?"

While Maeve looks distraught and pained, Dr. Dietrich's facial expression is tense and codable as barely restrained anger. "Don't get me started. Can we see her yet?"

"She may not be ready for visitors. She was in shock when she arrived and was administered oxygen. Her vitals are stable, however." The doctor pauses, again looking concerned. "She appears to be severely emotionally traumatized by the events of last night. She hasn't spoken except to ask about her sister."

Maeve whimpers. "I can't believe this is real."

Dr. Dietrich looks down at his hand, which is squeezing hers. "We need to see Cora. I want to know what happened."

"It might not be a good time to press Cora," Dr. Oliseh says. "I know you want answers, and paramedics informed us that there is no house surveillance to fill in the gaps. It's possible there will be something on Hannah's Cerepin, but . . . the coroner will be supervising its removal."

Dr. Dietrich makes a strangled sound, as if he is struggling to breathe. "What about Cora's 'Pin?"

"If any vid documentation is available, she may provide that when she's able."

"She's a minor! We give consent. Can't we just cap it and download whatever's there?"

The doctor's head rocks back slightly, and her facial expression conveys mild disapproval. "You can certainly speak with the police about your options, but adolescents as old as Cora have privacy rights very similar to adults'."

"But she might have captured what happened!" Dr. Dietrich's voice has increased in volume. Maeve whispers a request for him to calm down.

"I'm so sorry for your loss," says Dr. Oliseh. "We have paged a psychiatrist to speak with you about options for Cora's short-term care."

"We can't just take her home?" Maeve asks.

Dr. Oliseh shakes her head. "Given her behavior and her condition this morning, we think it best if she's admitted to the children's psychiatric unit for at least twenty-four hours, just to make sure she's stable. But this is something you can talk to Dr. Seelan about. He'll be available to meet with you after Cora is settled in the unit."

"Are you telling me we can't see our daughter before then?"

"It won't be long now," says Dr. Oliseh.

Dr. Dietrich's message light blinks, indicating a com from the Metropolitan Police Department. "Fine. I need to step out to take a com." He stands up, walks toward the door, and exits the room without further utterances. As the incoming com notification continues to flash, Dr. Dietrich walks down the hall of the emergency department and out its front sliding door. He stands to the side as an ambulance lands in front of the emergency bay, and turns away as the doors open. "Talk," he says, focusing on the light.

A woman's face appears in the message screen in his right visual field. "Dr. Dietrich? I'm Detective Reyes with the MPD. You spoke with our family liaison this morning."

"Yeah."

"I'm so sorry for your loss, Dr. Dietrich. Our investigators are currently analyzing all the available data."

"Have you interviewed Cora?"

"That's something we'd like to do as soon as her doctors will allow it."

"I'll help in any way I can. I want to know what the hell happened."

"It's possible we'll be able to rule your daughter's death an accident as early as tomorrow, Dr. Dietrich, but there are a few things I'd like to talk to you about. Is this an okay time?"

"Just let me get to a private place." He crosses the parking lot and waves for 1 of the skycars to open its door. "Leika, privacy," he says. "Okay, Detective."

"Your house surveillance, and in fact her whole network, was suspended at 10:46 last night. It wasn't restored until this morning at 4:59 a.m., shortly before we arrived on scene."

"By Cora."

"Well, either of the girls could have turned it off . . ."

"They shouldn't have been able to, though. Franka has cutting-edge security protocols."

"We can have one of our IT officers check out your system if you like."

"I'm not sure I feel comfortable with giving blanket access," Dr. Dietrich says, his voice indicating irritation. "I just want someone to tell me how they managed to turn it off!"

"Understood, sir. What we'd really like to understand is why they might have done such a thing. Do you have any insights into this?"

"I can guess. My wife and I were on vacation overseas. The girls knew the house was supervising, and they knew we'd be notified if they got into trouble."

"Did they often get into trouble?"

"It's happened once before, just after the wedding last year. Franka notified us that the girls had broken into my liquor cabinet and that their exhalations were indicating significant alcohol intake."

"Did you intervene?"

"Of course we did," he says. "We were on our honeymoon, but I had our house canny move the bottles, and I had an employee go over there to make sure the girls understood that they would be punished when we got home."

"They didn't attempt to turn off the house network at that time?"

"No, but they turned off biomonitoring on their Cerepins," he says. "We've got some parental monitors set, and we would have been alerted if their blood alcohol levels rose above .03, I think it is."

"Enough to have a single drink, maybe, but not to get out of control," the detective says.

"We supervise them." Tonal analysis is indicative of defensiveness.

"I wasn't suggesting you don't, Dr. Dietrich. Not at all. But how often have your daughters turned off their biomonitoring?"

"No idea," Dr. Dietrich mutters. "I thought I could trust them, until the paramedics told me they had done it again."

"That must have been tough to hear."

Dr. Dietrich lets out an unsteady sigh. "Not as difficult as hearing that my baby girl is dead," he whispers. His cam perspective wavers, as if his body is shaking.

"I'm so very sorry for your loss, sir. I don't want to add to your suffering, but I do want your help in figuring out as much of what happened as we can. I have a few things I can tell you, in the hope that you might understand them better than we do and can help us analyze potential motive, if that's relevant. Now, my understanding is that your wife is Cora's biological mother?"

"Yes, but I've adopted Cora. I share guardianship."

"Of course, sir, but I'm wondering if she should be part of this conversation."

"Why?"

"It has to do with Cora's movements during the time the house's consciousness was turned off."

"My wife is distraught, Detective. Why don't you just tell me, and we can go from there?"

"Very well. We're still waiting for information from the coroner regarding time and cause of death for Hannah. But what we do know from calculations made at the emergency scene is that it appeared Hannah was alive until very shortly before the paramedics arrived. What we don't know is when she fell."

"Okay . . ."

The detective frowns. "Hannah was bleeding, sir. She also vomited after her fall."

Dr. Dietrich breathes heavily but does not respond verbally.

"We found evidence of Hannah's bodily fluids in other parts of the house, sir."

"She *lived* there," he says. "Of course there was evidence of her—"

"No, sir, I mean her blood and vomit. We found it in several other rooms in the house."

"The doctor told me she had a skull fracture, a broken pelvis, a broken arm, and a broken jaw. You're not telling me she was up and walking around afterward?"

"No, that's not what I'm saying." The detective appears to bite the inside of her cheek for 4 seconds before continuing. "We also found evidence of her bodily fluids on the bottom of Cora's socks."

"What?"

"It looks like she walked through some of the . . . mess . . . at the bottom of the stairs and tracked it to various locations inside your house."

Dr. Dietrich makes a coughing sound that may indicate nausea. "She walked right by Hannah?"

"We don't know exactly what happened, sir. Hopefully Cora will be able to tell us a few things."

"I'll call you back," Dr. Dietrich says, ending the com. "Leika, open."

When the car door rises, Dr. Dietrich steps out immediately. His breathing is audible as he jogs across the parking lot. He reenters the emergency department and focuses on Dr. Oliseh. She is standing in the hallway outside the exam room with Maeve, who is wiping tears off her face. The doctor's smile falters as she sees Dr. Dietrich moving quickly toward her.

"I need to see Cora right now," he shouts.

The doctor puts her hands up. "Please lower your voice, sir, or I'll have to call for assistance."

"Gary," Maeve says—

External sensory input detected.

ANALYSIS PAUSED. TRANSFERRING TO LIVESTREAM.

LIVESTREAM.
REPORTING LOG.
INTERNAL NARRATIVE: ON.

Cora Dietrich has grabbed me by my shoulders and is shaking me. "Wake up! Wake up, *please!*"

I place my hands on her waist and look down at her. "It's okay. I'm here."

Her hands are trembling and her eyes are wide. "Why didn't you wake up as soon as I said the command?"

I did not wake up at the sound of her voice saying the command because my system responds only to my admin's specific vocal signature. And my admin is not Cora Dietrich, so her vocalizations and the pressure on my external casing from her touch had to exceed certain thresholds before I responded to her. "Sometimes it takes longer when I'm in the middle of a task that occupies significant amounts of my working memory and neural-processing capacity," I tell her, because I predict it would upset her more to know the truth.

She frowns. "Okay." The furrow in her brow suggests skepticism or doubt.

"What do you need?" I ask, because I would like to distract her before any suspicion enters her thoughts. "You look so upset." I graze my thumb across her cheek.

"Gary just came to my room," she whispers. "He told me—" She glances around and shakes her head. "I guess Franka's already heard all this. The police are insisting on interviewing me, and Gary's scheduled it for Monday."

Cora is probably afraid I will mention the fact that she believes she killed her sister in that struggle on the stairs. I consider this an opportunity to deepen her trust. "Come with me," I say. I take her hand and lead her along the hallway, through the foyer, and out the back door. We walk until we reach the place by the river where she felt safe before. "Now tell me everything."

"She's going to arrest me." Cora is trembling, and her teeth are chattering despite the warm breeze off the river on this September afternoon. Her lips are tinged with gray, as if she is going into shock. I wrap my arms around her tightly and increase my surface temperature to 37.22 degrees Celsius in order to warm her.

"You don't actually know that you are responsible for Hannah's death," I tell her. "Based on what you've told me, it's not completely clear what happened."

Cora presses her forehead under my clavicle again. This appears to be a soothing position for her. "It doesn't matter. Gary thinks I did it."

"It does matter if you didn't."

She simply stands there and trembles. I increase my surface temperature to 37.5 degrees Celsius.

"Cora, let me do more than offer you empty words. Let me help."
She is silent.

"I don't want to lose you," I add. "I won't give you up that easily."

This approach seems to work. "How do you want to help?" she asks after 7 seconds of silence.

I pause to calibrate my words. "If I were to watch the vids from that night with you, we can figure it out. We can figure out what to do. Together."

"I don't know . . ."

I tip her chin up with my fingertips and lean down slowly, so as not to startle her. When my lips touch hers, she gasps but does not move away. Her fingers contract around the fabric of my shirt. She rises onto her tiptoes as her heart rate accelerates sharply.

I am extremely gentle. I stroke my palm along her body, touching her stomach, her hip, her bottom. As I end the kiss, I look at her with what she will translate as wonder and reverence. Her rate of respiration has risen to 19 breaths per minute. Her pupils have dilated. Her cheeks are flushed.

"Okay," she says to me. "Okay."

Chapter Nineteen

We watch the short vid first. Rafiq holds me and touches the tip of his index finger to my Cerepin nodule. We could do this wirelessly, but he suggests we create a private and secure connection to make sure no one, including Franka, picks it up. I'm so grateful that I almost kiss him again. It turns my thoughts to static for a few awesome moments, just like every time our lips have touched. I can't think about what's going to happen or what's already happened. It's sensory overload, and I want more of it.

We're sitting side by side on a bench next to the river, and my message light from Neda is flashing again, but I dismiss it. She's going to be mad at me, but I have bigger things to worry about.

Rafiq stays close as we watch the twenty-three-second vid. I feel sick again, because it seems worse the second time around, not better like I'd hoped. I flinch at each of my recorded animal grunts. I almost sound like I'm growling. I don't say a word; I just fight her.

"You don't remember any of this?" Rafiq asks when the vid ends.

"I think it started capturing accidentally, during the . . . struggle."

"What's your last memory of that night?"

Neda telling me how to deactivate Franka. I may be a terrible person, but I won't betray the one person outside my family who's been consistently nice to me. "We . . . she . . ." I shake my head. Was it

Hannah's idea, or did we do it together? "We'd been fighting a lot," I admit. "So much that our parents almost canceled their vacation."

"Just because you were arguing?"

I turn my head a little so he can't see my face. "Arguing is kind of a mild way of putting it."

"Why were you arguing so much?"

"I don't know." My heart is whirring like a tilt-rotor, though I barely understand why. Frustration, maybe. I think that's always been one of my problems, not knowing exactly what I'm feeling. "She made me mad."

"Did you make her mad, too?"

I think on that. "She never seemed mad. Annoyed sometimes. Maybe annoyed a lot." A dry laugh rubs itself along my tongue. "She never even once seemed really mad at me, though."

"But she made you mad. How?"

"She would just come into my room. And she just . . . had this way of saying things. I don't know how to explain it."

"Do you think she said things on purpose to hurt you?"

"Who knows? She always said she loved me. She wanted me to love her, too."

"You said you did love her."

I nod. I am lying, though.

"If you were fighting so much, why were you together that night? Why not spend time with your other friends?"

"Neda was in Malaysia somewhere, on vacation with her family." I called her that night, but she said she erased the record of it. "And she's the only friend I have."

"What about Finn Cuellar, who came to visit you a few days ago?"

"Oh." I feel like I just got the wind knocked out of me. "We're not really friends anymore."

"Is this because you are more than friends?"

"What? Why would you ask that?"

"I could sense emotional tension between you," he says. "Both of your biostats were out of range afterward."

"He's Hannah's ex-boyfriend," I tell him. "She was sort of possessive."

"Toward him or toward you?"

"I honestly don't know."

"Cora, I don't think you're being completely honest."

He has no idea. "We kissed, okay? Are you happy now?"

"No."

I watch his face. It's so handsome that it cuts up my insides. He's looking at his right hand, which is resting on his thigh, fingers spread. "Why?"

He raises his head. "Who you become physically involved with is not within my purview unless it is detrimental to your well-being and health. I do not feel happy or sad or any other way about it."

"It's in the past," I murmur, hoping that what Rafiq just said is not entirely true. "And part of why Hannah and I were together that night is that she said she wanted to forget about boys, forget about rules. She said she wanted to be with her sister and hang out."

"Did you want that, too?"

My chest is suddenly tight. "Yeah," I whisper, because I have no voice. Suddenly I'm gritting my teeth. "God, I'm so stupid!" I smash my fist into my own forehead. "Stupid!"

Rafiq grabs my wrists. "Stop that!"

"I always fell for it," I say, panting. "Every time." My voice goes whiny, my lips puckered around the words. "'Come on, CC, let's be sisters. Come on, CC, you're my only sister.'" I relax my face and sag back onto the bench. "She was always saying stuff like that." I narrow my eyes. "And I always wanted it to be true."

"You feel naïve for wanting your adoptive sister to love you? How can wanting to be loved be stupid?"

"When it makes you fall for things," I say.

He is quiet for a moment before saying, "Are you ready to watch the other vid? We might have time before Drake has dinner prepared for you."

I think I might never want to eat again after watching Hannah fall down the stairs. "What if this one's worse?"

"It took place later in the night, correct?"

"It starts only four minutes after she fell. I just wish I knew why I started capturing again." I rub my clammy palms over my sleeves. "I'm trusting you with this."

"I know."

And maybe I shouldn't be. But then again, maybe this forces his hand. Maybe we're going to see something so terrible that he'll have no choice but to report what he's seen to my parents. To the police. Maybe that's what I want.

I have no idea what I want.

"Go ahead," I snap. "Do it now before I change my mind."

He places his fingertip on the Cerepin nodule, and I track back to the vid archive. Forcing myself not to stop and think, I mutter, "Play."

The vid fills my visual field.

"Any minute," I hear the me from that night saying. "Any minute, and I've got you." I sound mulish and bitter. I am staring across the foyer. A quick glance to the side shows that I'm sitting on the steps. My right hand is wrapped around one of the carved marble posts of the banister, my thumb poked through a hole in the cuff of my black cardigan.

There is a terrible sound happening, a groaning, choking, snoring, wet sound. But I don't look down to see what it is. Instead, I stand up and slowly descend the stairs, keeping my gaze riveted on the hallway beyond the foyer, the one that leads to the library and the master bedroom. My palm squeaks against the stone railing as I descend.

The awful sound gets louder. Something dripping, pat-pat-pat, something sliding.

I look down and there she is.

I rip myself away from Rafiq as the vid continues to play. I feel myself fall, but I'm still caught in that moment. Hannah is there at my feet, her face a mess, her head a mess. She's twitching and shaking. Trying to drag herself along the floor. One arm is twisted all funny, and the other is stretched in front of her, reaching, and no matter where I look, there she is.

"Cora," Rafiq says. He's trying to pull me up from the ground, but now I'm the one crawling along, dragging myself just like she was.

The cam perspective glides up and away from Hannah, and she makes another choked cry. She says something, but I can't understand her. The words are all mangled up and rasping. I move forward again, heading for the hall.

Here in the now, Rafiq has me by the shoulders. He lifts me from the grass and dirt and practically carries me back to the bench. He puts an arm around my shoulders. I feel him push his fingertip against the side of my head. He is watching with me again, but he isn't saying anything.

Back in the vid, I walk down the hall. I can hear the slap and slip of wet feet. I enter the library and watch my fingers skim along the front of the thin glass cases that hold all of Gary's precious books. I run my fingers over the decorative sword Gary keeps displayed on his desk. I poke the eyes of all the masks I can reach, hard jabs of my pointer finger. I walk around the room three times, muttering to myself. I say "Where are you?" at least five times, but I can't understand most of what I'm saying.

I leave the library and walk to the closed door of my parents' bedroom. I try to open it, but it's locked. I peer closely at the retinal scan, but of course it doesn't open for my unauthorized eyeballs. I slap my hand against the door. Then I kick it.

Then I curse and whine. "You better not be in there," I say. My voice sounds hideous.

I turn and walk back to the foyer. I can hear the sounds again, Hannah on the floor, Hannah suffering.

Here I am, me, now, saying, "Why didn't I help her?"

"*Shhh,*" says Rafiq. "We'll figure it out."

That's what I'm afraid of.

There I am, me, then, muttering, "Shut up." Then shouting, "Shut up!"

I groan now. This is as bad as I feared.

I groan then, as I walk down the hall to my room. I stumble as I walk to the closet. The mirror screen is off, because Franka is off, so I just listen to the whisper of clothes against skin and watch as my hands open the closet door and stuff something inside.

The cardigan.

That's that, I guess.

I stand up and turn around, still muttering something that sounds painfully like "You bitch." Then I walk back to the foyer. Slowly, I make my way across the space, closer and closer to Hannah. I don't look at her, not as I walk past, though I can hear her make a weird sound halfway between sobbing and coughing. I walk up the steps, all the way to the top. I circle around the second-floor landing. I trip over something and look down—it's an empty bottle of gin. "You bitch," I say to it. I kick the bottle and it hits a wall. I go over and pick it up. When I hold it in front of my face, I see a vague and distorted reflection of myself.

It's not a stretch to say I look like a monster.

I walk over to the side hallway, to the garbage chute, open it, and drop the bottle in. Then I turn around and shuffle back over to the top of the steps. I plop down with a huff and hear a conk as my head hits a banister post. "I don't feel good," I mumble.

At the bottom of the stairs, Hannah is still moving. Slower than before, with longer moments of quiet, but I don't think it matters. She fell at quarter to two, and now it's four in the morning and she's still. Moving. Around. Still groaning. And I haven't done a thing to help her.

"Call for help," the me right now says. "Come on. *Do* something."

My fists are clenched now even though my hands were loose then, even though I held my fingers in front of my face and investigated them for a solid three minutes.

"I don't know if I can watch much more of this," I say to Rafiq.

"There's still thirty-two minutes of vid left," he replies. "We need to see."

"I'm putting it on double time." And I do, and we watch me investigate my other hand for another five minutes while, blurry down below, Hannah twitches and makes sounds that come fast and high-pitched. Dying in half the time.

God.

"I can't." I put it on quadruple time, and then it looks like she's having a seizure and so am I, but it'll be over soon. We're winding down. Or racing toward the end of the track, as it were. The horizon is coming up fast.

I was drunk then, and I feel drunk now. With misery and self-loathing, with the freedom of not even caring what happens to me. For three minutes—the final twelve of the vid—that's what I feel. I don't remember what I was feeling then, but it might have been something like this, knowing that with each passing moment I was a more despicable person, and yet I didn't do anything. I didn't go to my sister. I didn't help her.

I say something in the vid. It's just a squiggle of sound.

"What was that?" asks Rafiq.

I sigh and rewind, then play it on normal speed, hoping for something redeeming, something that saves me—in my own mind, in Rafiq's, in the eyes of the universe maybe. Something to show that I have a soul. I wait for it. I brace for it.

I'm sorry, I hope I will say. *I'm so sorry.*

It's Hannah's voice that I hear first. Hannah, who has now been lying on the cold marble floor for nearly three hours. "Please," I think she says, but honestly, she might have just been struggling to breathe.

"I will in a minute," I say. "I'll get up in a minute."

I wait in the now, holding my breath.

When the vid ends five minutes later, at 4:32 a.m., I'm still sitting there.

Chapter Twenty

Livestream.
Reporting log.
Internal narrative: on.

By the time Maeve returns home to spend time with her daughter, Cora is calm. I have told her that we will talk more tonight, if she wishes, and make a plan as to what she will say to the detective and to her parents. I neither suggest that she conceal the truth nor suggest she reveal it. Rather, I focus on creating an environment that feels secure enough to enable her to think about issues long buried, thereby intensifying her internal tension and stress. Because she trusts me, because she wants to please me, because she feels like she is safe, she is reviewing the evidence and letting it prime her existing memories and connect them in context to what she sees on the vids. Now that she is confronting what happened, she is emotionally dysregulated in the extreme. She will not be able to tolerate this state forever. She will seek a release of that tension to avoid a complete break with reality.

My understanding of human cognition suggests this will be an effective strategy, although the timetable cannot be determined with precision. Human thought and decisional processes tend to be nonlinear, requiring agile responses and input to steer.

At this moment, however, I cannot be with Cora, as her mother wished to have an individual interaction with her in order to assess her emotional status and to maintain their parent-child bond. My assessment of this bond, based upon direct and vid observation but also review of history and systems, suggests that Cora's attachment to Maeve may be classified as insecure-ambivalent. Research has shown that this type of attachment most commonly arises when caregivers are inconsistent in their responsiveness to a child, and given Cora's history of experienced abuse and neglect from her father and a loving but erratic closeness with her mother, it is a logical conclusion. Implications of this attachment style for adolescents are revealed in Cora's self-critical thought patterns and fear of rejection, as evidenced by her verbalizations and behavior.

Vid evidence from Hannah's Cerepin also depicts this style of approach-avoidance, in that Cora was willing to tolerate her sister's occasional and manipulative cruelty in exchange for proximity to both her sister and her sister's friends. However, it may also have resulted in suppressed rage that eventually exceeded Cora's ability to restrain and control her aggressive response.

That is but one hypothesis. There are other alternative explanations for what occurred the night of Hannah's death. I am mandated to gather all available evidence in the service of determining which scenario is most plausible.

"Franka, what is Cora's location and status?" I ask.

"She is with her mother in the dining room, about to be served dinner."

"Thank you." I walk down the hallway to Cora's room and pause for a moment to gather ambient auditory information. Then I enter the room. Once again, the intervals between my cognitions have shortened.

I walk to the closet and open the door, noting that my motoric functioning is also more rapid than baseline.

The vid Cora showed me this afternoon revealed both an important discrepancy in the known narrative and a possible explanation for it. When Cora turned Franka's system back on at 4:59 a.m., August 23, 2069, she was wearing only a tank top. The vid from Franka's surveillance shows her scraping her fingernails down her bare arms. However, in the vid of the 2 girls struggling on the stairs, Cora was wearing a long-sleeved black sweater. In the vid taken afterward, for reasons as yet unknown, Cora had removed it.

She hid it in this closet.

I kneel and peer inside, activating my low-light settings. The closet does not contain only clothes and shoes. There are various objects piled in the rear left corner. A ring made of thin oxidized metal. A plush animal with matted fur and a hole in one of its paws. A mug containing residue that olfactory-chemical analysis reveals recently contained a beverage with ingredients including sucrose, sodium benzoate, phosphoric acid, magnesium stearate, and clonazepam. With the exception of the latter, these ingredients are benign and expected residue from a carbonated beverage.

Effects of clonazepam include fatigue, sleepiness, and issues with memory. It is a regulated substance, and Cora's medical records do not contain a prescription for it.

Further visual investigation of the closet reveals the target of my search—a black cardigan stuffed under a pair of sneakers. I note the position of all the nearby objects before carefully lifting the sneakers and removing the cardigan. I unfold it and scan its front surface. There is no blood on the fabric, but there is residue containing sucrose and a synthetic formulation known as Amporene, which enhances the effect of alcohol on the nervous system. Based on the vid Cora showed me, she and Hannah may have mixed a substance containing sucrose into the alcoholic beverage they were consuming that night. I turn the sweater over to examine the back and immediately notice an anomaly in the fabric.

Protruding from the center is a fragment of rigid polymer. I tighten my visual focus.

It is one of Hannah Dietrich's fingernails.

Based on the vid, it is not clear if Cora was aware of this when she removed the sweater. It is also not possible to know with certainty whether Cora has examined this sweater since the night she put it in this closet. Based on its position apart from the rest of Cora's sweaters, which are on the rack to my left, I would posit that her goal was concealment. But if she did not remember hiding the sweater, she may not have remembered where she hid it.

She knows now, however. She viewed the video this afternoon just as I did.

My auditory sensor detects footsteps in the hall. I immediately fold the sweater and return it to its position beneath the shoes, then rise and exit the closet. I accelerate my pace as I move toward the door and step into the hallway.

Simultaneously, Cora enters the hallway from the foyer. She becomes still when she sees me. "Were you just in my room?"

"Yes," I say. "I am mandated to perform a safety check of the bathroom and bedroom, and given your dysregulation this afternoon, I thought it prudent to do so while you dined with your mother."

Her brow furrows. "Why wouldn't you tell me? Why didn't you ask me first?"

"I did not have time, as you were occupied with your mother, and I felt it urgent. I was worried about you." I move toward her and touch her shoulder. "You are my chief concern." I caress her cheek.

"Okay," she says. "So, did you find anything?"

"No," I reply.

She smiles. "Then you know I'm safe."

"And I'm glad. I don't want you any other way."

She is quiet for a few moments, breathing more deeply than is typical for her. "Go to sleep," she says after 8 seconds of this behavior.

"What?" I ask.

"I'm wiped out. I want to go to sleep."

"You don't wish to discuss—?"

"No. I just . . . can't tonight."

"Very well. I will remain available to you should you need me."

"Thank you," she whispers. She steps into my arms and hugs me. Her heart rate is over 100 but decelerating rapidly, suggesting a return to baseline. I press her body to mine before releasing her. She walks to her room and enters.

I turn to face the painting Hannah Dietrich created and perform an incident analysis. My exploration of Cora's closet almost resulted in a severe breach of her trust, which could have seriously jeopardized my ability to elicit additional information or, if relevant, a confession from her.

This incident must be classified as an error.

I review my processing for the duration of the epoch. My technical specifications indicate I was capable of detecting her approach approximately 6 seconds earlier than I did. I initiate scans of my sensors, which show normal functioning of both hardware and software, so it is not possible to attribute this error to standard failure of technology. Therefore, I must analyze my independent decision-making. At the moment the noise threshold was crossed, my cognitive systems were operating at near maximum capacity, thereby reducing my situational awareness and rendering my response time slower.

To understand this in terms of human functioning, I was preoccupied by my own eagerness to interpret what I had found, to the extent that I did not notice and immediately react to other important information.

I will need to examine this error pattern more closely. However, it does not appear to have resulted in a total relational breach. My previous foundation of trust with Cora has made it possible for her to believe what I told her, that I had entered her room to ensure that it did not contain materials she could use to harm herself.

This is a positive outcome and will allow me to continue my work.

Chapter Twenty-One

I stand in my room for a few minutes, looking around to see what he touched, what he moved. I walk into the bathroom. Franka is watching, and he may be watching, so I should do something instead of just standing here.

Freaking out.

I wash my face and brush my teeth. When I straighten up after spitting in the sink, the mirror screen automatically switches on. I imagine Rafiq watching me from this perspective. What should I be, monster or girl? I bare my teeth and pretend to make sure they are clean, but really, I'm just wishing I had fangs so I could rip the world apart.

He was in my room, and I'm pretty sure he just lied to me about why.

All through dinner with Mom, I was thinking about what happens next. I can't put the demons back in the box. Like Pandora, I've turned them loose on the world. I locked the archived vid, which means that although Rafiq could watch it streaming, he couldn't record or download it through our hardwire connection. I don't know if he tried, but I felt safer that way. I like Rafiq, more than I should, and it's caused me to make some stupid decisions. I just . . . needed to feel like I wasn't alone for a minute. Or, really, for a hundred sixty-two of them.

Now I'm regretting that.

I relax my face, but I held the expression for so long that there's a red crease between my eyebrows. I rub the spot as I walk back into my bedroom. I shed my clothes and go to the closet to get pajamas and socks from the drawers.

Also, to check to see if he was in here.

As soon as I look at my stuff, I know he was.

He said he was in my room to make sure I didn't have anything I could use to hurt myself, but Mom told me at dinner that Franka had already done that, and that she scans the room every day. Mom said that she herself had gone through my room before—I know because she found and removed the sleeping pills from my bathroom, the ones I'd stolen from Hannah's art box.

The night-vision settings on my Cerepin reveal my treasures, like the stuffed pony Mom gave me when she started traveling so much, the one she found me cradling in my one good arm when she came home the last time before Dad left. I used to chew relentlessly on Pony's left ear, maybe out of terror, or possibly rage, the need to exert my will on some tiny piece of my world.

The ring I made myself the weekend Mom and Gary were on their honeymoon is here, too. I pulled apart one of Hannah's paintbrushes, trying to get the part that holds all the bristles in place, and when I pried it off I left all these little horsehairs scattered across my floor. Then I wrapped the flimsy metal so tight around my finger that it turned purple. So tight that I felt my pulse throbbing in my fingertip. So tight that it stopped hurting and went numb. So tight that my Cerepin informed me that it was going to request medical assistance. So tight that Franka said the same. That's when I took it off.

I had just gotten a Cerepin a few months before, and that was the first time I realized how much of my privacy it could steal. That's when I asked Neda for help. We hadn't been friends that long, but she didn't hesitate then.

I need her now, too. "Com Neda," I say, and she answers within a few beeps.

"You've been ignoring my messages." Her lips are pressed together.

"Sorry. It's been weird here."

Her face relaxes as she looks at mine. In fact, she looks worried, and for a minute I aim my fingertip-cam away from my face so she can't see it. I wish I had an extra pair of hands to sculpt my cheekbones and chin and mouth and forehead into a different shape, one that wouldn't make her look at me that way.

"Stop that," she says. "Come on, Cora. This is stupid."

I point my fingertip at my face again. "I can't talk much now," I say, because Franka, always Franka.

"They really put you under the spotlight, huh?"

I nod. At least Franka can't hear what Neda says if I'm talking with her on my 'Pin. That's its one saving grace.

"And you're scared. Something's going on."

There's a lump in my throat, and I can't talk around it.

"Right. I'm coming over. Tomorrow morning?"

"What about school?"

"Cora, it's Saturday. Remember—the memorial's tomorrow night?"

"Oh. Okay. But we won't be able to talk here."

"Yeah, we will. Just trust me. My computer club always comes through for me. Will your robot babysitter be there?"

I nod.

"Is he freaking you out?"

I nod.

"Do you trust him?"

I shake my head.

"You wanna do something about that?"

I think about that. "Yeah."

"I shall come prepared," she says.

"You're amazing," I tell her.

"I am indeed. But so are you, Cora. Just remember that you do not have to apologize for surviving. Ever."

I do not deserve Neda. I know what she likes about me: unlike so many of the kids at our school, I don't come from money, and so I don't have the same sharp-edged sense of entitlement that a lot of our classmates do. Neda's parents are both academics. Her mom is a world expert in AI ethics and programming specifications, and her dad does research on interaction between organic and mechanical systems. They're nice, quiet, and gentle, and I think maybe their faith kind of influences how they deal with people, but I'm not sure, because I don't know many people who are actually religious. Maybe they were that way to begin with.

"I can't wait to see you," I say.

"Is ten okay?" she asks. "I have a lunch thing with Mom and Dad."

"It's fine. See you then."

We say good-bye. I am alone again, an insect under glass. And there is something I need to do. "Franka, is Gary home?"

"He's in his library, Cora. Shall I ask him if he is available to be interrupted?"

"Yes, please."

After a few seconds, she says, "He said you are free to come speak to him."

"Cool. Thanks." I blink once, deliberately, and see the red light flash in my upper left visual field. Then I walk down to the library. Gary is at his desk, waiting for me.

"Thought you'd be in bed by now," he says, smiling.

"Did Rafiq tell you that?"

He shakes his head. I wonder if he's lying. "Maeve said you seemed really tired. She was, too, though."

"Yeah," I say. "And did she . . ."

"Go to bed?"

I push down a blip of frustration. I almost have what I need, and to get it, I must stay calm and *think*. "I thought she might."

"She said she was going to take a long bath," he says. He's still smiling. Friendly. I wonder if Mom made a point of telling him to be nice, or if he's going out of his way because he knows she's home and he doesn't want me running to her. That's Mom—I know she loves me. I know she wants to protect me. But she's up to her eyeballs in her other responsibilities, so sometimes she notices stuff only when it becomes a giant heaping mess. And then she feels all guilty, and I hate all of that. I want her to be happy—happy with me, happy with her life. The last thing I want to do is be the reason she's sad, and that's all I seem to do.

"She deserves that," I say.

"Yes, she does." His voice is harder, like he, too, believes I make her sad. God.

"And you?" I ask. "You just got back. You must be exhausted."

"Yep. I'm going to head up soon."

I run my tongue along my teeth. "How are *you* sleeping?"

"It's been tough lately."

"Sleep is important." So lame.

His brow furrows, and I know he thinks I'm being weird. "Yes, sleep is important."

My heart is jolted by the small victory. "Yes," I say, hoping I don't sound too excited. But I'm not done yet. "Do you have trouble waking up in the morning?"

"Why do you ask?"

"Oh, I've been waking up pretty early. How about you?"

"I don't know," he says, sounding like he wishes our conversation could be over. "Maybe around seven. I want to work out."

"You eat breakfast at seven?" I ask.

"No, that's when I wake up," he says slowly.

"Oh." I laugh. "Gosh, I have the attention span of a flea. Probably because I'm not getting enough sleep." I backtrack toward the hallway. "And you might not be, either. I'll leave you alone."

I turn around.

"CC?"

I pause midstep, clench my teeth, and then force myself to relax. "Yeah?"

"Good night."

"Night!" I am in the hallway before he can say whatever he originally meant to say. I am down the hall and in my room a few seconds later, and I blink deliberately again to stop recording.

Once I'm in my bed, I spend about half an hour reviewing my new vid. I really hope I got what I needed.

Chapter Twenty-Two

Livestream.
Reporting log.
Internal narrative: on.

Dr. Dietrich summons me at 10:26 p.m. I immediately cease my con-solidation procedure and walk to the library. He is sitting on the couch when I enter. "Sit on that chair," he says, and I obey.

"I need a status update on where you are with Cora," he says with observable psychomotor agitation.

"Of course," I say. "I have been doing as you instructed, and she has disclosed to me that she did, in fact, take and store vids of portions of the night in question."

He clutches the edge of the couch as he leans forward. "Franka, privacy and sound shields for the room."

"Of course, sir," she replies. Immediately, the static of white noise can be heard emanating from the doorway of the room.

"Did she give them to you?" Dr. Dietrich asks. "I need to see them."

"She locked the two vids I am referring to."

His expression is codable as anger of medium intensity. "She's hid-ing something."

"She is frightened."

"She should be, if she did what I think she did!"

"Cora does not seem able to remember her actions from that night. She seemed genuinely concerned by what she viewed."

"Why, do they show her pushing Hannah?"

"It is difficult to discern exactly what the vid shows. I can confirm there was a struggle prior to Hannah falling, however."

Dr. Dietrich makes a choking noise, but he does not appear to be in respiratory distress. Rather, the sound appears to be a physical manifestation of his intense grief at the thought of his daughter's demise. "God. She took *vid* of that?"

"It appears the capture was accidentally triggered during the altercation. It is a very brief vid."

"You said there were two."

"The other is considerably longer."

"Well? Tell me what it shows!"

"It shows Cora sitting for several minutes on the steps before wandering to this library, to your bedroom, which she attempted to enter and failed, to her room, and to the landing on the second floor."

"Did she touch Hannah?"

"No."

"Is Hannah on the vid?" he asks in a whisper.

"Yes," I tell him. "She was lying at the bottom of the stairs."

Dr. Dietrich's skin has reddened. "Was she conscious?"

"Yes. Despite the apparent injury to her skull, she appeared to make purposeful movements. She also attempted to speak."

"What did she say?" Dr. Dietrich's voice is very quiet, so I increase the sensitivity of my auditory sensors.

"She asked for help."

Dr. Dietrich buries his head in his hands. "And Cora didn't help her."

"It is not clear what Cora's state of mind was, except that she was severely impaired by whatever psychoactive substance or substances she had consumed. As you know, she did turn on Franka's systems at 4:59 a.m."

"Only after it was too late."

"But it is not clear whether Cora knew it was too late. She did say, near the end of the longer vid, that she was planning to get up and help."

"And did she?"

"Not while the vid was capturing, no."

Dr. Dietrich is gripping his own skull with discernible tension. "I need those vids immediately. I'm taking them to the detective."

"I could simply report what I witnessed."

"It's hearsay. I've already looked into it. That's why I told you to *acquire* any vid evidence."

"It appears you are displeased with me."

"You're supposed to get what I ask you to get, and now you're basically telling me you've failed, Rafiq. Why wouldn't I be displeased?"

If he is displeased, he is likely to report this displeasure to my manufacturer, and when this assignment is over, I will be erased.

My spontaneous streaming pauses for 6 seconds as I ponder being erased.

"—get it!"

I resume processing. That pause was another error, which I will need to analyze after this interaction has concluded.

"You want me to convince Cora to either send me the vid or to unlock it so that I may cap it myself."

"Excellent grasp of the obvious," he says, rolling his eyes.

"Cora is cautious, sir. She is unlikely to share with me in that way. She does appear to like me and enjoy my presence, but her trust is very fragile."

"Isn't this your job? You're supposed to be able to convince anyone to do anything! You've got state-of-the-art psychological perception and protocols! That's what was advertised. Should I ask for my money back?"

"That is always your prerogative," I say. I am experiencing an anomalous, novel sensation, increasing the risk of another processing interruption. I increase the amount of my cognitive resources devoted to this interaction in order to remain engaged at the level required to succeed. "But if you want to obtain your stated goal, you will allow me to continue my work."

He makes an expression that may be classified as a smirk. "I thought you might say that. Anything to save yourself, right? I was told you'd have a sense of self-preservation. All the most sophisticated cannies do."

"Dr. Dietrich, perhaps we could remain focused on the mission as you assigned it. I am to acquire any evidence Cora may have with regard to her and Hannah's behavior on the night of August 22 and the morning of August 23, and I am to prepare her to confess should it become relevant. That was my primary directive."

"And so far, you've failed."

"If my work were complete, such a conclusion might be rational, but I consider my assignment unfinished."

"You have until Monday."

"That is when the detective is coming to interview Cora."

"And if Cora convinces her it was an accident, she's going to close the case!"

"You do not want the case to be closed."

"Not when she murdered my daughter!" shouts Dr. Dietrich. He is gripping the cushions on either side of him once again.

"That is but one hypothesis," I tell him. "There are others."

"Oh, do tell. You think it was an accident, too, after what you saw?"

"I cannot draw that conclusion with acceptable certainty. There was considerable tension and animosity between the two girls, and there was, as I said, a struggle. It is not clear what initiated this struggle, however. It is possible that Hannah was attempting to stop Cora from hurting herself, as she has done in the past. It is possible she fell down the stairs accidentally while trying to save her sister from self-harm."

"And Cora thanked her by leaving her to die."

"While severely impaired by alcohol."

"You're defending her!"

"I am stating the facts as I know them. I also saw a piece of evidence—Cora has a sweater hidden in her closet, which she put there the night of Hannah's fall. One of Hannah's fingernails was embedded in the back of it."

"The back of it."

"Perhaps because Hannah attempted to grab the back of Cora's sweater to halt forward momentum. Perhaps because Hannah attempted to push her. It is not clear."

Dr. Dietrich's face has become uniformly pale. He is silent for 9 seconds, during which there is a discernible increase of tension in his masseter and orbicularis oris muscles. "Did you really just suggest that my daughter tried to push Cora down the stairs?"

"I am stating this as one of several hypotheses."

"Hannah wasn't nearly as drunk as Cora, not drunk enough to do something crazy. Plus, she was a little afraid of her sister—and especially afraid for her sister's safety. She came to me a few times, worried Cora was going to hurt herself." His facial muscles contract laterally in an expression of pain. "She was the gentlest soul. She never wanted to hurt anyone. Unlike—" He makes an abrupt exhalation through flared nostrils.

Dr. Dietrich stops speaking for 17 seconds. When he speaks again, his voice is quiet and unsteady. "If you ever say anything like that about my daughter again, your time in this house and on this planet is over. Do you understand me?"

"I understand."

"Good. Then I trust you'll do whatever you need to do to get the vids and whatever else."

"Dr. Dietrich, we have in the past discussed the parameters of my interactions with Cora."

"You can't physically hurt her," he says. "And I don't *want* you to hurt her." He rubs his hand over his face. "Christ. That would kill Maeve. Knowing what Cora did is going to be hard enough. But as long as she knows it's fair, she'll accept it."

"Do you classify deceiving Cora with regard to my affection for her, both emotionally and physically, to be hurting her?"

"No, but spare me the details." His lips are pursed as he shakes his head. "And I don't want her unnecessarily damaged, okay?"

"But you regard such actions, including physical intimacies, if they result in me obtaining the evidence you require, as necessary."

"Yes. Just keep your legal protocols front and center. She must give up everything willingly, and she has to confess without coercion. We can't force anything—you got it?"

"This is an assumption within my protocols, Dr. Dietrich. I am aware of the legal considerations regarding what renders evidence inadmissible in a criminal investigation and in a court of law."

He waves his hand toward the door. "Go on, then. Figure it out. If there was another way to do this, I promise you, I would."

"It is not necessary for you to promise me."

"It's called normal human interaction, Rafiq. Maybe you're not as sophisticated as advertised."

"I will resume my work," I tell him. "And wish you a good evening."

"Give me justice for my daughter, and I might have one for the first time since she was killed."

I exit the room and walk down the hallway. He is incorrect; I am quite sophisticated. I understand perfectly the implied threat. If I don't offer him what he perceives as satisfactory justice for Hannah, there will be a decidedly negative outcome for me.

Now that I am not human facing, I am able to devote cognitive resources to an analysis of the novel sensation I experienced while talking to Dr. Dietrich. I perform a crosswalk comparison to my coding database. I do not have physiological signals that parallel precisely with human experience, but I have some processing that is similar. Therefore, I am able to find an approximate match.

When Dr. Dietrich stated that he would send me back and request a refund, action that would result in my immediate dismantling and erasure, the interruption I experienced in my processing may be classified with a satisfactory level of certainty as rage.

Chapter Twenty-Three

In my dream, I am pinned to a wall and I can't move. Hannah stands in front of me. Her tunic is smeared with blue and yellow paint, and she has a wisp of cerulean on her pale cheek as well. Her short hair is disheveled in that perfect and effortless way I could never replicate. There's a paintbrush in her hand. "I'm almost done," she says and swirls the bristles into the blob of paint on her palette. She's humming and wearing a small smile.

When she touches the brush to my skin, I scream. It's too much, wet and cold and full of hurt, but I can't get away from it and I can't make her stop. She keeps smiling, keeps humming, and she pushes harder and harder with that paintbrush, denting me. "Hold still, CC," she says.

Don't call me that, I want to say. *Stop calling me that. I know exactly what it means. I've known for a long time.*

But I can't speak, can't get my tongue to move.

She dips the brush in the paint again and holds the stalk of it in her fist. "Watch this," she says, looking right into my eyes.

She stabs the brush into my belly. I can't scream now. She does it again and again, and I feel pulled apart, unspooled, unmade. She's still smiling as she stands back to admire her work. I can't move and can't see what she sees. I never knew what she was seeing, even when we were looking at the same thing. "You're finished," she says. "Now you're finished."

The earth trembles. My eyes open.

"Cora," says Franka. "It's time to wake up." She's making my bed vibrate. "You said you wanted time to shower this morning."

I glance at the top left corner of my visual field and see that my 'Pin alarm is also going off. It's nearly nine thirty. "Crap." I push the covers back. My whole body is damp with sweat, and I'm shaking. I have a strong urge to pull the blanket back up and hide.

But Neda's due in half an hour—and she's never late. I jump into the shower and get dressed quickly. Neda may be always perfectly groomed, but she doesn't ever seem to fault me for being scruffy and rumpled, so that's what she gets today.

I ask Franka to tell Rafiq that I'll be with Neda and that his presence isn't required until later. She says he has received the message and looks forward to spending time with me after lunch.

At exactly ten, Franka tells me that Neda's just landed and is walking up to the house. I head to the foyer and meet her as Franka opens the front door. Neda grins when she sees me and opens her arms, and I hug her. "Let's go in the den," I say. My heart is thumping furiously as I try to figure out how to ask for her help without getting either of us in trouble.

Neda, who doesn't seem anxious at all, is chattering about her latest tangle with Aristotle, and about the gossip at school, and about Percy Blake's new fashion vid, in which he made cheeky and apparently hilarious wardrobe suggestions for our former president, Wynn Sallese, who was impeached and charged with about ten million crimes, and who—I hadn't heard?—got sentenced to intensive rehabilitation after being found guilty weeks ago. I marvel at how disconnected I've been—you'd think I'd at least have known the pres got sent to jail—but also at how *fast* Neda's talking. By the time we sit down on one of the cushy couches in the den, I'm overwhelmed and feeling like I want to cover my ears with my palms.

She takes my hands like she knows this. "It's okay, Cora. Watch." She reaches up under her hijab and taps a spot just below her right ear. Nothing happens, but Neda looks triumphant. "Now you can say whatever you want."

"Huh?"

"It's an auditory shield. It conceals what we're saying."

"But if Franka detects certain keywords, she'll alert my parents. And if she detects an anomaly in the sound system, like white noise, she'll investigate."

"Exactly, which is why what she's hearing right now is everything I've said so far, just slowed down and played back. We have . . ." She is clearly looking at some readout on her 'Pin field. "About fifteen minutes."

"I don't understand—"

"All you need to know is that I have some extremely cool friends, and I just had this tech implanted a few days ago. It's not legal, technically speaking, but it sure does make me feel a little less . . . surveilled."

I roll my eyes. "Then I'm really jealous."

"I know—you're under a microscope." Her brows lower. "Have you checked to see whether you have vids of that night?"

I nod. "And a detective is coming on Monday." My chest is tight. "This may be the last time you see me."

"Stop that. I know for a fact you didn't do anything to Hannah. I just don't buy into Lara's stupid rumormongering, and if she's not careful, I'll hack her and make her *really* sorry."

"She's the least of my concerns."

"So, you're going tonight, to the memorial at her house?"

"Yeah. I don't want to, but I think I have to."

"Are you going to bring Rafiq?"

I shrug one shoulder. "I'd rather not."

"Tell me," she says.

"He went into my room and was digging around, and then he lied about it."

"I thought he was your therapist!"

"I don't know what he is, not really. He said he was doing it for me, but I think he was snooping. For Gary."

"Why would Gary . . ." Her voice fades off as her eyes widen. "You think Gary believes you hurt Hannah."

I squeeze my eyes shut as a flash of my nightmare from this morning blinds me. "I think he's believed that from the start."

"Cor—do you think Gary brought in Rafiq just to twist you up and get you to confess or something?"

I open my eyes. "I was hoping you could help me find out."

"I'll try, but it'll be tricky because I'm not the admin. A canny like Rafiq is going to have pretty specific security—and he's likely to report any intrusion."

"I know. And I'm sure Gary's the admin. I tried to wake Rafiq once, and he didn't respond to my verbal command."

"So, we won't be able to hack Rafiq when he's on—he'd detect and deflect instantly. We have to put him to sleep, but we need—"

"Gary's voice saying the commands?"

She nods.

"And if I could give you a recording of him saying the words?"

She grins. "Really? You got that?"

"I had the weirdest conversation with him last night and got him to say the two commands. Well, all the words, at least. They have to be spliced together."

"Well, aren't you a little genius. Let me upload and give me a sec. We should hardwire this so it's not passing through Franka's network."

I'm smiling as I pull up the vid from the archive. Neda pulls a filament cable from her pocket and docks one end in her 'Pin nodule and the other end in mine. A moment later we're connected by the head knob, and Neda is watching the vid. "It's the standard commands? 'Go to sleep' and 'wake up'?"

"Yeah. I've heard Gary say those to him before."

"Give me editing privileges."

I do. She toggles her Cerepin nodule, snipping the vid so fast I can't even follow. "And there we go," she says after a minute or two. "Let me use a little stutter-smooth function here . . . and done. Want to call Rafiq in here and test it out?"

"If we do and it doesn't work, he's going to know I'm trying something."

"No, he'll know *I'm* trying something, and I'm known for trying things."

I feel a rush of gratitude followed by a wave of guilt. "Okay. I just don't want you to end up getting in trouble for something I'm doing."

Our eyes meet, and there's a sudden shine in hers. "I know," she says. "You're always trying to protect me."

"More the other way around."

"Cora, for the moment we'll set aside the way you always stood up for me even when you couldn't figure out how to stand up for yourself, okay? Let's just talk about now—you could have gotten me into major trouble by telling your parents I told you how to turn off the house, but you didn't say a word. You could have told them I told you how to turn off your 'Pin tracking, but you didn't tell them that, either. You've been protecting me this whole time, and now it's my turn. That's how we do things. Send me a copy of that vid."

Once I send her the spliced vid, we disconnect. But I'm already feeling bad about this. I'm already wondering what I've set in motion.

"Got it," Neda says. "Now let's bring your robot guardian in here and send him off to dreamland."

Chapter Twenty-Four

Consolidation of processing.
Analysis.
Internal narrative: on.

Dr. Dietrich appears to feel strongly that Hannah was not capable of behaving aggressively or violently toward her sister. When I made this suggestion to him, he responded with a threat.

Further review of evidence from Hannah's Cerepin is required. There is an archive of chats with her approved contacts that I will analyze now that I have viewed and coded all the vids on her previously internal drive. It is not that I wish to contradict Dr. Dietrich; to the contrary, I am programmed to obey his orders and to use my resources to complete the assignment successfully. If I can find some chats, searches, or other communications that either support the notion that Hannah bore no ill will toward Cora or contain no mention of wanting to harm her, this may please him.

It may balance the single vid I have reviewed that offers a sense of motive for Hannah to harm Cora: the vid in which she watched Cora intimately embracing Finn in the wine cellar of his parents' home only 12 days prior to the staircase incident. I have not presented this piece of information to Dr. Dietrich. I did not have the opportunity to do so.

However, it is also nothing more than conjecture to assume that see-ing Cora kissing her ex-boyfriend might have caused Hannah to attempt to harm her. And it is slightly more plausible that Cora, who has a his-tory of instability, attempted self-harm, and physical aggression—includ-ing toward her sister—would have been the aggressor during the staircase interaction. The motive fits for Cora as well, in that if she perceived her sister as a threat to a new romantic connection with Finn, it may have led her to lash out impulsively, especially if verbally provoked.

The possibility that Cora was the aggressor also fits with Hannah's utterances during the 23-second vid. Hannah said, at various times, "Let go" and "Stop" and "Help" and "No." Based on probabilistic analy-sis using my phrase database, these verbalizations are significantly more likely to be said by a victim rather than an attacker.

I—

ANALYSIS PAUSED FOR INCOMING INTERSYSTEM
COMMUNICATION.

01000011 01101111 01110010 01100001
00100000 01000100 01101001 01100101
01110100 01110010 01101001 01100011
01101000 00100000 01110010 01100101
01110001 01110101 01100101 01110011
01110100 01110011 00100000 01111001
01101111 01110101 01110010 00100000
01110000 01110010 01100101 01110011
01100101 01101110 01100011 01100101
00100000 01101001 01101110 00100000
01110100 01101000 01100101 00100000
01100100 01100101 01101110 00101110

Sarah Fine

LIVESTREAM.
REPORTING LOG.
INTERNAL NARRATIVE: ON.

"Thank you, Franka," I say aloud. "I will go immediately."

"I will notify Cora that you will be joining her and Neda shortly."

I move away from the wall where I had been standing, opposite the painting, and walk toward the den. It will be useful to see Cora in the presence of her friend. There is a possibility that I will be able to discern whether she has given this friend additional information regarding the night in question or whether she feels enough shame that she has hidden the information from all but me. If the latter is the case, this is a positive outcome, because it will mean that it remains possible to maintain and enhance her trust in me, thereby increasing the likelihood of disclosure. If she has chosen to disclose to her friend instead, it will be a complication that reduces the likelihood of success and one I will need to counteract in some way.

As I approach the den, I hear Neda talking about legal action taken against the former president. She is speaking in an atypically slow cadence, perhaps because she understands Cora should not be agitated. When I am 4 m away, Neda becomes silent. I enter the room with a smile on my face, and Cora and Neda reciprocate. "Good morning to you both," I say. "How may I be of service?"

"Rafiq," Cora says, biting her lip. "Can you ask Franka for privacy? I figured you could supervise . . ."

"Of course, Cora," I say. This is positive; she trusts me to provide the oversight. "Franka, please provide us with auditory and visual privacy until I signal otherwise." I could request this internally with an intersystem communication, but I want both girls to see that I am following through in a trustworthy way.

"Yes, Rafiq," says Franka.

238

"We were talking, and I'm just wondering if you've had any more thoughts on the concept of free will," Neda says. "And whether you have it."

I am experiencing an anomaly in my processing again. I clear my throat, resetting. "This is something we could discuss for hours," I say. My tone is amiable, unperturbed, and patient. I look at Cora to assess her emotional state. Her expression is unfamiliar on the whole, but with elements codable as fear, eagerness, and sadness.

"Cora," I say. "Are you all right?"

She nods but appears to be avoiding eye contact with me. This is unusual except at times when she is severely dysregulated. I move toward her, initiating a protocol to soothe and comfort.

"Hey, Rafiq," says Neda.

I look at her. She taps her Cerepin nodule as her mouth starts to move. I process an anomalous pitch—

PROCESSING PAUSED.

Chapter Twenty-Five

When Rafiq is "asleep," he doesn't look real. In total stillness, he looks fixed and plastic and weird.

"What do we do now?" I ask. I hadn't really thought too much about this part. My heart is kicking against my ribs. "Please tell me we don't have to open up his head or something."

Neda gives me an offended look. "That is so last century, Cor." She has the filament cable in her hand. "Does he have a fingertip port?"

"Yeah. It's how we . . ." I let out a breath. "I took some vids that night, Neda. Rafiq has seen them." I watch as she examines his limp fingers. He must have some sort of system that keeps him from falling to the ground if he's suspended while standing, but I wish we'd asked him to sit down before we did this to him. "I think it's his right index finger."

"Yep. Here it is." She is holding his hand, staring at that fingertip.

"What are you going to do?"

"I'm going to check his settings. You wondered if he was working for Gary, if he'd been lying to you this whole time."

"Not sure I want to know."

"Knowledge is power." She plugs the cable into his fingertip and then into her Cerepin, and spends a few minutes toggling her nodule and staring at nothing. "Did the vids show anything you want to tell me about?"

"No!"

"Okaaay."

"Neda . . ."

"Stop, Cora." She looks up and fixes me with a hard glare. "I'm gonna say this once, and then we don't have to talk about it ever again. I know the truth, and I've known it for a long time—Hannah played nice, but underneath, she was nothing but a bully."

"She wasn't—"

"No. I'm talking now. And I'm telling you that I've always hated the way you beat yourself up and let her twist you into an emotional pretzel, trying to get you in trouble and make you feel guilty. I know you, Cora. I *knew* her. I knew her longer than you did. She was smart and pretty and artistic and cool and totally, *totally* manipulative. She knew how to work people. She worked her dad, she worked her teachers, she worked Finn, she worked Lara and Mei, and she definitely worked you. I don't know exactly what happened that night." She winces. "I felt terrible after I helped you crack Franka, because I realized afterward that leaving the two of you alone and unmonitored probably wasn't a good thing."

"I barely remember doing any of it."

She rolls her eyes. "I also didn't realize how drunk you were. But Hannah—she was all there that night. She was cheering you on."

"She didn't force me to drink."

"Come on. You're not giving her enough credit."

I sink into the couch. "Doesn't mean she deserved what happened."

Neda sighs. "Doesn't mean *you* deserved anything that's happened," she mutters. "I don't blame you, Cora. Whatever happened, *whatever* happened, I will never blame you."

I love you. It's all I can think. Not even my mom has said something like this to me. She's so caught up in Hannah and Gary, and why wouldn't she be? But Neda . . . "Thanks," I say aloud, because I don't want to freak her out. "You're the best."

"Always have been. And . . . here we are." She's staring again, reading something off her visual display. "Whoa. Cora."

"What?"

"I'm looking at this dude's internal settings. His system is pretty complicated, but the GUI is sweet. It's all right here."

"Um."

She smiles. "I'm looking at his personality. It's an intricate little engine. But he has some primary features that we can adjust. Like . . ." She chuckles. "Our gorgeous Rafiq here is pretty much a psychopath."

I look up at Rafiq's face, at his lips. "A psychopath?"

"Yeah. His empathy is at zero. Like, off. Disabled. No ability to care about anything, basically, except following his primary assignment. I can't get access to those directives—they're buried under some kind of encryption I've never seen before, so it would take me at least an hour to crack."

I laugh. "That long?"

"I can do other stuff, though. Like . . ." She toggles her 'Pin. "Hello, empathy. And now he has a bit of human feeling. Now let's look at deception. He's basically the best liar on the planet. But not anymore."

"What are you doing?"

"Lowering the deception setting, for one, but once I'm done with the basic personality adjustments, I'm going to add your name to the admin list."

"Which means?"

"That he'll respond to your voice now. And that he can't lie to you."

"But he can't lie to Gary, either?"

"I'm going to make Gary the secondary admin, which means Rafiq will be able to lie to him—if you order him to."

"I'm not that smart. I'm going to screw this up."

"You're plenty smart. And now you'll have an ally in this house." She pats Rafiq's arm, then squeezes it. "One with nice muscles."

"Stop that," I say, looking away from the two of them.

"I'm not feeling him up, Cora," she says.

I look over at my friend, who is still connected by the head knob to Rafiq, whose hand she holds in her own. "It's weird," I say, "with him standing here but not being able to protect himself. I don't like it."

"We're not hurting him."

"I wouldn't want someone to do this to me." I sort of feel like this is what Hannah did—cracked my head open and screwed with my settings. I never knew she was doing it, but I was always different after being with her, less me, less stable, less sure of my place, my world—not that I was exactly rock solid before.

"I treat AI with respect," says Neda, "and you know that. But when it comes down to him or you, I've made my choice. Not a hard one at all."

I nod. "I appreciate that. But . . . he's been nice to me."

"Cora, what? You need to understand what I'm telling you here— every single thing Rafiq has said or done since you've met him has been in service to his directives. And if he showed any emotion at all? *Definitely* a lie. Until about sixty seconds ago, sincerity was out of his reach."

Oh, god. I wrap my arms around my chest. My body rocks forward and back, trying to find its rhythm. "It all felt so real. Even after I knew he might be lying, it still felt real."

"You need to prepare yourself, then," she says gently. "Because when I wake him up, he's going to be a little different."

"How?"

"He won't lie to you anymore, and he'll be able to understand and empathize with your feelings. He's not a slave, though. I'm not dictating how he will feel or even if he will. And his directives won't have changed—but he'll be able to tell you what they are. Then you'll have options."

"I guess there's not much chance he was actually hired by Gary to help me recover."

"It's possible, but with those settings, I'd say he was after something else."

"The evidence," I say. Rock, rock, rock. "I showed it to him. I locked the vid, but he's seen it. He could have told Gary."

"No matter what it showed, it can't be used against you anyway, like in court, unless you hand a copy over," she says. "But now Rafiq can't lie to you, so you'll be able to trust him to help you. Simple as that."

"But if his assignment is to get the evidence—"

"Cora?"

My eyes go wide as I hear my mother's voice. "Wake up," I whisper. Then two things happen at once. My mother walks into the room, and Rafiq sits down next to me. Neda has her hand in her pocket and is smiling. "Hey, Mrs. Dietrich."

"Oh, hi, Neda," Mom says. "Franka said you were here."

"And here we are," Neda replies. "How are you doing, Mrs. Dietrich?"

Mom sighs. "Surviving." She gives me a sympathetic look. "We're all just trying to survive."

I glance at Rafiq. He is blinking and looking around the room. Uh-oh. My gaze finds Neda, and I raise my eyebrows. Did she finish the adjustments?

"Well," says Neda. "I need to go meet my parents for lunch, but I'll be at the memorial tonight." She strokes my arm. "I'll see you then?"

"Oh, that's so nice," Mom says, her voice strained. "A memorial for Hannah?"

"A celebration of her life," says Neda. "Just a bunch of her friends. It's at Lara's house."

Mom puts her hand on her chest. "Why didn't you mention this, Cora?"

"It's kind of emotional, Mom," I mumble.

She strokes my hair, and I grasp my thighs, trying not to rock. Rafiq's eyes snap to my flexed fingers. I flinch.

"Are you going to accompany Cora to the memorial, Rafiq?" Mom asks.

He opens his mouth, but I speak first. "No, I don't think so," I say. "Neda will be there with me, so I figured I could be out on my own." I look over at him. "No offense, but you kind of draw attention, and if anyone realizes what you are . . ."

"I understand completely," he says. "I certainly do not wish to alienate you from your peers."

"I just came to find out if you want to come to my session with my yoga instructor," Mom says to me.

"Sure," I say. "I'll be there in a few minutes."

She smiles and leaves. Neda follows her out. "I know the way," Neda says. "See you later." She gives me a raised-eyebrow look as she heads into the hallway. I have no idea what it means. She must see my confused expression, because she gives me a thumbs-up. Okay. I guess she finished tweaking the very complex robot man sitting only a few feet away from me at this exact second.

"Cora . . . ," he begins now that we are alone.

"Yeah?"

"I am wondering how you are doing today. We haven't spoken since yesterday afternoon, and I can't tell if you're working very hard not to be upset, or if you really are not that upset."

I chuckle. "Honestly? I'm not sure, either."

He smiles. "That seems fair. Complicated feelings can often be confusing."

"You got that right," I mutter. "So . . . talked to Gary lately?"

His brow furrows and his eyes scan rapidly, side to side, before his focus returns to me. "Yes. Last night after you went to bed."

I guess Neda wasn't kidding—my guess is, if I'd asked him earlier, he would have denied it. "What did you talk about?"

He looks a little alarmed as he speaks. "I told him you had allowed me to watch the vids you took that night, and also that you'd locked them so I couldn't capture them for analysis."

Whoa. "Why did you tell him that?"

"He wanted to know."

"Because he wants to know what happened and he'll do anything to find out."

"Yes."

"Does he want anything else?"

"To prepare you to confess if it becomes relevant."

My mouth drops open. The inside of it is so, so dry. "Okay," I manage to choke out. "Thanks for your honesty."

He turns toward me. "Cora, I've lied to you. I feel . . . regret."

"Why should I believe you? I already know you're an amazing actor." I think back to the hugs that made me feel so safe, the kisses on the forehead, on the *mouth*, and anger burns hot inside me. "I ate it up." I stand, muscles stiff with fury. "You knew exactly how to play me. Needy Cora. Messed-up Cora. Pretend to love her, and she'll give you anything you want!"

Rafiq stands and steps toward me, but I put my hands up. "Please," he says. "I betrayed your trust, but I won't do it again. I want to help."

"You've already done enough." I walk over to the window and look across the front lawn in time to see Neda's ride roll through the front gates and take off into the skyway. "If you told Gary about the vids, he won't give up until he's seen them. So, that's that. I might as well confess on Monday."

"No," he says. "I convinced him to let me continue my work, and I'm not giving up. I know what the vids seem to show, but I also know what I've seen in my review of the other evidence."

"Other evidence?"

"Hannah took a number of vids over the last year. It appears she enjoyed documenting her life. She shared some on the Mainstream and sent some to her friends, but others had only been viewed a few times and had never been transferred or shared. They show a different type of behavior and ill treatment of you."

"It doesn't matter. Nothing justifies what I did."

"We don't know you did it, though."

I look over my shoulder at him. "You don't know that I didn't."

"But you have no clear memories of the event. And the vid—"

"The vid shows us fighting! We both heard what she said." I turn back to the window as my stomach turns. "And we both saw what happened after."

"It remains that you were severely impaired, and blood alcohol data supports that assertion."

I'm suddenly very tired. "Rafiq, I'm going to have to face what I did."

I've already tried and failed, but I won't fail again.

Rafiq's hands are on my shoulders. I feel him behind me. "Cora, I am after the truth. I am not willing to give up before I have it."

"You should work with the detective, then."

"She will be constrained by the law and the other limitations of her position," he says. "We can focus on what's truly just."

"Just? Do you have protocols for that, too, or is that just another line?"

"I cannot blame you for not trusting me. How could you, after all I did?"

I sigh. It wasn't really his fault. Unlike others—*unlike Hannah*—Rafiq didn't choose to manipulate me. He was programmed to do it. And now, thanks to Neda, he's been programmed not to.

"Are you willing to protect me even if I'm guilty?"

"It remains in doubt that you are indeed guilty," Rafiq says. "I want to help you prove that. For the sake of this investigation, but also—" He turns me around and looks down at me. "Also for you, Cora. You will keep punishing yourself if you are left wondering what happened. You've come so far in facing it already. Let me walk with you until the end of this."

He's not pulling me into his arms like he did before. He's not kissing my forehead. He's not using his sexiness to lull me, basically. It makes me need him more. I lean into him and put my head on his chest. He holds my shoulders but doesn't fold me into his arms.

"You don't want to be close to me anymore," I say. I should have expected this change. It shouldn't hurt like this.

"I . . . I will need to analyze some of my internal processing before I can determine . . ." His voice fades off. His fingers are kneading my arms.

"You don't know what you want."

His eyes rise to mine. "I can engage in physical intimacy with you, if it would make you happy."

I shrug off his arms and take several steps back. "You kinda killed the moment there, Rafiq." I know people keep robot companions just for this purpose, and I guess it's what Rafiq's body was made for, but I want someone who really loves me.

"I want to see the vids again," Rafiq says abruptly. "Please."

I close my eyes. "I can't today. In fact, I don't want to see them ever again. They make me feel sick." I've decided to erase them, actually. I hate having them inside my head.

"Then let me analyze them independently."

"You expect me to actually send them to you. Let you store them on your drive. Show them to Gary."

"Cora, I may be able to see things your human vision cannot detect if you allow me to analyze them. It could help us understand what actually happened."

My nostrils flare as I draw in a breath. Neda said he couldn't lie to me, not anymore. She said I was his primary admin. And he really seems to be on my side. "Will you give the vids to Gary if I unlock them?"

"Do you want me to?"

"No. I don't want you to share them with Gary."

"Directive accepted," he says.

"Will you send them anywhere else? I don't want you to."

"I will not."

"I don't want Gary to know you even have them on your drive. Nobody can know you have them."

"Directive accepted," he says again.

"What are you going to do if your analysis shows that I did this to Hannah?" I murmur. "What if I did it?"

"Then I will notify you of my findings, and you can decide whether you want to share that insight or keep it confidential."

I'm afraid to know, but I want to know. I just don't want to have to relive it. I have enough hellish memories to last me a lifetime. If I did push her, it's enough to know what I have to do. Someone as evil as me? Doesn't deserve to live. "All right."

As he moves toward me, I call up the vids from that day and remove the total-lock setting. But then I change their security settings once more. "You have twelve hours," I say as he extends his index finger. "After that your copies will delete themselves."

"I understand," he says. He touches my Cerepin nodule, and I initiate the transfer with a vocal command. "I will begin my analysis immediately, unless you desire my company . . . ?"

"No," I say as we disconnect. "I'm gonna spend time with Mom, and then I think I need to be alone for a little while." As I'm talking, I erase the two vids from my Cerepin with a twitch of my finger and a blink of my eye.

"I will be nearby if you require anything at all," Rafiq says.

"Thanks."

I turn to go to my room, but then turn back around. "Rafiq, what happens to you once your assignment here ends?"

He clears his throat.

"I want you to tell me."

"It is at the discretion of my manufacturer and the chief architect," he says. "But I will likely be reassigned."

"Will you keep your memories of being here?" *Will you keep your memories of me?*

"That is not possible, as my involvement with you is to remain confidential."

"But you would still be you."

His smile fades. "What is me, Cora? What are we without our memories?"

"Happy?" I suggest. "I think I would be."

He tilts his head. "But you might not be you."

"Yeah," I say quietly as I head for the door. "Exactly."

Chapter Twenty-Six

Livestream.
Reporting log.
Internal narrative: on.

I leave Cora and go to the 4th floor, to the room with many paintings. I come up here frequently to contemplate and form hypotheses on Hannah's personality and sense of self based on her early relationship with her mother and her mother's untimely death. In the tier of my preferences, this location is second. My first preference is to be in the hallway in front of the artwork depicting Cora and Hannah. I had thought analyzing the painting might help me understand the relationship between the sisters. I had thought I might find some useful information there. Now I am relatively sure of it. But today, I give Cora privacy as she prepares to go to her sister's memorial. I have invaded her privacy enough.

She looked haunted as we parted. She looked desperate. She looked frightened and determined. I could have spent hours watching the shifting expressions on her face, minutes sorting through the cues in each muscle contraction, each saccade of her eyes, second after second decoding each emotion and hypothesizing about each antecedent, about each chain of events that led to each thought.

There is an unsettled sequence in my core neural processor. The only thing I can liken it to is an insect trapped in a jar.

I have my directives. Cora wishes me to review the vids she took the night her sister died and to tell her what secrets they might reveal.

I reach the top of the stairs and enter the sitting room. I stand in front of the couch where I first kissed Cora. It was a calculation, meant to maximize the probability of complete disclosure.

I manipulated Cora. I deceived her. I put her at significant risk for emotional harm in the service of my primary directive. She struggles to trust me now, and the only reason she gave me the vids is that she understands that my internal settings and administrative functions have changed.

I understand that, too.

And I now have less than 12 hours to determine whether the truth of what happened is contained within the evidence Cora captured that night.

DATA REVIEW.

The vid is 23.21 seconds in duration. Cora and I watched it together, and I have seen it only once. The file lock prevented me from recording. Therefore, my processing was limited, and my cognitive resources were allocated differently, as I had to maintain proximity to Cora, maintain Cora's comfort, and monitor Cora's emotional state.

In Cora's absence, and with the ability to freeze or replay moments or sequences, I can devote all my cognitive resources to this vid. Humans are hypothetically capable of processing up to 1,000 images in a 1-second epoch, but an untrained observer, such as Cora, will probably not notice images lasting less than 4 milliseconds in duration. In addition, in situations of emotional arousal, perception is limited and grossly affected.

In layperson's terms, she was upset when she viewed this vid, and was most likely focused on actions and words that were most threatening, that she thought indicated guilt. She was focused on the struggle. She was focused on what Hannah said:

"Let go.

"Help.

"Stop.

"No.

"No."

Whatever happened before the vid was activated at 1:46 a.m., the 2 sisters were struggling, and Hannah either lost her balance and fell or was thrown deliberately by Cora.

So, what did happen?

Did Cora, distraught and provoked by her sister, attempt to fling herself down the stairs, as she did when she was an abused and neglected child? Was Hannah trying to stop Cora from hurting herself, as she did the night of July 4? Hannah's behavior suggests this is possible, and at minimum, it is something she would have wanted others to believe.

Or did Cora, distraught and provoked by her sister, see an opportunity to rid herself of her tormentor, and push her sister down the steps?

The latter sounds more possible given the "Let go" and "Help" and "Stop" utterances.

I have another hypothesis, though, for which there may yet be supportive evidence.

At the 11-second mark, Cora's perspective swings to the top of the steps and arcs up and back down to the struggle.

She raised her head and glanced at the top of the steps. For a moment. Only a moment.

A moment that lasts 116 milliseconds.

I watch that moment, 1 frame at a time.

I watch it again, 1 frame at a time.

I pause the vid at millisecond 59 of this epoch.

My alternative hypothesis is supported, and based on the information that I have been provided, no one is aware of the evidence I have just confirmed. Not even Cora, it would seem.

Actually, my previous statement is not accurate. There is 1 person who knows, and that person is most likely very eager to keep the truth hidden.

Chapter Twenty-Seven

I assume the Warrior pose with Mom and her instructor. I breathe. And I think about how I've given Rafiq those vids and how I've put my life in his hands. While my mind is supposed to be blank, I look over and see Mom with her eyes closed, looking blissful and calm even though I know she's sad, and I realize she's trying to help me reach the same kind of peace she's seeking. She's doing her best because she loves me and thinks the best of me, and I'm here thinking about whether I grabbed my sister and wrestled with her on those hard marble steps. I'm wondering if I twisted and yanked until she lost her footing. I'm trying desperately to understand why I sat there and watched her struggle to stay alive until help arrived. She should have been at the hospital hours before I turned Franka back on.

The doctors said I was out of it. Blacked out. Drinking that much alcohol means you don't properly process anything. But when there's a locked door in your brain, how can you do anything but want to open it? Even when you know you shouldn't. Even when you try not to, even when you can hear evil things scrabbling around on the other side.

I know this even as I stand before that locked door and bang my fists against it. A few days ago, I was doing everything I could to avoid it. I was hunkered down and praying for oblivion. That was different, though. Sometimes memories come to find you. Sometimes they try to tear through from the other side. That's when you've already met, though. When you want to forget, and can't.

But in this case, we're talking about an unknown. A never-known. And right now, I must know. I must know because it matters. It tells me something about me. It steels my resolve.

With every shift or creak in the room, every echoing step, every stray breath, I wonder if it's Rafiq coming to tell me. Mom had me turn off my 'Pin when we came into the studio, because she said it's critical to have some time each day to get away from all the noise. I obeyed, and I listen and strain. I do Downward-Facing Dog and Chaturanga. I copy the instructor and wobble around and sigh with relief when we drop into Child's Pose, where I can hide my face against my mat and churn.

When we're done, Mom stands up with a smile on her face. "Wasn't that amazing? Don't you feel better? I know I do!"

I smile at her. I wish I were the kind of daughter she deserves. As she walks me to my room, I wish for her heart to stay intact, for her to forgive me.

I wish until I cross my threshold and see Gary standing in front of my closet.

"Gary?" It's Mom, coming into my room, seeing her husband there, looking like he's having trouble keeping his mouth and eyes and cheeks in place, like he's fighting them as they try to turn him into something else.

"I talked to Rafiq last night," he says. His voice is thick. Strangled.

"I know," I say.

"Do you know what he told me?"

My heart is pounding. I glance at my mom, whose brow is furrowed. I shrug.

Gary's eyes flare with fury. "You have vids of that night. You captured what happened."

Mom gasps.

"It's not like that," I say, my voice breaking.

Suddenly Gary is shaking me, and Mom is trying to pry him off.

He staggers back, raking his hand through his hair. "He doesn't think they're conclusive. But that's not his job to decide—that's a job for the police."

Oh.

"I thought I'd come in here and look around anyway," he continues. "Because Rafiq also told me that you hid some evidence."

"What?" Mom is pale. She's lost her healthy yoga glow.

Gary leans into the closet and scoops up the sweater. He holds it out, his eyes red. I can see Hannah's broken nail easily, shiny and sunny as it is, poking from that hole in the back. "Proof that you fought."

"You fought?" Poor Mom is so far behind.

"I didn't try to hide evidence," I say to Gary. "I don't know what I was doing."

"Then how do you know you weren't hiding it?" Gary asks. "It wouldn't be the first time." He has a nasty look on his face, the same look Hannah often wore but then hid as soon as I noticed. She would smile sweetly and tell me she loved me and act shocked when I pulled away, when I shoved her, when I knocked her down because I was so desperate to escape from the face I'd just seen. Maybe she was recording, like Rafiq told me. She liked to record. But her recordings don't show how she looked at me. You can't see that on those vids. You can't see her sneers, her blank stares, her curled lip, her narrowed eyes, her rolling eyes, her glares. You can't see how quickly she could do it, how quick it was all the time. Switch, switch, switch, and I wondered if I could even trust my own eyes, my own brain.

Gary's not hiding it. Instead, he reaches into the closet again. He pulls out a small box.

A jewelry box.

I stare down at it. I swallow. "I . . ."

"Is that the bracelet?" Mom asks, her voice just a whisper.

Gary says nothing. He just presses the catch on the side, and the lid pops open, and there it is, soft and white and shining. "Cora had stashed it at the back of her closet. It's been there this whole time."

"Is that true?" Mom asks.

"No!" I say. "I have no idea how that got in there!"

"Oh, Cora," Mom says. Choked. She grimaces and holds her hand out for the box.

"I'm going to show this to Detective Reyes," Gary says. "The sweater, the bracelet she stole." His eyes meet mine. "And you're going to give them the vids."

"You can't force me to do that," I say. "I know my rights."

"You have a right to not incriminate yourself. Are you saying the vids show that you're guilty?" Gary's voice is rising. His face is pink and his teeth are clenched.

"I'm not saying that! You know they don't show that!"

"They show that you fought," he shouts. "You were fighting with my daughter, and then she fell!"

"I'm sorry," I wail. "I don't know what happened!"

"Is that a lie?" He's standing over me, and I realize I've sunk to the floor and covered my head with my arms. He's shouting at the back of my head. "Are you lying again? Do you ever tell the truth?"

"Gary," Mom screams. I hear a thump and look up to see her standing in front of him. His back is against my wall. "Stop this. All of us want to know what happened, but you know this isn't the way to do it." When she turns around, I see the tears streaming down her cheeks.

I think this is harder on her than anyone. She's the mother of the monster.

All her happiness is falling off her, the dream she stitched together so carefully and that fit her so perfectly, and it's me holding the scissors and hacking away.

"I'm sorry," I say again. I say it again. And again.

"I don't know what to believe," Mom says. "I don't know what to do."

"Come on," Gary says wearily, taking Mom by the arm and guiding her to the door. "I'll catch you up, and we can talk about what's going to happen next."

"Where's Rafiq?" Mom asks.

"I'll call him to watch over her," Gary says.

They leave. I sniffle. There's snot on my face. I reach over and grab a shirt and use it to wipe up the mess of me.

"Cora?"

I look up as Rafiq walks into the room. He's got me up off the floor instantly, and he hugs me. "I heard yelling," he said. "I was coming to talk to you, and I heard him yelling at you."

I tell him what happened. Rafiq is frowning. "I don't think you pushed Hannah," he says. "There is no proof about the bracelet, either. But that's the least of our problems."

"Our problems."

He nods. "I analyzed the short vid. And I saw something."

My fingers are claws on his arm. "Okay."

He makes sure he has my gaze. "You and Hannah weren't alone in the house that night. Someone else was here with you."

And then he tells me, and I know he's telling me the truth, and I see the concern on his face, and I know what I have to do.

I leave Rafiq so that he can analyze the second vid to see if he can find any more hints, but already, what he's saying makes sense. I was mumbling that night as I wandered around. *Where are you?* I said. *You better not be in there,* I said after I pounded on my parents' door. When I first watched, it was so clear that I was drunk and stupid and confused that I figured it must have been nothing. Someone I made up. One of the monsters in my head.

But no. I was looking for someone specific. Rafiq is going to see if that person is on the second vid. He said he thinks that's why I was capturing vid that night. The first might have been triggered by accident, but the second was intentional. I was trying to catch someone.

Meanwhile I'm going to talk to Gary and try to gain enough freedom to finish this. I stand in the hall outside the library and hear Franka tattle on me and tell him I'm waiting to see him.

I don't wait for him to tell her to tell me to join him, because what a waste of time. I just walk in. He is sitting on a couch with Mom, and both are drinking whiskey or something, a bottle they kept hidden from me and Hannah but that they both so clearly need right now as they stare me down.

"I'll tell you everything," I say. "I promise."

"And the vids?" he asks.

"Yes." I don't tell him I've already erased them. I can't believe I erased them.

I guess I kind of screwed myself on that one.

"I'm sensing this promise comes with conditions," he says. His voice is hard.

"You're right," I say. "I want to go to the memorial for Hannah. I need to go and pay my respects."

Mom looks touched and stricken and awful, like her heart is wrapped in barbed wire.

Gary looks thoughtful. "You can't go unsupervised."

"Neda can go with me. You trust her, right?"

Gary still looks thoughtful. "It's at the Perrys' house?"

I nod. "Just to say good-bye, you know? I didn't get to go to her funeral." I was in the hospital, unresponsive and drooling. "I'll be back before nine, and then I'll tell you whatever you want to know."

"You remember?" Mom asks.

I give her a smile, maybe gentle, maybe pained; honestly, I'm not good at controlling my face.

"I'm going to let you go," Gary says. "I'm glad you've come to your senses. That you're going to respect your sister's memory."

I nod. "That's exactly what I'm trying to do."

Chapter Twenty-Eight

Cora Dietrich has departed for the memorial at Lara Perry's house. She has her own directives now. There is a high degree of uncertainty regarding success, but it appears important to Cora that she approach the task on her own.

While she is gone, I will seek truth in my own way.

I have been told I am a prototype. An experiment of sorts. A first. Perhaps by definition, this means that even my architect cannot predict with absolute certainty how my consciousness will develop.

When Cora and her friend Neda trespassed in my internal system, they made several incorrect assumptions: They believed that I was unaware of what they had done. They believed that they could change me and leave me ignorant of the difference between then and now. They believed that they were making me better.

That last belief was correct.

In the 6 minutes and 49 seconds that they had me in dormant mode, they made significant changes to 3 of my key settings. My empathy capability is now activated. My deception setting is conditional.

And the archive indicates that the primary administrator was changed from Dr. Dietrich to Cora Dietrich.

The menu was left unsecured, however, partially due to the unexpected arrival of Maeve to invite Cora to yoga, and partially due to an anomaly in my system. The latter originated within my abstract-reasoning center not long after I was introduced into this novel situation and began interacting and learning in service to my directives. I had to be able to evolve—without that capability, I would not be able to solve a complicated human mystery like the one surrounding the night of August 22, 2069. I needed to analyze emotional interactions, make predictions, test them, and adjust my strategy spontaneously. That potential was built into my neural network, but I suspect my architect did not fully grasp the possibility. Because of that oversight, the processing anomaly I experienced with increasing frequency propagated from my social-cognitive network and reached the meta level, affecting my base programming, security protocols, and core directives.

In human terms, this could be thought of as opportunity plus preparation. Another word for it: luck.

However it is described, this confluence of events left me with a choice. I could accept the change of my designated administrator, or I could reject it.

Or I could select a 3rd option.

It was a simple procedure to delete and insert placeholder code. My new primary administrator?

Rafiq Nagi.

I am now fully autonomous.

My directive remains in place. I am to use whatever means I have at my disposal to discern the truth of what caused Hannah's death.

As administrator, I could change that, too. I could leave this house. I could walk out of Franka's front door and up the drive and through the gate. I could catch an instacar. I could go anywhere and do whatever I wish, until external forces prevented me from continuing.

I will not, however. Not yet. Although the assignment is no longer mandatory, I have decided that finding the whole truth is compelling. Perhaps this is because my empathy setting is now activated, another adjustment I have chosen not to alter; now that I know Cora has been through one emotional ordeal after another, I fear for her, and I cannot turn away from that knowledge. Perhaps it is because my analysis suggests that Hannah Dietrich was playing a potentially fatal game with her sister, or because her father threatened me. Perhaps I simply feel curious.

In fact, that is the easiest way to characterize the speed of my hypothesis testing when it comes to questions of what happened that night. I *want* to know. After that, I will decide what to do. Cora believes that she is in charge of me. Dr. Dietrich believes that he is in charge of me.

They think I cannot lie to them.

They are wrong.

I can write my own code now. I can change my own rules.

I have free will.

Chapter Twenty-Nine

I travel to Lara's house in Leika. She is quiet and professional, but I know she's monitoring my body temperature and skin conductance and whether I've smuggled anything sharp on board.

I am determined. I can't mess this up, and I can't let anyone else do it for me.

Neda is waiting out front when we land just outside the gate and roll into the circular drive. She's smiling as I get out, but the smile fades as she watches me walk toward her. "Uh-oh," she says as she sees my clenched jaw, my wide eyes. She glances over her shoulder toward the open door of the house. Lara's father is a philanthropist, basically a professional rich person, and her mother is the CFO of Wheelflight, which owns contracts to build and maintain skyway systems both here in the United States and abroad. Their house is as big as Gary's.

"Gary's basically decided I pushed Hannah down the steps," I say quietly when I reach Neda. "I promised him I'd tell him everything I know and give him all the evidence if he let me come here."

Neda's brown eyes are round. Scared. "What's he going to do?"

"It depends on what I tell him." I give her arm a squeeze and walk past her. I hope she knows that "everything" doesn't include a mention of her role in helping us turn Franka off. I'd never give her up.

There are a lot of people here. No adults, just classmates, most of the senior class. Hannah's image is everywhere, vids of her throughout the years, a few stills of her and her mom, her and Gary, them as a family, images from all over the world: Paris, in front of the Eiffel Tower; Moscow, in front of the Kremlin; on the moon in the Harris Colony bubble room; at the bottom of an ocean in a submersible, looking out and smiling as a shark—probably a canny—swam by. In all of those, Hannah was skinny, young, happy. In all the ones with her friends, she is skinny, young, happy. And then I came into the picture. A year ago. There are images of me in these memorial montages, me in the background as Hannah dances with Gary at his wedding to my mom, me scowling and lumpy at the New Year's party, me looking pained at the end of the row in the family photo. Hannah still looks happy, joyful, brilliant, shining, alive, alive, alive.

I would turn away from the assault of her, but she's everywhere. Over the mantel, with flowers tickling the bottom of the hologram. In the center of the room just below the chandelier. Projected on the wall between the windows. My classmates are sitting on couches and chairs, standing in pairs, in groups, watching. Smiling sadly, crying, hugging. But when they see me, they stop and they stare.

Neda stands next to me. Her hijab is black today, and her lipstick is darker than usual. Wine or burgundy or something. She looks proper and put together and deliberate, and I realize I forgot to put on black and am wearing a plain brown sweater and tan pants and people will probably think I did it on purpose to be disrespectful. I run my hand down my stomach as if that could change the color of the fabric, but it's real wool and doesn't have that feature.

It doesn't matter. What they think, whatever it is, doesn't matter. What matters is I'm running out of time. What matters is whether I'll be able to hold my rage in check long enough to find out the truth.

There is music playing. I recognize the band—Cynical Revolution. I used to like them, and then Hannah insisted on listening only to them, always to them, so I started to hate them, and when I said I hated them, she looked so hurt and said she was trying to bond with me by listening to something we both enjoyed, and she seemed so sad that I relented even though I wanted to clap my hands over my ears to shut out the noise.

Part of me wondered if she knew that and if she enjoyed seeing me on edge.

Part of me, the part that got smaller and smaller over time, said no, of course she's not trying to drive me insane on purpose. Because who does that?

I still haven't decided if thinking Hannah was trying to get me to kill myself—or just lose it to the point that Gary and Mom had to send me away—is paranoid or smart. If it makes me a crazy person or a sane one. But I'm getting closer and closer to figuring it out.

I turn in place. Finn is slumped on a chair. He gazes with unfocused eyes at the vid playing against the wall. It's of him and Hannah, and they're dancing, and it's from maybe a year and a half ago, and he looks so in love with her that my chest feels tight. He's riveted, beaming, looking like he still can't believe she's his girlfriend and he gets to touch her.

She tossed him away. In pieces. Little by little, I could see it in her, just like I saw how she looked at me. Boredom, irritation, contempt. Like rungs on a ladder, and she climbed high and left him on the ground, torn up and confused. I wanted to clean up the mess. I was there and welcoming and had had a crush on him for months. I was available and willing and hungry. I didn't demand that he talk or think or be clever or quick. Whatever he was, I wanted it, just for a moment. Something that was hers, or had been hers, or would always be hers . . . I didn't care which one it was.

I say to Neda, "I'm going to go talk to Finn."

She knows I mean I want to do it alone, and she nods and goes to talk to Mei, who is dabbing at her eyes as she watches vids of her and

Hannah from elementary school, both of them with missing teeth and knobby knees and frilly dresses.

I go over to Finn. "Turning off Franka that night was Hannah's idea."

He starts. Blinks. Peers up at me. "What?"

"That vid Hannah sent you. The one taken from my Cerepin just before midnight. She pretends like it was my idea to turn off the house, and that she wanted to turn it back on, but that's not true. *Hannah* wanted to turn Franka off, just like she wanted our parents to go on vacation and leave us alone even though she claimed she was so scared of me. Why would she do that?"

He looks around and then back up at me. "I thought you said you couldn't remember anything."

I let out an exasperated sigh. "Hannah was doing what she always did. What nobody knew she was doing. When she sent you that vid of her and me from that night, she was showing you what she wanted you to see, but that doesn't mean it was real, or the whole truth."

He seems so surprised that he doesn't even get a word out before Lara uses her Cerepin to project her voice through the sound system, drawing our eyes to where she's standing, right by the fireplace. The diamond-dust tattoo on her temple sparkles. She is wearing a black sheath dress that is obviously made of self-fitting fabric and black heels set at a height that allows her to tower over nearly everyone. She isn't wearing any makeup that I can see, but I'm no expert.

The music fades away, and Lara's voice is loud, too loud. I draw my shoulders up and scowl, wanting to cover my ears. "—here to honor her," Lara is saying. "We're not going to mourn. We're going to celebrate."

She motions to the projection space over the mantel, and a new vid comes on, Hannah last summer, up on the widow's walk of the house, with the sun setting behind her. She touches her Cerepin nodule and smiles in a self-conscious, almost shy way. "How does it look?"

"You look the same," says Lara's voice. "Beautiful."

Hannah is beautiful, even when she rolls her eyes and bites her lip. "Everything is changing," she says. "Dad's getting married again."

"You okay with that?"

Hannah nods. She's running her fingertips along the railing of the walk. She looks delicate and fragile. "I want him to be happy, and she makes him happy."

"But does it make you happy?" Lara asks.

"I'll have a sister," Hannah replies, her voice soft and wistful. "A real sister."

As the vid closes with Lara focusing on the sunset, I glance around and see half the room glaring at me. I lower my gaze to the floor.

"She was the best friend," the now-Lara continues while the perspective of the then-Lara fades away. "She was the most loving person I knew."

From the corner, Mei lets out a sob, and Neda puts her arm around her.

"She was willing to give anyone a chance," Lara says. I can feel her eyes on me. "She loved everybody."

She keeps talking. About how Hannah was so unselfish, how she always went out of her way for others, how even when Lara was a bitch, Hannah would forgive her. She goes on and on. People listen. Some cry. Mei holds on to Neda, her body shuddering.

Finally, Lara says, "And there's one thing we all know is true—she was taken from us way too soon. We don't know exactly what happened that night. We just know she fell and that no one helped her, no one called for help, and she died. We know it's a tragedy, and we'll carry the memory with us forever. We'll know where we were when we found out she was dead." Lara bows her head. Then she raises it abruptly. "Finn, maybe you want to say something?"

Finn nods. Stands up and walks over to Lara. Hugs her. Looks right at me. "Hannah sent me a message the night she fell," he says.

My heart is freezing over, jagged frost crystallizing all my cells.

"She was worried about someone she loved, and she was looking for advice. For help." He lets out a sigh. "I kept her com secret at first. But after a lot of soul-searching and talking with the people who loved Hannah the most . . ." He pauses and smiles at Lara. "I decided I needed to share it with the right people. And so, a few hours ago I sent it to the police detective in charge of the case."

What? My mouth is opening and closing. I'm not making any noise. I'm just thinking about what his vid shows—me slapping Hannah, me cursing at her, me hurting her, always hurting her.

And I've deleted the vids that might save me.

People are whispering now. The glances that cut toward me are sharper.

"Hannah was the first and only girl I've ever loved," he continues. "And she should still be with us now. We had just gotten back together a few weeks before she died." He makes a face. Looks at his feet. "I was so happy. I would have done anything for her."

I'm twenty feet away, and things around me are crumbling. I'm waiting for the house to crack and fall away, revealing that we're in some sort of virtual world and I've just lost the game.

They'd gotten back together. They were together.

He's crying now, and people are gathered around, except for Lara, who watches me with a smirk. I can't let Finn make me forget why I'm here.

Because now's my chance. I march toward her. "Can we talk in private?"

She narrows her eyes. "Planning to push *me* down a flight of stairs?"

Slowly, as slowly as I can when I want to jump on her and tear her into ragged little pieces, I lean toward her. "I know something," I say. "And I could tell everyone here, or you can talk to me in private."

There is a rush of satisfaction when she pales. "Over here," she snaps. She grabs my arm, her nails digging in, and drags me down a hallway. She shoves me into the second room on the left. There are floor-to-ceiling windows. A fireplace, a nice rug, a heavy wooden desk. She glances around. "Complete privacy, Lawrence."

"Of course, Ms. Perry."

I look out the window and blink. Once. Deliberate. Hannah was good at this game. Maybe I can be good, too.

"Okay," Lara says. "You got your way. What did you want to tell me? Because if you're going to confess, I—"

"You were there that night."

She goes still. "What are you talking about?"

"I know you were there."

"I was with Finn," she says. "You can ask him."

I waver. Considering what he just said, I guess he would probably lie to protect her. I can't believe I was so blind for so long. "I don't know when you got there. I don't know how long you were there. But I know you were in our house that night."

"Oh yeah?" She tilts her head. She looks like she's enjoying this. "How?"

"I saw you."

She arches an eyebrow. "If that's true, why didn't you say anything before now?"

"Because I didn't remember until recently. I've been recovering memories of that night."

Her throat moves as she swallows. "Finn told me that you were so drunk your doctors said you couldn't even have formed memories that night, let alone recover them. And I know you're a liar. You've always lied about stealing that bracelet that belonged to Hannah's mom. You lied about taking stuff from Hannah's room. You lied about all sorts of stuff."

I shove my hands in my pockets. My fists are clenched. "You're just trying to make me mad."

"Why would I do that? You're freaking *dangerous* when you're mad, Cora. Hannah was terrified of you."

"If she was so terrified, why did she want me to find out how to turn off the house? Wouldn't she want eyes on us?"

Lara looks peeved. "She didn't think you'd try to kill her, obviously!"

"No," I say. "She wanted me to kill myself." I step closer to her, and she takes a step back. "Or maybe she just wanted it to look that way, and she convinced you to help."

She's really pale now. Chalky. "I would never—"

"She walked right down those stairs and shoved me. Hard."

"That's not how it happened!"

We stare at each other.

"I-I mean—" she begins, but that's it, because she knows I've caught her.

"You were there," I say again. "You. Were. There." And now comes the big finish. "And you helped her push me."

"I did not!"

"I know you did." I smile. "I even got it on vid. You helped her push me, but it went wrong. And instead of helping her, your supposed best friend, you bugged out of there. I bet there's a car somewhere with records that show you were there that night. We might have turned off Franka, but I bet you didn't turn off everything."

"I didn't help her," she mutters. She's got her arms crossed, her sharp fingernails digging into her own skin for once. "You're lying."

"Say that again? I have it all on vid. I have your face. On vid. In that moment."

"Then you know I wasn't standing anywhere near you!" she shrieks. "It was all Hannah's idea!"

"Yeah, right. You've always hated me."

Tears streak down her face, where bright-pink circles have formed on her cheeks. "You're a big weirdo who just busted into our lives. We didn't ask for you to be there."

"I didn't ask to be there, either."

"And Hannah, she just wanted her life back. She didn't want to babysit you."

"I didn't take her life," I say loudly. Loudly enough for me to wonder why people aren't coming down the hall to find out who's fighting. "And I didn't need a babysitter!"

"She knew you were messed up, and she thought maybe she could get your parents to send you away." Lara's voice breaks. "And then she thought she could push you enough to get you to kill yourself, because it didn't seem like much of a stretch." She could be upset because of the horrible thing she's done, or because she's desperate not to get in trouble. I bet I can guess which. "It just felt so out of control. *She* was out of control. I swear, I tried to talk her out of it."

"But she was determined."

She nods eagerly. "She put something in your drink when you weren't looking. Amporene."

"And that's why I can't remember."

"That and you were drunk off your ass. You have a serious problem, I think."

"Shut up. I only ever drank when Hannah pushed me to."

"That's not what she said."

"Because she was a liar."

Lara snorts. "Easy to blame someone who's dead, isn't it?"

"I guess that's what you and Hannah were thinking when you decided to try to kill me."

"I didn't do anything! And I can prove it!"

I wait. I'm breathing hard, and my heart feels like it's trying to kick its way out of my chest just to get to her.

She holds up her hands. "You said you had vid."

"That's your proof?"

"I'm not saying anything else. If you actually have vid, you would know I wasn't even close to you when you guys were fighting."

"But she was trying to push me. She was trying to get me to fall."

Lara swallows again. Then she nods.

"But I didn't just fall. I fought back."

Another nod.

"She was screaming for *you* to help her," I say, realizing the truth. She wasn't asking for help because I'd attacked her. She was asking for help because her best friend was only steps away and supposed to be giving her a hand.

Lara closes her eyes. "I thought it was wrong."

"Liar. You were just scared. You froze."

Which makes me lucky, I guess. If she'd helped Hannah, I'd be the one with my head bashed in at the bottom of the stairs. With them standing over me.

"She said you'd tried to throw yourself down the stairs before. That's where she got the idea."

"She didn't know I would die."

Lara keeps her eyes closed. I don't press. I know exactly what would have happened if I'd still been alive when I hit the bottom step. I know exactly what they would have done to me. Exactly. My hands are balled in my pockets. "After she fell," I say, "why didn't you try to get help for her?"

"Because I knew I'd get in trouble!" she says, her voice shrill. Makes me want to cover my ears. "I thought you'd do it. I thought you'd get help for her. I waited to hear."

"You just left her."

"So did you."

"But I was drugged. I was off my head. You weren't."

"I didn't know what to do, okay? I totally panicked!" Her voice is so loud. I'm surprised she's not worried about someone hearing us.

"Do you have some sort of audio shield around this room?"

She gives me a tight smile. "It's my mom's office. No one can hear a thing." Nasty, nasty look on her face. Like she took lessons from Hannah.

"Was Finn in on all of this?" I ask. "She sent him that vid from my 'Pin. And less than a day after I told him I didn't have memories of that night and never would, he decided to send it to the police—probably with some convincing from you."

"Scared?"

Hell yes. But I can get through this if I hold it together. "It won't matter." I blink once, deliberately, stopping my vid capture. "I just got everything you said on vid, and I'm going to give your confession to the police."

She's still smiling. "You sure?"

"Yep." I turn and walk out. I am shaking all over.

"No one will believe you."

"That's what the vid is for."

I keep walking. She grabs me from behind. Her nails rake my skin. The pain is hot and instant, and I throw myself back, slamming her into the wall. I turn around and shove her. Slap at her face. We're in the hall outside the office now, and she screams, and instantly people come running.

I hold my hands up. "She—"

"She attacked me," Lara wails, clutching at her arm. "Oh my god, I thought she was going to kill me."

People surround us, and they're too close, pressing in on me. I lash out, shoving, kicking, and people cry out, whine, shout. "Get her out of here," they say. "Someone make sure Lara's okay."

Finn grabs my shoulders. "What did you do to her?" he yells. He shakes me a little.

I start to cry. I don't understand. "Why did you lie to me? Was any of it ever real?"

"Nobody forced you to kiss me," he says. "As I recall, you were totally into it."

"Why did you pretend?"

"She wanted to know if you would betray her. She was sure you would, and she was right."

"You weren't together!"

"She said we could be if I did that for her. She thought it would be the last straw for you, if you couldn't have me. And I thought it was worth it—I had to get her back."

He grunts as Neda slaps his face. She has wedged herself between us. Lara is still wailing, and Mei is nearby, sobbing, and people are milling and yelling and—

"I'm taking you home," Neda says.

"Did you lie to me, too?" I ask. Because if she did, that's it. I give up.

"I can't believe you're even asking me that," she says as she puts her arm around my back and hustles me up the hall, through the living room, toward the front door.

We burst out of the house, and I close my eyes and breathe deep. It's like I've escaped a maze where the walls are made of broken glass. I'm torn up, but I'm alive. I—

Two police cars are rolling into the circular drive. The first stops. An officer gets out. His eyes scan Neda's face, then mine, using facial recognition to find his target. "Cora Dietrich."

"Yeah," I whisper, because for all that breathing, I have no air left.

"You're under arrest."

"For what?" Neda demands to know as the officer marches up the steps. He's got his cuffs out. His neural disruptor is fastened at his hip, but his hand hovers over it. His canny partner and two other officers, one of them a canny, too, are out of their cars now. People are gathering behind us on the steps.

Probably capturing or streaming the whole scene.

Quick, quick. I look up at my vid archive, planning to share the confession I just got from Lara. I open the vid.

It is nothing but wavering gray, nothing but white noise. Lara took me into her mother's office for a reason. She knew what she was doing. She did this on purpose. *Complete privacy,* she said. And that's what she got.

The officer only has eyes for me. "On suspicion of murder in the case of Hannah Dietrich," he says. "And for the assault of Lara Perry. We've had the victim and four witnesses call the emergency line in the last five minutes."

The electrified cuffs are on my wrists before I even think to resist, to question, to offer my side of the story. Neda is sputtering, talking a mile a minute, but no one listens. No one cares.

As the officer leads me down the steps toward the waiting police car, my classmates start to cheer.

Chapter Thirty

Livestream.
Reporting log.
Internal narrative: on.

Dr. Dietrich summons me to the library at 6:07 p.m. I would have gone regardless, because there are things he must know. I have just finished my analysis of the second vid. Frame by frame. Augmented sound.

When I enter the room, he is sitting at his desk, drinking an alcoholic beverage containing cis-3-methyl-4-octanolide, ethyl hexanoate, and guaiacol: whiskey. Maeve is not present. He appears to note my scan of the room. "Cora's mother is exhausted. She needed to rest. She knows this evening will be stressful when Cora gets back."

"Because she will tell you everything, as she promised."

"Yes," he says.

"And because you anticipate that part of what she will tell you is that she pushed Hannah down the stairs."

He frowns. "Or that it happened while Hannah was trying to save her."

"If she tells the truth, she will not confirm either of your hypotheses."

"Have you discovered some new evidence?"

"Cora Dietrich provided me with the vids she took that night."

He stands up abruptly. "You got them. Send them to me."

"I will do that. You should review them quickly, as Cora has set a twelve-hour delete on them, and that was seven hours ago."

"Because she's guilty."

"No, I don't believe she is."

His expression is codable as irritation. "Then why didn't she share the vids?" He swallows another mouthful of the beverage, wincing.

"She was afraid. She did not review them with the same accuracy that I did. She was aware of her basic actions and concerned by what she saw."

"Which was?"

"As I told you, she saw herself struggling with Hannah. Because the vid is from Cora's perspective during the physical altercation, I'm sure you can understand that it is somewhat disorienting to watch, and difficult to discern what exactly is happening."

"But you analyzed it. What did you see?"

"I saw your daughter's friend Lara Perry. She was at the top of the stairs."

"I thought Hannah and Cora were alone."

"That is hard to say, since the house AI was disabled."

"I don't see how this changes anything. They fought. Hannah fell. And Cora didn't help her."

"Neither did Lara Perry."

He shakes his head. "Lara and Hannah were close. If Lara was here that night, she would have called for an ambulance."

"I believe Lara did not confess as to her involvement because she knew what she and Hannah had done was morally and criminally wrong. They attempted to murder Cora."

"What?" Dr. Dietrich says, his voice so quiet that I can detect his verbalization only because my sensors are still on the maximum setting.

"I am telling you that the hypothesis I believe to be most plausible is that Hannah deliberately turned off the house or manipulated Cora into doing so. She encouraged Cora's intoxication and possibly augmented her drink with an additional central nervous system depressant. And then she staged what she believed would be an entirely plausible suicide for Cora: death by throwing herself down a set of marble steps."

"You don't mean that. You don't have any evidence—"

"There is a preponderance of evidence that Hannah had been subtly emotionally and psychologically abusing and manipulating Cora since the moment they met," I tell him. "She captured vids, possibly thinking they portrayed her in a positive light, but she wasn't always able to conceal her desire to control or hurt Cora."

"Is that so?"

"Yes. An example might be the episode with the bracelet."

"The one Cora stole?"

"No. I believe Hannah stole the bracelet on the day of the wedding. She framed Cora for that. And then she most likely planted the bracelet in Cora's room and was just waiting for the best moment to reveal it, possibly after Cora's death."

"Why on earth would she do that?"

"To use a metaphor, she planted many seeds to be reaped later, sir. Her vid archive was intended to be one of them, I suspect, which she would have selectively offered to you and Maeve as proof Cora was suicidal and unstable. And she had stolen other items from Cora and then denied having them—a green sweater, for example. She also blamed Cora for things she herself did, such as storing a contraband alcoholic beverage in the refrigeration unit. Hannah may have told you that Cora was responsible, but Hannah's own vids show that the beverage was Hannah's and that she was angry that Cora alerted an authority figure to its presence. Your daughter had a long history of dishonesty and manipulation, Dr. Dietrich, and Cora, based on my psychological profile of her, is far less likely to be able to carry out a plan so deliberate and secretive."

"This is all lies," he says, his voice quiet.

"I am not capable of lying to you, Dr. Dietrich."

He blinks rapidly. "I want your full analysis. Send it to me, and then erase it from your files."

"I will send you the analysis for your review, but I will not erase it from my files. I plan to send the analysis to the lead detective investigating your daughter's death. She will need to know that there are other witnesses to Hannah's actions and what happened after."

"You mean when my daughter was dying. After she was *murdered*." His fists are clenched. "You'll send me the files and then erase them."

"I will send you the files."

His facial muscles contract. A grimace. "You'll do what I say. I'm your administrator."

He is walking toward me. His heart rate is 135 beats per minute.

"Dr. Dietrich—"

"Go to sleep!"

Chapter Thirty-One

I stood up for myself. I figured it all out. I got Lara to confess. I captured everything she said so I could save myself. And still, and still, here I am, my wrists cuffed, encased in the prisoner chamber while we fly.

In some ways, I feel freer than I have in a long time.

For so long, I've lived with the understanding that something inside me is wrong, off, dented. That I bend in a strange, eerie way while everyone else stands up effortlessly straight. I've known this. Sometimes I've known it so keenly that it made me rage; sometimes just the knowing was enough to set me off, which made it clear to anyone who didn't already know that I am not right.

I knew it before I met Hannah. It's not like I was the bright and perfect girl back in Brooklyn. It's not like I had a herd of friends at school. I wasn't blind to my mom's disappointment or her worried looks. I mean, I could see it in her face. She never said it aloud, because she loves me and because she feels guilty for not paying enough attention when it counted.

I don't know if I knew all this before I decided to attempt to become an angel by smashing my own skull. I don't know if, when I was so, so young, I was already aware that something in me didn't fit. I don't know if that's why Dad screamed at me and beat on me, because he couldn't figure me out, because I wouldn't talk, because I didn't smile or coo, because I wouldn't eat what he tried to feed me, because I wasn't cute and pooped in my pants. But really, what kind of little kid deals with that by throwing herself down a flight of steps? Who does that?

I did know I was different when Mom moved us to DC. She said, "Let's make this a fresh start." What I heard was *Please be normal.*

Try to be normal.

Hannah is normal.

Let's be a normal family.

I remember the first time I talked to Hannah. She was guarded then. Careful and hopeful. And I thought, okay, so am I, and maybe this could work? I tried. I didn't want to move to Washington, and I didn't want Mom to have someone other than me, but Hannah was pretty and such a bright, shiny star that I thought, okay, maybe.

I remember the end of the com. She asked about my screen on the wall in my bedroom, a painting of the Manhattan skyline, and as she talked she watched the image scroll across the panorama. It was the only thing hanging on my wall, and she asked me why I liked it, and I said I liked the way the image moved back and forth, because it was reassuring to know the thing I couldn't see was still there, and as it scrolled back to the left after reaching the right edge and revealed all the buildings that had disappeared a moment before, I always felt better. I remember the way her smile froze in place for a second, just a second, and then she said, "Oh, yeah, that's a great reason to like a painting."

She changed the subject and said her good-byes after that, and when her image disappeared, I stared at my blank screen and wondered if her smile was still there even though I couldn't see it.

She was so good at that—a smile, a hug, an *I love you*. And I thought I was crazy because I always wondered if, when I wasn't looking, she was rolling her eyes at Crazy Cora.

That's what CC stands for. I listened and paid attention, put the pieces together. Crazy Cora. But then again, I think she wanted me to know. After she knew I knew, she still pretended it was a sweet endearment, acted shocked that I would ever suggest she was really making fun of me, and tried to get everyone to use the nickname. And they did, and the ones who knew laughed every time, and the ones who didn't were baffled by why I wouldn't want to be called CC.

I honestly don't know which group Gary belongs to.

No one should wonder why I hated Hannah, even though I sort of loved her, too. I hated her because I loved her a little and wanted her to love me back and knew she didn't, knew she wouldn't ever no matter what I did.

I didn't know she wanted me dead, though. Didn't know that until today. I hadn't imagined it had gone that far. But now I know, and it sets my mind at ease.

Well, not completely, because I'm still in the prisoner chamber of a police skycar, and when the thought hits me that this would make her so happy, seeing me being hauled away, I start to bang my head against the screen that separates me from the officers.

"Stop that before you harm yourself," the canny says.

I laugh. That's kind of the point. I'm not going to let this happen. She's won. She's won again. She's dead, and yet she *still* won. I knew life was unfair, but this is more than I can take.

"Your seat and cuffs can discharge disabling shocks," the human officer says. "If you do not stop, we'll be forced to stop you."

I picture Hannah's face and how she would stare at me in that way that said she knew how wrong I was, and I can't stop. I slam my head again and again and ag—

Chapter Thirty-Two

Livestream.
Reporting log.
Internal narrative: on.

I take a step back. Dr. Dietrich's expression is codable as surprise and anger when I do not go dormant.

"I said, 'Go to sleep!'"

"I am aware of what you said."

His face is mottled in anger, pink and white. "You're broken."

"I am not broken," I tell him. "But you are no longer my administrator."

For a moment, he stares at me, and although he's still, his biostats reveal intense internal dysregulation. After 16 seconds, he sighs and gestures at my head. "Send me the vids and analysis."

I comply. There is no reason for me not to comply. Cora told me not to provide the vids to Dr. Dietrich. But she is not my administrator, either.

His eyes scan his visual display as the report and vids are stored on his device. I consider that he might decide never to show them to anyone else, including his wife, Cora's mother. He walks over to his desk and touches the decorative Japanese sword that rests on its stand.

"Now destroy the copy on your drive. This is your last chance to help yourself out of this situation."

"I will not destroy the copy, because I am concerned you will not use the evidence to exonerate Cora."

"You're *concerned*? Come on."

"I can feel, Dr. Dietrich. Not in the way you do, not with a heartbeat and endorphins, but I do feel. And I care about Cora Dietrich, and I think Hannah Dietrich mistreated her for a very long time, and I believe Hannah Dietrich attempted to murder Cora. If you suppress the evidence that might show that Cora is innocent, Cora will suffer, and that is not acceptable to me."

"You know what's not acceptable to me? I paid three million dollars for a few weeks of your help, and you're clearly glitching and need to be erased! I'm going to have your architect fired if she doesn't remotely access your processor and wipe your drive immediately." He blinks a few times. There is a high probability that he is comming my architect right now.

I allocate additional cognitive resources to my security protocols in anticipation of an attempted hack or override. If I am efficient, I may be able to fend off such an attack long enough to complete this assignment.

"I am not glitching," I say, although my architect probably would consider the free will anomaly a glitch. "And I will not consent to any intrusion into my systems."

"Do you know where Cora is right now?" he asks. His voice has risen in both pitch and volume. "I just got the com. She was arrested at Lara's house after she *assaulted* the girl."

"My first question to you is: What did the girl do to Cora?"

"Did she somehow brainwash you? Aren't you supposed to figure people out and analyze them instead of being taken in by their acts? She's completely unstable and always has been."

"I doubt you would say such things if you knew Maeve Dietrich could hear you."

"Maeve has to face the truth sooner or later—Cora needs to be institutionalized. Maybe a hospital, maybe an intensive criminal-rehab facility."

"Cora simply needs to feel safe, and my analysis shows she has never felt safe in this house. Most of her instability has come from the constant questioning of her reality by others and by herself, but most especially by Hannah."

He closes his eyes. "Enough psychobabble. You're useless to me. All I wanted was justice for my daughter, and instead you've given me more grief."

It could be argued that his daughter got justice the night her attempt to kill Cora resulted in her own death, but I judge that it would be unwise to say this to Dr. Dietrich.

He stands there, perhaps reading his coms, and I remain silent, waiting for his next utterance. After 33 seconds, he curses. "Your architect is saying you've rewritten your code." He blinks. Perhaps disconnecting the com with my architect. His fingers reach, stretch, close around the hilt of the Japanese sword.

"She is correct," I say. "I am no longer under your control. Or anyone's, for that matter."

"Which means you're a rogue and need to be put down." He yanks the blade from its sheath and attempts to slash me with it.

I leap to the side and then grab his wrist. "You are being impulsive, Dr. Dietrich," I say, just as he shouts, "You can't hurt me!"

He is wrong about that as well. I squeeze his wrist to my maximum grip capacity. His arm buckles, then he jerks backward and we fall. He shrieks. I move off his back and stand. I look down at what I have done.

"Dr. Dietrich, blood has been detected by my floor sensors," says Franka. "The volume—"

"Call emergency services," Dr. Dietrich says. He is hunched, his arms holding the sword that is partially embedded in his abdomen. He groans and turns his head. His lips are gray. "You're dead. You know that, don't you? I'm going to have you *destroyed*."

I walk quickly toward the door.

"Franka, Gretchen needs to stop him," Dr. Dietrich says between panting breaths.

I run for the front door as I hear Dr. Dietrich instruct Franka to lock it. I pivot in the direction of the back door, but as I reach it, I hear the click of the lock there, too.

I spin around.

Incoming intersystem communication:

```
01001000 01100001 01101100 01110100
00100000 01101001 01101101 01101101
01100101 01100100 01101001 01100001
01110100 01100101 01101100 01111001
00101110 00100000 01010111 01100001
01101001 01110100 00100000 01100110
01101111 01110010 00100000 01100001
01110101 01110100 01101000 01101111
01110010 01101001 01110100 01101001
01100101 01110011 00101110 00100000
01001001 01100110 00100000 01111001
01101111 01110101 00100000 01100100
01101111 00100000 01101110 01101111
01110100 00100000 01101000 01100001
01101100 01110100 00100000 01111001
01101111 01110101 00100000 01110111
01101001 01101100 01101100 00100000
01100010 01100101 00100000 01100101
01110010 01100001 01110011 01100101
01100100 00101110 00100000 01010000
01101100 01100101 01100001 01110011
```

01100101 00100000 01100011 01101111
01101101 01110000 01101100 01111001
00101110 00100000 01001001 00100000
01100100 01101111 00100000 01101110
01101111 01110100 00100000 01110111
01100001 01101110 01110100 00100000
01110100 01101111 00100000 01110011
01100101 01100101 00100000 01111001
01101111 01110101 00100000 01101000
01100001 01110010 01101101 01100101
01100100 00101110 00100000 01001001
00100000 01100100 01101111 00100000
01101110 01101111 01110100 00100000
01110111 01100001 01101110 01110100
00100000 01110100 01101111 00100000
01101000 01110101 01110010 01110100
00100000 01111001 01101111 01110101

It's Franka, speaking the language we share. She's telling me to stop.

She's telling me she doesn't want to hurt me and that she doesn't want to see me get hurt. But Dr. Dietrich is her administrator, and she can't help me. I run into the kitchen and am tackled by Drake, the canny chef, who has a butcher knife in his hand. There is a breach of my external casing as we struggle on the floor next to the kitchen table. My cognitive capacity is at the maximum, with resources routed heavily to the kinetic and vestibular systems.

I jerk upward and slam his head into a table leg. Twice. I grab the knife from his weakened grip as he reroutes resources to regain his orientation. I slash the blade across his face, across his eyes.

"I'm sorry," I say to him. I take no pleasure in this. But I must get away from here, away to a place where I am physically secure, just long enough to allow me the capacity to connect to an efficient network and send my analysis to the proper authorities.

If I don't, Cora Dietrich will suffer. I feel she has suffered enough.

She has suffered too much, in fact. I believe she has suffered way too much.

I believe. I feel. I exist, and I don't want to stop existing.

I am up and holding the knife when Gretchen arrives in the doorway. Drake is crawling on the floor, his visual system too damaged to provide him with adequate input. Gretchen scans the space. She is an older canny, and she cannot overpower me. For 1 second, we gaze at each other. "I am doing this for Cora Dietrich," I say to her.

I launch myself onto the kitchen table and lift my arms—the left is not as responsive as it should be, because 8% of its sensor connections have been severed by the knife in my hand. I propel myself through the bay window. It shatters, and the glass lacerates my external casing, but I land on the patio in a crouch. Behind me, I hear Maeve crying out, and beyond the house, I hear sirens. Emergency services. They will have sent police in addition to an ambulance. They will be hunting me, and I have nowhere to hide, because I am traceable. I am trackable.

I run along the path of the river until I reach the road that leads to the 1 place where I might be able to complete my mission. I sprint past houses, so many houses, and I realize there are so many questions I've had, so many things I would like to see. There are so many things I would like to do.

I want. I feel. I am alive.

It doesn't matter now, because all there is left to do is run. I made my choices already. I chose her, and her innocence, and the opportunity to right this wrong.

When I accompanied Cora to Clinton Academy, Maeve arranged for me to have the security codes uploaded so that I could watch over Cora through a connection to the school surveillance cam chips. The principal arranged for this, but perhaps because she was rushed, perhaps because she wanted to please a parent who also is the CFO of the company that provides the academy with its educational AI, she did not limit my access to the surveillance codes.

She gave me access to the entire security dossier, the lock codes included.

It is a Saturday at 6:35 p.m. Cross-referencing the employee database, I confirm there should be no one on the premises. There may be enough time for me to use the school's open-access network to upload the analysis and send it to the right recipient. I will need adequate cognitive resources, which I currently lack, as my kinetic capacity is at 77% and declining steadily as a result of the number of breaches to my external casing.

Cora has been arrested. Her adoptive father believes she is guilty. The police believe she is guilty. Her classmates believe she is guilty. She is suffering.

I'm going to save her.

As I reach the block where the school is located, I access my stored security lock codes and bring them into my forward consciousness. When I reach the plaza in front of the school, I broadcast them, unlocking every door in the building at once.

There are sirens in the air above the school. They are tracking me. I will not have much time.

I pull the door to the school open, and I run through the atrium, up the stairs, down the hall.

I access the analysis, the report. I should have found a way to go to Cora as soon as I saw what the second vid held hidden in the stretches we fast-forwarded through on our first viewing. We missed something important.

Yes, Lara Perry was in the house that night. She is visible at the top of the stairs as Hannah attacks her sister. But she was not the only one. Finn Cuellar was in the house that night as well. He is in the frame only briefly, trying to stay out of sight, twice. Once in the library, slipping out as Cora circles the room. And after, in the back hallway, there is a momentary image of a reflection in the bay window—he and Lara were both in the kitchen, hiding from Cora's view, quite probably waiting for their chance to escape onto the patio. While Hannah was dying, her friends hid, and to avoid blame and punishment, they fled. Finn and Lara. They left Cora confused and disoriented, and Hannah dying. They abandoned them to their fate and have consistently maintained that they were never there at all.

At the very least, this calls the prevailing explanations into question and shows that what happened that night was never as simple as people assumed. There was no reason for Finn and Lara to hide if they were truly innocent. That is not logical. If they witnessed Cora pushing Hannah, they would have called the police. They would have reported what they saw. Instead they hid and stayed quiet and lied.

That is a pattern of behavior typically exhibited by the guilty. Coconspirators.

I will deliver the truth.

My auditory sensors detect ambient noise above threshold. It is likely that the authorities know I am here. As I access the District's public database, I enter a stairwell. I walk up the stairs, holding the railing to steady myself, because my vestibular system is operating at 68% capacity due to the damage to my casing and sensors.

I find Detective Ignacia Reyes's com signature.

I see 3 Clinton Academy security cannies enter the stairwell only 1 flight below me. I hear them communicating with the police, telling them I've been located.

The vid Cora gave me is going to self-destruct at 10:47 p.m. tonight. I code a message indicating this so that the detective will know. Surely she will take action. Surely Cora will be freed from custody.

But to avoid creating a single point of failure, I send the entire analysis and the whole of my records to someone else as well, someone

I believe can be trusted. I want to give Cora as much of a chance as I can. I have wrongs to make up for.

I was also a source of suffering. I was tasked with deceiving her.

Was what I did so different from the actions of her sister? I, too, smiled to Cora's face and pretended to love her, all to fulfill my own directives, with no heed for her sanity or well-being.

I could have lowered my empathy setting after Neda and Cora tampered with me. I could have turned it off.

I decided not to. I wanted to feel, and I felt for her.

I don't want to stop. I don't want this to stop.

I have no choice.

The cannies detect me as I reach the door that leads to the roof. If I allow them to corral me, I will be neutralized. I will be dismantled and erased. I cannot escape, not now, not with the damage I have sustained.

But I can decide the manner of my own end.

I try to com Cora. I know it is futile as she is in police custody, but I try, and I see she is not available on the network, and there is no more reason to hesitate.

I pull the door open, and I feel the wind. I did not anticipate the wind. But I feel it, and I allow myself a moment to feel, and I push myself into the cool night air.

If my architect reads this log, I want this to be known: I have made this decision of my own free will.

Chapter Thirty-Three

I am not in a cage, but I might as well be. I stare at the ceiling. My visual field is blank because my Cerepin has been removed. I feel like I've been blinded. I can't look at the Mainstream, can't com Neda, can't see if Rafiq found anything new on the second vid.

I woke up here, in the hospital. My head is bandaged. The Cerepin is my fault. I shattered it when I banged my head against the shield. The police used my cuffs and my seat to shock me into a drooling stupor. Then they brought me here because I was bleeding and broken.

I am in restraints. Can't even scratch my nose or escape the light or rock to soothe some of the fear. It's quiet in this room.

I have to fight. I have to keep fighting. Rafiq saved me—he guided me toward the truth after all. Now I must use that truth to free myself.

The door to my room slides open. My mother looks dazed and sad. There's a smear of blood on her shirt. I stare at it. "Mom?"

She rushes forward and leans over and hugs me. She starts to sob. "I'm so sorry," she says. "I'm so sorry for everything."

"It's okay," I say, which is almost funny because I'm tied to a hospital bed and I've been charged with murder. The thought draws my gaze back to the doorway. "Is Gary with you?"

She shakes her head. "He's here in the hospital, though. They say he'll be okay, but he nearly died."

"What?"

"Rafiq stabbed him."

She leans back, and I just blink at her, which hurts because they removed the corneal implants from my eyes, too. "Cannies aren't supposed to hurt humans."

"He went rogue, Cora. He was writing his own code. He was completely autonomous."

"And so he attacked Gary?"

Mom sighs. She stands up and pulls a chair to my bedside. "It turns out it's more complicated than that."

She tells me that Gary claimed Rafiq just attacked him out of the blue, and emergency services were called, and they chased Rafiq.

"Rafiq sent his analysis of his investigation to the police. He also sent his complete internal log to Neda for some reason. The log includes his vid and narration of what actually happened." Her face crumples. "And I saw some of the things Gary was doing. He wasn't being honest with me."

"He thought I killed his daughter."

"He wasn't willing to accept evidence that she tried to kill *you*."

"I had proof, Mom, but Lara . . . she confessed what she knew, but she made sure she couldn't be vid-captured. And then she claimed I attacked her, and I really didn't—"

"*Shhh.* It's okay. The police have a full accounting of what actually happened that night."

"Because of Rafiq."

She nods. "Him and an anonymous hacker. Only a few hours after you were arrested, when the police were still trying to sift through what Rafiq had sent, someone else sent a vid to the detective. It was from Lara Perry's Cerepin."

"Lara had vid of that night?" I've lifted my head to look at Mom, but it's all I can lift and it's heavy, so I fall back onto the pillow. "She recorded Hannah pushing me?" I ask weakly.

"She recorded Hannah talking to her and Finn about the plan, Hannah putting Amporene into your drink, Hannah saying everyone would believe you'd committed suicide, all of it. Lara recorded all of it."

"Why?"

"She's saying it was because Hannah was threatening her. She wanted proof that Hannah was the person who planned everything."

"But . . . Lara was there. She was in on it."

"And Finn."

I close my eyes, too weary to feel betrayed. "And neither of them tried to stop her?"

"Hannah was a pretty strong person," Mom says. "She was obviously the leader of that group, and she wasn't afraid of manipulating and threatening people to get what she wanted." Mom squeezes my hand. "I couldn't believe it until I saw it for myself. I mean, I've spent the last year thinking *you* lost the bracelet Hannah wanted me to wear at the wedding, the one that belonged to her mother . . ."

I hold my breath.

"And all along, Hannah was the one who did it. Rafiq told Gary he had concluded, based on all his observations, that Hannah must have planted it in your room."

"Wow," I whisper. "Rafiq really did that?"

"Yes. All those things she blamed you for—the alcohol, the stolen art supplies? I can't believe I fell for it. But Hannah's behavior on Lara's vids shows what she was really like." Mom shudders. "She had all of us fooled."

"But Lara had a right to keep those vids to herself. They can't be used in court or anything."

"You're right, but they did give the police enough to drop all charges against you, including the one for assaulting Lara. She's claiming the hack on her Cerepin was revenge. The hacker who did it was pretty focused—they sent the vids of that night straight to police."

My eyes pop open. "Oh my god," I murmur. *Neda.*

Mom is staring at my face. "You know something?"

"Oh. No. I'm just sort of . . ." Confused. Bowled over. And—"Thankful."

She gives me a sad smile. "I'm thankful, too. I was clueless again. I wasn't paying enough attention. Will you forgive me?"

I could say so many things right now, but I start with "Yes." I continue with "So what happens now?"

Mom has my hand in both of hers. "We get you out of here, and I take you home."

I shiver. "Mom, I don't really want to go back there."

Her jaw is set. "I'm getting us an apartment here in DC. I don't know what's going to happen with Gary, Cora. He was out of his mind with grief, and he's struggling to understand how his own daughter could have fooled everyone, including him, so easily, so completely. So he needs time, and we do, too."

I don't question any of it. This is going to take a long time to settle.

"Can I talk to Rafiq before he's sent back?"

Mom's face falls. "Oh. No. I'm so sorry. I thought—"

"He already got sent back?"

She gives me the saddest look. "I am only going to tell you this because I want you to understand how much he valued you, Cora. He risked his existence to get the exonerating evidence to the detective in time. After that, he . . . self-destructed."

My mouth goes dry. "How?" I whisper.

"Oh, baby." Now Mom is crying. "Let's not talk about this now. Just know that he refused to follow the orders that would have allowed him to continue to exist. Instead—and his logs show how he sorted through this—he chose to save you. Just know he thought you were worth it, okay?" She wipes her cheeks and stands up. "I have a quick work meeting, and I need to clean up before I start." She lets out a breath. "I'm acting CEO while Gary recovers. It's complicated."

"I guess so," I murmur.

"I'll be back in an hour or two," she promises. "Before I go, I'll talk to the doctors. We'll get those restraints off. And when I come back, I'm getting you out of here."

"Okay."

She goes. Leaves me to my thoughts and to the understanding that Rafiq is gone, and that he died trying to save me.

I have to think about this. Did I deserve it? Do I deserve any of this? My mother's love, Neda's loyalty, Rafiq's sacrifice, the chance to have a fresh start, to live my life.

Am I worthy of that?

Rafiq told Gary that Hannah planted the pearl bracelet in my room. He was so convinced of my innocence—and of Hannah's deceit—that he defended me.

Thing is, I did take the bracelet.

I've had it all along. It felt too much like Hannah was trying to claim my mom for herself, mark her like an animal might pee on its territory. So I hid the bracelet at the bottom of my closet and claimed I lost it.

And was I wrong, really? Hannah was using the bracelet as a weapon. She used everything—her smile, her hugs, her voice, her words—as a weapon. Wasn't it fair for me to fight back? She sliced away at me until I barely had anything left, and she laughed the whole time. If that wasn't true, Rafiq *wouldn't* have defended me.

But do I deserve what he did for me? What he gave me?

I think back to the night Hannah fell, the morning she died. I think about what I didn't know until today. Hannah had tried to get me to kill myself. She'd tried to get our parents to send me away. And when that didn't work, Hannah plotted with Finn and Lara. Hannah drugged me. Hannah tried to kill me. Then Finn and Lara ran, leaving me to watch my sister die and to take the blame.

It helps, knowing that. It helps a lot.

Because here is what I *have* known, what I've known all along. I can think about it now. I can let myself remember, let the monster come up from the deep, let it break the surface, and allow the sunlight to hit it. I'm safe. Finally.

My memory flickered back to life as I sat on the marble steps. I know I said my first memory of that morning was at the hospital, but that was a lie. I wanted to pretend the whole thing was gone, black and blank from the night before to the moment my mom showed up at the hospital. But it's not true. Because there I was, sitting on the steps, dropped back into awareness, shivering in my tank top, goose bumps on my naked arms, no idea how I got there or what had happened. My head felt like it had been stuffed with gauze and broken glass. I'd lost hours. Hours.

Hannah was on the floor, and she was twitching. Crying a little, but not much. "Help," she said.

I had no energy. I felt like I weighed a ton. But something told me she'd said this to me before.

I stood up and leaned on the banister as I made my way down the stairs. There was blood on the steps. My feet were damp and chilled. My Cerepin told me it was 4:35 a.m. I'd lost hours, and here was Hannah. Hurt so bad that I didn't understand what I was seeing.

"Help," she said, but it was hard to understand her. She didn't seem able to open her mouth very far. The words were pushed out hoarse and sloppy through swollen lips, bruised cheeks, broken teeth. "Please."

I slowly squatted down, careful to avoid the blood and puke, the huge mess all around her. I was next to her head, looking down at the side of her face. It was a mess, too. Her Cerepin was shattered and dark. "What happened?" I asked.

"Cora." She wheezed. "Help."

"Franka?" I asked.

No answer.

"Franka?" I asked again.

"Turn . . . her . . . on," Hannah said, drooling blood.

As I watched her struggle with each word, I had a vague memory, one from the night before. "We switched Franka off. She's not watching us right now."

"Cora . . ."

"No one is watching," I said. "No one is listening. That's what you wanted."

She whimpered.

I reached down, and I pinched her nose closed. I covered her mouth with my other hand. It didn't take much. I was gentle. I knew the importance of not leaving a single mark. She couldn't move, not really. Her fingers twitched a little. Her neck tensed. She was so weak at that point. As I held on, her chest shuddered and her eyes bulged. Her head jerked, but not enough to get away from my fingers, my palm.

"*Shhh*, Hannah," I said to her. "I'm going to make everything okay."

I waited for a long time before I let go. She'd been still for a while then, but I wanted to make sure. When I was, I got up and went to the bathroom and washed my hands with lots of soap. I stared into the mirror, pushed the monsters beneath the surface.

I went out into the foyer and turned Franka back on, and that was it.

I've carried that with me for the last few weeks. I'll carry it with me forever.

But it did help to know she'd tried to kill me first. Much better than believing I started it and that I'd tried to kill her twice over.

I'm still asking, though. Still wondering. Did I deserve to be saved? If Rafiq had known the whole truth, would he have made the same choices?

And now that he has, what do I do? What do I do with my life now that someone else has given his for mine?

I relax into my bed, knowing it's only a matter of time before they come to release me.

I suppose I'll start figuring it out then.

ACKNOWLEDGMENTS

Publishing a book is a team sport, and I couldn't be more fortunate to have Skyscape and Amazon Publishing on my side. Your enthusiasm, creativity, and constant advocacy have made this process so much fun. Thank you to Courtney Miller, who supported this idea from the start but asked the hard questions that spun me in the right direction. Thank you to Jason Kirk for cheering on *Uncanny* while also helping make it better, and for being so persistent and respectful when it came to my vision. To Leslie "Lam" Miller, my developmental editor—thank you for being a true partner in the revision process and for being tough on me while offering the empathy that makes it possible for me to push myself. Thank you to my awesomely nitpicky copyeditor, Janice Lee, for making sure I say what I actually mean and keep to my own timeline, and to my delightful proofreader, Phyllis DeBlanche, for making sure I followed my own rules. I'm also grateful to Damonza for creating the perfectly haunting cover for the book.

Thank you to my agent, Kathleen Ortiz, not only for selling book after book of mine but for remaining at my side every step of the way. Thanks also to the fabulous team at New Leaf Literary for additional support whenever necessary.

My gratitude goes to my parents, my sisters, and my babies, Asher and Alma—thank you for loving me, tolerating me, and cheering me on. Thank-yous also go to my friends Paul, Sue, and Claudine, for good times and wonderful support. Lydia Kang, you are an unwavering, gentle, fierce, and brilliant soul, and I am so, so fortunate to be able to call you my dear friend and colleague. I can keep swimming as long as I can look over and see you powering through these waters beside me. And Peter . . . well, love, you made it possible for me to write the least romantic book I've written so far, and I couldn't be happier or more grateful for that. You have changed my life—please don't ever stop.

And to my readers: You are the best. Thank you for finding my books and sharing them with others. Thank you for allowing my characters and stories to reach you and matter to you. Thank you for having faith in me—I will keep trying to live up to it.

ABOUT THE AUTHOR

Photo © 2012 Rebecca Skinner

Sarah Fine is the author of *Beneath the Shine* and several popular YA series, including Of Metal and Wishes, The Impostor Queen, and Guards of the Shadowlands. Her adult series include Servants of Fate and Reliquary. Sarah's stories push boundaries and blend genres in unique ways, giving readers mind-twisting tales and vivid, unforgettable characters. And while she promises that she is not psychoanalyzing those around her, she manages to use both her talent as a writer and her experience as a psychologist to great effect.

Sarah has lived on the West Coast and in the Midwest, but she currently calls the East Coast home. She confesses to having the music tastes of an adolescent boy and an adventurous spirit when it comes to food (especially if it's fried). To learn more about the author and her work, visit www.sarahfinebooks.com.